Blood and Fog

Buffy the Vampire Slayer™

Buffy the Vampire Slayer
   (movie tie-in)
The Harvest
Halloween Rain
Coyote Moon
Night of the Living Rerun
Blooded
Visitors
Unnatural Selection
The Power of Persuasion
Deep Water
Here Be Monsters
Ghoul Trouble
Doomsday Deck
Sweet Sixteen
Little Things
Crossings

The Angel Chronicles, Vol. 1
The Angel Chronicles, Vol. 2
The Angel Chronicles, Vol. 3

The Xander Years, Vol. 1
The Xander Years, Vol. 2
The Willow Files, Vol. 1
The Willow Files, Vol. 2
How I Survived My Summer Vacation,
   Vol. 1
The Faith Trials, Vol. 1
Tales of the Slayer, Vol. 1
The Journals of Rupert Giles, Vol. 1

The Lost Slayer serial novel
   Part 1: Prophecies
   Part 2: Dark Times
   Part 3: King of the Dead
   Part 4: Original Sins
   Onmibus Edition

Child of the Hunt
Return to Chaos
The Gatekeeper Trilogy
   Book 1: Out of the Madhouse
   Book 2: Ghost Roads
   Book 3: Sons of Entropy
Obsidian Fate
Immortal
Sins of the Father
Resurrecting Ravana
Prime Evil
The Evil That Men Do

Paleo
Spike and Dru: Pretty Maids
   All in a Row
Revenant
The Book of Fours
The Unseen Trilogy (Buffy/Angel)
   Book 1: The Burning
   Book 2: Door to Alternity
   Book 3: Long Way Home
Tempted Champions
Oz: Into the Wild
The Wisdom of War
These Our Actors

The Watcher's Guide, Vol. 1: The Official Companion to the Hit Show
The Watcher's Guide, Vol. 2: The Official Companion to the Hit Show
The Postcards
The Essential Angel
The Sunnydale High Yearbook
Pop Quiz: Buffy the Vampire Slayer
The Monster Book
The Script Book, Season One, Vol. 1
The Script Book, Season One, Vol. 2
The Script Book, Season Two, Vol. 1
The Script Book, Season Two, Vol. 2
The Script Book, "Once More With Feeling"

Available from SIMON PULSE

Blood and Fog

Nancy Holder

**An original novel based on the hit television series
by Joss Whedon**

SIMON PULSE

NEW YORK LONDON TORONTO SYDNEY SINGAPORE

Historian's Note: This story takes place in the
sixth season of Buffy

First Simon Pulse edition May 2003

™ and © 2003 Twentieth Century Fox Film Corporation.
All rights reserved.

SIMON PULSE
An imprint of Simon & Schuster
Children's Publishing Division
1230 Avenue of the Americas
New York, NY 10020

The text of this book was set in Times.
Printed in the United States of America.
2 4 6 8 10 9 7 5 3 1
Library of Congress Control Number 2002115626
ISBN 0-7434-0039-9

Somebody saved my life tonight.
—For Kym

Acknowledgments

O wonderful world, that hath such usual suspects in it! A big thank-you to the cast, staff, and crew of *Buffy,* especially Joss Whedon, Marti Noxon, and Sarah Michelle Gellar. Thank you, S&S Lisas: Lisa Clancy and Lisa Gribbin, and others—Efraim Salzberg and Paula Reedy. For Howard Morhaim, my wonderful agent and friend, and Ryan Bilstein, his assistant, my gratitude. Thanks to Debbie Olshan at Fox, long may you wave. My buds, Von, Wes, Dal, and Deb—*muchas gracias*. Steve Perry, aka Veiny-Armed Dude, thank you for your friendship and your *duende*.

Prologue

The cavern was dark, deep, and overflowing with the bad.

Adrenaline rush, fear rush . . . Willow had it all. It was almost as bad as the day she threw up on Snoopy backstage after the ice show.

Only younger then, and having no idea weird creatures with heads far, far larger than their bodies actually existed.

As if to illustrate her point, a grunt and a squeal from such a creature echoed across the cavern. From her position behind a stalactite, Willow flinched; then an enormous, grotesque head spewing green blood from its neck sailed past her and landed splat into a bubbling mud pot in the bone-strewn floor. Overripe pumpkins came to mind as hot mud splashed from the cannonball splat. Willow ducked behind a large rock, covering her head with her hands, and did a quick warding spell to save her dry-clean-only top. *Stupid, only go for the washables when one is on patrol with the Slayer.*

Especially if one is trying to cut down on the magick use. Which I am.

She looked between her fingers as she rose, seeing only flashes of light in the yawning maw of shadow that was the entrance and egress to the huge cavern. That was where she had dropped their flashlight; it was on the ground, canted slightly toward the ceiling, and as Buffy battled whatever she had taken on next, their shadows danced like Bizarro World Fred and Ginger overloaded with caffeine.

Not a pretty sight, that, so Willow concentrated on conjuring a fireball to throw across the cave. But while she was putting her spell together, something smacked her over the head and sent her facedown in the muck. It hurt, and if there had been time she would have seen little birdies; but she had a lot of hours on her slayage clock and her reflexes were pretty good. Not as stretchy as the Slayer, but bendy still, she flipped over on her back and sent the three-quarters-formed fireball from her hand. It caught a hairy, hunchbacked demon in the face. Its skin began to sizzle as it staggered backward, shrieking and clutching its head, and then it slammed very hard into the wall.

Chunks of ceiling shot downward, and Willow flipped back over, this time taking a deep breath and clamping shut her mouth. She contracted into a ball and, pushing back onto her knees, she scuttled out of the range of the cascade, and plopped behind a boulder.

Catching her breath, she watched the demon's throes of agony as the flames ate up its face. Now she was thinking baked pumpkin pie. Its clawed feet twitched. Then, with one final roar, it bolted to a sitting position, froze there for a moment, then collapsed stiffly onto its side. It didn't move again. It appeared to be dead in the extreme.

"Yay," Willow whispered. She rubbed the back of her head as she held on to the boulder, feeling very wobbly. A knot was already forming just above the hollow at the base of her skull. She felt drained and incredibly sick to her stomach, but she could indulge her maladies later. She needed to help the Slayer.

Who is not here . . . Willow thought, confused. Then she realized that Buffy and her opponent must have moved out of the cavern and into the tunnel. The ground shook, and she felt a little better because the battle was still on, which meant that Buffy was still more or less okay. Then she realized that something that could make the ground shake that hard had to be really big.

Really dangerous.

Really able to maybe kill the Slayer.

"Buffy?" she shouted. Her own voice echoed the only answer she got. *"Buffy? Buffy? Buffy?"*

There was another quake; this time it seemed that the entire cave tilted. More chunks of ceiling detached, one narrowly missing her shoulder.

"Buffy!" she yelled again.

And still no answer except her own voice.

Buffy's good at the big battles. It's who she is and what she does, Willow reminded herself as she staggered backward, accidentally running into the remains of the headless demon. *Day in, day out, she slays. And what I do . . . is what I'm not supposed to do. Magick. And, okay, I did a couple of small spells to keep the Slayer from dying . . . again . . . but that's magick for a good reason . . . so even Tara should be okay with that . . .*

. . . if she knew . . . which she won't, unless Buffy narcs on me. . . .

"Buffy!" she shouted into the darkness.

"Out of the way, Will!" Buffy shouted back.

Willow jumped to the right as an enormous demon with a ridged back and furled head shot backward into the cavern from the tunnel. It was a Riencosta, very bad, very evil. It was mostly a blur, its bulk too large for the watery beam from the small flashlight to fully illuminate.

Then Buffy came after it, and Willow thought, not for the first time, *Wow. Buffy's got the moves.*

With a fresh burst of strength, the Slayer made a rip-cord leap at an angle toward the monster, jamming her boot heel into its ear. She zinged backward, then leaped into the air again, executing a perfect one-eighty. As she landed on her right foot, the black leather outlined her quads as she pulled in her left thigh, then let the package explode into a sidekick that sent the Riencosta demon slamming across the chamber. As it hurtled through the air, the ridges on its back collided with and crushed a line of stalactites suspended from the ceiling. It roared in pain, then slammed into the wall.

The ground shook again as it landed. Another huge chunk of rock above its head vibrated free and landed on its skull. Willow distinctly heard bone crushage.

It roared once more and then collapsed, hopefully dead, definitely unconscious. Buffy smiled briefly, registering a moment of satisfaction at having taken it out. Then she saw Willow, and the smile faded.

That was not a good sign, in Willow's opinion, of her own physical condition.

"Willow, you okay?" Buffy asked, rushing toward the Wicca.

Willow smiled wanly and held out her hand. "I will be," she assured her friend. "Just a hot bath and a whole lotta—"

Then Willow caught a flicker of pale blue-white in the flashlight beam behind Buffy and shouted, "Wraith!"

Cued in by Willow's warning, Buffy pushed Willow away. Then she whirled around, bouncing-on-her-heels ready to face yet another assailant. There had been plenty tonight. More than usual on a Saturday night.

No rest for the wicked . . . not on my watch.

Whatever was coming had moved out of the light, but Buffy Summers knew that seeing was not a necessary component of successfully defeating. She got ready to rumble. No stupid evil creature could resist a fight, even if the better part of survival would be to run away. She knew from experience that retreat was a difficult concept to love, yet there were definitely times when it beat dying.

And I should know. I've died twice already, and I'm not even old enough to drink legally.

Sure enough, a phantom of tissue-thin membranes and half-decomposed bone whirled at her, a terrifying wash of terror and death, a hideous mask of decay and horror . . .

. . . *yawn* . . .

. . . and Buffy made short work of it. With a fist full of undercuts, she caught the thing in the center of its rib cage and thrust in and up. Each rib disconnected from the sternum with a *sprong* like a broken guitar spring, then flittered upward, a deck of shuffled cards let loose from the hands of a horribly inept magician.

"That'll teach you to mix up your similes and metaphors!" she boasted to the rest of the wraith as it clattered to the ground. "Or rather, mine."

"Another one!" Willow shouted at her, and Buffy nodded as the second wraith flew at her, determined to also die the final death.

"On it!" she cried.

"And you were probably thinking in similes!" Willow added.

"Got it! Thanks!"

And she did get it, pressing her heels hard into the dirt and then springing at the creature, whose elongated face reminded her of the mask in *Scream*. The distorted mouth made a boomerang "V" as it tried to dodge Buffy's trajectory, but the Slayer made contact, rammed a fist into that mouth, and felt the entire creature crumble like a ceramic cookie jar of doom . . . leaving crumbs of wraith behind instead of chewy deliciousness.

She shook off the crumbs. Boots and black leather were a good battle-gear combination, even though she and the Willster had planned to catch a chick flick, not battle demons and monsters. *Cheaper evening, this way. We could have dropped twenty-five bucks easy, if we'd bought refreshments.*

She remembered watching Hindi TV together long ago, Willow offering a comment about making their own fun as they watched the heroine wailing about her podiatrist. Willow had been the fun-discovering Wicca tonight; it was she who had gotten bad vibey on the way to the Sun Cinema, way before Buffy's spider sense went a-tingling. Heeding her instinct, she and Buffy had followed the scent, discovering a rat's nest of the bad.

If those rats happened to be Rodents of Unusual Size.

"Curtain call!" Willow shouted, pointing over Buffy's shoulder.

Buffy spun around as a third wraith rushed her from the shadows. She took it on with ease; then, as soon as that one was down, she scrolled down to a club-wielding troll—the green, flesh-eating kind—and then the not-quite-so-dead Riencosta groaned and sat up.

Buffy assumed battle position, ready to handle—make that manhandle—both attackers, when a small glowing orb erupted from Willow's palm and smacked the Riencosta in the back of the skull. With an impressive display of green sparks, the demon's head erupted. The headless corpse flopped back onto the floor, and vast quantities of green goo burbled from its neck.

Another point for our side.

Willow looked pleased with herself. Buffy gave her

a quick nod of thanks, snatched the troll's club from its grimy fists, and whacked it over the head with it. The troll snarled once, twice, and fell to its knees. Buffy gave it another whack at the same time that another ball of magickal energy whizzed across the cavern. It caught the troll in the face and then . . . no face.

Down it thudded.

Buffy reassumed battle stance and scanned the perimeter.

"And then there were none, finally," she said, lowering her arms. She and Willow were alone at last. *Except for goo and bubbling mud.* "Right? Seeing anything else? Feeling anything?" She gazed at her witchly bud.

"It's all good, except for the feeling anything," Willow announced. As Buffy looked concerned, she got herself up, dusted her hands together, and walked toward Buffy. "No rift in the force that I can feel, anyway."

"I had the troll, but thanks," Buffy said. She hesitated. "You didn't need to use up your energy, Will. I know all that . . . stuff . . . makes you tired."

Willow gave her a don't-try-to-coddle-me look and said, "I thought you needed help. It was just a couple of little spells. Or maybe six," she added guiltily.

"But I could have done it all my . . ." Buffy began, then mentally zipped up her mouth and pocketed the key. "You're right. I could have gotten overpowered," she added peppily. "And there you were, just like the Energizer Bunny, saving the day. Boom, boom, boom with the fireballs."

"The Energizer Bunny being such a scary thing," Willow said with her customary gentle wryness.

"Anya thinks so," Buffy retorted, and they shared a smile. "Seriously, thank you."

"It was nothing." Willow's voice was a bit strangled.

"I know . . . I know you're trying to . . . not use so much magick," Buffy said jumbily.

Willow said nothing.

They had just entered a different sort of dangerous territory, and Buffy knew it. Tara had recently left Willow because Willow was using so much magick. Willow hadn't even been able to go a week without trying a heavy-duty spell that had given everybody amnesia and almost cost them their lives. Willow was easing off, but Buffy thought she was still using magick when she didn't really need to.

But I'm not one to judge her, Buffy reminded herself. *She can't stay away from magick, and I can't stay away from Spike.*

Ew, ew, ew.

At the images that rose into her mind, she blanched and wiped her forehead. She muttered, "So, well, speaking of battery-powered objects." She crossed to the flashlight, picked it up, and smacked it hard into her own palm. "We need new D-cells. These are seriously compromised."

"Worn out," Willow agreed. She flicked her fingers, and the beam glowed more brightly. Traces of magick sprinkled off the circumference of the flashlight face like teeny-weeny fireworks.

"Willow," Buffy murmured, then zip, zip, zip with

the mouth, throw away that nasty chatterbox key.

"I'm thinking latte now, or maybe a frothy, high-octane Frappuccino. And some of those chocolate-covered graham crackers," Willow said. "We so deserve it."

"We so do." Buffy smiled, remembering many happy times at the Espresso Pump, another casualty of life in the postmodern age of too much responsibility and no relief in sight. They hardly ever went there anymore. They hardly went anywhere anymore. Life was grim and filled with obligations. Most of the time, anyway. There were exceptions.

When I'm with Spike. Then I forget it all . . . I forget who I am and where I was . . . that Willow and the others yanked me out of heaven, and dragged me back here, to be the Slayer, to this endless battling . . . with demons and bills and trying to raise Dawn and it's all too much.

She did it with her magicks, which she can't stop using. And I'm glad I'm a good enough person that I don't think that's some kind of poetic justice. Willow is my friend, and she was just trying to help me.

But why did she assume I would be in some kind of trouble in my afterlife? Yet . . . not assuming, just covering my bases. Better to suffer in this earthly coil than go through what Angel did. She had no way of knowing I was in a kinder, gentler place. For all they knew back here, Glory was torturing me for thwarting her.

She swallowed hard and raised her chin. "Seriously, Willow. I'm glad you were here to watch my back."

She smiled as Willow trudged toward her. The red-head looked tired. Her goo-splattered black velvet blouse hung on her—Willow had been losing weight—and her ebony wool skirt hung lower on her hips than when she and Buffy had first bought it on a rare outing to the Sunnydale Mall. Shopping was rarer than even movies these days, for two reasons—little free time and less money, and what's a mall for when you're over sixteen?—but it had been a necessary thing to spend some friend-time with Willow. She was so down since Tara had moved out.

And to think when I first moved here, she was so down because Xander wouldn't look at her twice.

And then she was so down because Oz left her.

Jeez. Poor Will. So much with the leaving. She's almost as unlucky at love as . . . me.

"You okay, Buffy?" Willow asked, as the two walked toward the maze of tunnels that led into the cavern. Subterranean activity was up lately; it had been noticed by the Scoobs, and no one knew why yet. Buffy wished Giles were still here. He'd probably remember that it was Night of the Seven Hundredth Evening of the Convergence of the Apocalypse of the Ananda Marga Yoga Society. Or a chess club, at least. Instead, he was off in England, probably frittering away his time at a pub, drinking beer, playing darts . . . *having fun.* . . .

"Buffy?" Willow said again, raising her brows as she peered at the Slayer.

"I'm fine. Just a little low on the blood sugar. I skipped dinner so I could gorge on palm kernel oil and popcorn," she said.

"They don't use that anymore," Willow offered.

"But it still tastes just as good." She smiled. "Nothing says 'movies' like the smell of popcorn and margarine product."

Buffy nodded. Then she sniffed the air around Willow, enjoying the pleasant fragrance of Willow's new scent. "Speaking of . . . nice perfume, which I can detect above the rancid stench of demon blood. Smells like strawberries."

"Huh." The Wicca raised her forearm to her nose and inhaled as if she were smelling her perfume for the first time. "It's patchouli, though," she said half to herself. "Not known for a fruity base."

"And yet," Buffy said. "I'm smelling strawberries."

"Shouldn't," Willow insisted.

"Well, it smells good, whatever it is." Buffy glanced over her shoulder at the carnage. "A lot better than it's gonna smell in here in a day or so. So"—she looked at Willow—"there's been a definite increase in belowground demon sightings, and they're not taking the weekends off. Comments, Mr. Spock?"

"Not a clue," Willow admitted. "Maybe it's the same guys who froze the guard at the museum."

Buffy shrugged. "I can't say. Maybe our diamond thieves are demons after all. Stirring things up to distract me so they can rebuild Adam or something." She moved her hands like a robot. "What do you think?"

"Could be." Buffy could almost see the wheels turning in Willow's head as the red-head thought through the possibilities. "We hadn't seen a troll for a long time, you know? Maybe that's significant. Or it could be an anomaly."

"Nope. It was definitely a troll," Buffy quipped, then crinkled her nose as Willow looked seriously embarrassed for her and added, "That was a joke, Will. I know about anomalies. After all, I got to take freshman math for, oh, about two seconds." She flashed a brief grin to signal Willow that, hey, joke, not bitterness. "Or was that covered in freshman English?"

"Could be either," Willow offered. She looked sad. "I'll bet there's a late show," she said with faint hope.

I'll probably fall asleep, Buffy thought, a trifle dismayed that Willow assumed they were still going. "Movies good?" she asked brightly.

"Movies good." Willow covered a yawn, saw Buffy noticing, and said, "I'm fine. Really." She walked a little faster to prove it.

"Good." *We're both too tired, but what the hey.*

Buffy strolled along, trying not to look like she was checking Willow out, but she was. Something was troubling her friend, and she wasn't telling Buffy about it.

We used to share all our secrets, she thought, *over half a decade ago. As soon as she found out I was the Slayer, we did the whole best-girlfriend thing. Bunny slippers and Mr. Gordo and talking about boys who turned out to be vampires. When did it all get so hazy and confusing?*

Will our lives ever be simple again?

Willow walked beside Buffy, remembering a short time when the Slayer had possessed the ability to read minds, and she kind of wished her friend could read her mind now.

Because Willow Rosenberg was scared. She was into stuff she wasn't sure she should be into, but there was no one to force her to stop. Tara had left her because of the magicks, and it didn't seem that she was coming back anytime soon.

And it's escalating. I can feel the need rising inside me; it's almost like the magicks are a separate entity, and they're hungry.

There's an old story about a shaman who is about to initiate his son into the secrets. He sits him down in the sweat lodge, and from the sacred smoke of the alder logs he conjures the images of two wolves, squaring off in battle. They fight each other savagely, but they're evenly matched.

"These are the two sides of you," the shaman tells his son. "One side is your shadow, operating out of aggression, envy, and hatred. The other side is your light, working from a foundation of courage, wisdom, and integrity. These two sides of you will war with each other until one of them wins."

The battle rages. The son is repelled by the savagery of the two wolves as they fight on, drawing blood, attacking each other mercilessly. Man and boy watch as the smoke fills their lungs and sweat pours down their foreheads.

Finally, the son tears his mesmerized gaze away and says to his father, "Please tell me now. The battle is so long. Father, which one is going to win?"

And the shaman looks at his son, taking the measure of his own blood, perhaps wishing to ask him the same question. And at last he says, "The one you feed."

My shadow side is starving, and I so don't want to feed it, but I need help . . .

. . . and to tell the truth, I sure don't want help.

Buffy had said she smelled like strawberries. Willow had read that some magick-users carried with them an unusual scent. For some, it was orange blossoms; for others, it was sandalwood. They reeked of it, the way people who smoke cigarettes or marijuana reek—and they didn't realize it. Though they showered often, took scented bubbles baths, and used essential oils and perfumes, their signature magick scent permeated their entire being.

Do I reek of magick? In a sweet, strawberry-scented way?

She swallowed back tears, raised her chin a little, and took a breath. She made herself look fine, act fine.

But she wasn't fine, not by a long shot. Secrets backfired; she remembered when everyone had caught her and Xander kissing—all the misery that had ensued. She thought about how Buffy had kept Angel a secret after he had returned from the hell dimension the Slayer had sent him to. She thought about Veruca, and Oz . . . catching the two werewolves locked in that cell together, with no clothes on. . . .

"Buffy," she blurted. *I'm gonna tell her I'm losing control. About how I'm tempted by the hard, black magicks and that I need someone to help me resist them. . . .*

"Yeah, Will?" Buffy's gaze was direct, ready. As if she knew what was coming next.

But here was the thing: The wolves inside Willow

still had plenty of fight left in them. Each one was convinced it was going to prevail, and all she could do was just sit back and watch.

"Um . . . you don't think Tara will be there, do you? At the Sun Cinema? Because she loves the movies as much as I do. . . ."

Buffy's face softened. She gave her head a little shake. "No, Will. I don't think she'll be there."

Willow twisted her hands, saw what she was doing, and dropped them to her sides. "Maybe we should just go to the Magic Box. Continue researching why so much increased activity of the *überbad*. Unless you think, um, Tara will be there. Because I know she's helping with that. . . ."

Buffy shook her head. "She checked in with me and Dawn before you and I met up tonight. They're really tight," she added, then said hastily, "but of course Dawn still misses you."

Willow flushed. It was like any bad breakup, any divorce—friends trying to stay neutral, friends trying to pretend that there wasn't a big, wide chasm in everybody's lives and in the fabric of their everyday world.

I made her go away, Willow thought. *I kept promising Tara I'd stop, and then I broke that promise. But she kept hers.*

She left me.

"Of course she still misses me," Willow echoed sadly.

"It'll get better," Buffy said. "Something will . . . work out."

Looking a little awkward—maybe because things hadn't worked out for her, and still weren't working out very well—Buffy gathered up her hair and pulled it away from her face. There were shadows under her eyes. Willow realized that she was being immature wanting Buffy to guess that something was wrong and fix it. Her friend had enough on her plate without taking on Willow's troubles, too.

"Everything's going to be better," Willow said. She smiled, but she could feel her cheeks practically freezing, the top half of her face not going along with the program because of the sadness. "Really."

"I know." Buffy tried for a smile, too, and did just as lousy a job of it. "It's all good."

The two friends walked into the labyrinth in order to get out of the labyrinth; and Willow flicked her fingers backward, willing the bodies of the dead they'd left behind to disintegrate into nothingness.

All's well that end's well, she told herself.

But she had a feeling this adventure was far from over. And from the preoccupied frown that had returned to Buffy's face, the Slayer felt the same way.

Bad times are brewing, Willow thought. *I hope they belong to someone else, selfish as that may be. But not Buffy. She's had more than her share of bad times. Way more.*

Same time, different dimension . . .

Sometimes history is written neither by the victors nor the vanquished.

Sometimes it's written by the only folks around who actually can *write*.

The ancient Romans—especially during the first two centuries A.D.—did an awful lot of writing. There being no TV and nothing much to do except figure out neat new ways to execute Christians and conquer strange foreign lands, they went nuts with the writing. Scrolls, monuments, clay tablets. Those busy Romans kept prodigious records.

They also got things wrong.

The fact was, anybody who wasn't Roman got vilified whether or not they deserved it. The way the Romans saw it, non-Romans deserved vilification, or worse. Crucifixion, at least. Or lion-chomping.

In one of those primitive, foreign lands that they conquered and then colonized, a group of magick-users called Druids were non-Roman in the extreme. Actually, the Druids could write: witness the Wurzburg Codex. But the Romans didn't like them, so they trashed that version of what Druids believed and did, and wrote their own.

Though human sacrifice played a minor role in Druid tradition, the Romans took artistic license with the popularity of torture and evisceration. They wrote fabulous, detail-loving accounts of how Druid priests constructed enormous figures out of oaken logs and caged living men and women inside, then lit the entire thing on Midsummer's Eve—the precursor to every bonfire since.

They also claimed that the Druids disemboweled

human victims in order to read the future in their entrails.

Which, okay, true.

And that they sacrificed virgins to clear the winter night of devils. That to drive away mists and fogs, said to herald the arrival of the *Tuatha Dé Dannan*—the evil faery born of fog and mist—they kept their virtuous girls screaming for as long as possible, secrets of prolonging agony passed down from father to son.

But the Druids didn't do all that much torture and sacrificing. Only on special occasions.

The Romans also insisted that the evil races dwelling on the benighted isles of Britannia had been completely and utterly destroyed—which, if one thinks about it, is redundant—you're either destroyed or you aren't. At any rate, according to T. Rexus E Pluribus or someone like him, the deformed and terrifying *Fomhóire,* who were the gods of night, and death, and cold, had clashed with the *Tuatha*. They went on to say that everybody died, except for leprechauns.

And that was wrong, and that was something the *Tuatha* took very personally.

A few Roman scribes had died miserable deaths for false reporting. The *Tuatha*—denizens of the air and movers of the mists—had actually won the Last Battle. They wanted people to know that. It was rather stupid of the survivors to make any effort whatsoever to announce that they were still alive, because no one wanted them around. But pride goeth before destruction, and faery were—and still are—prideful if nothing else. But they are plenty else. They are bloodthirsty, ambitious, and evil.

Additionally, the *Fomhóire,* deformed children of the waters, had not been completely destroyed. Their chieftains had been killed, as well as the heirs and heiresses of their crown. But the rest had been exiled, sent to an elsewhere no one else could contact. If they had known about the Phantom Zone of Superman legend, that was what they would have called their new dimension.

All ancient Ireland, not knowing about the exile, and not seeing any of the *Tuatha* around, had prayed that that was the end of faery. To that end, their Druid priests eviscerated innumerable girls and burned astounding numbers of boys alive as sacrifices to luck and destiny.

But no amount of deathdealing changed the facts. The Roman writers did that.

Then, lost in the ether of time and forgetfulness, the *Fomhóire* waited. The Druids got hunted by the Christians, and the *Tuatha* went underground as well. To the delight of the *Fomhóire,* the *Tuatha* became distracted, weak, and frightened. Human beings were making inroads into magicks that would reveal the existence of faery—and the *Tuatha* were terrified. Soon, their secrets would be discovered—spells and protections and the ways to kill them—and mankind would do what the *Fomhóire* had been unable to do: wipe out the *Tuatha*.

With the luxury of observing the situation without being involved in it, the *Fomhóire* grew wise in the ways of the humanity. They plotted for the day they would escape, obliterate first the *Tuatha* and then the humans, and reign supreme over the world, as had been their original destiny.

Distracted by the human menace, even the *Tuatha* forgot about the *Fomhóire*. Their terrifying enemies were actually protected in their distant limbo. Left to their own devices, they honed their powers and waited for just the right moment to return to the world and take what was rightfully theirs . . . which was everything that lived and breathed . . . and could die.

They had nearly succeeded in the nineteenth century, aided by the cursed shapeshifter, Jack. The madman—if man he could be called—was a misbegotten creature, even by *Fomhóire* standards. His parents, Thrial and Brak, had developed a forbidden lust—a *Tuatha* man who loved a *Fomhóire* woman—and she bore him the most hideous infant ever seen in the faery world known as the Hollow Hills of Sidhé.

Even as he was birthed, the baby shapeshifted and changed, his bones bending and molding as he struggled out of his mother. His eyes bulged wildly, the left one like a pox on his cheek. His mouth was enormous, and he was born with teeth. Blood oozed from his hair.

The labor killed his mother. And Thrial, his *Tuatha* father, would have killed him, too, except that the midwife took pity on the misshapen creature and spirited him away, telling his father that he was indeed dead.

She kept him in the cellar of her hovel, stuffing rags into his mouth when visitors came to see her.

There were many such; she was the village wise-woman. She could brew love potions and she could tell the future.

The future she foresaw for the *Tuatha* was very mixed; she tried to tell the elders that they ought to make preparations for war and to learn to live in harmony with human beings. But no one would listen to her.

Then she saw what the boy—whom she had named Thak, and whose name would eventually be pronounced "Jack"—would become, and she wept bitterly. For she knew that this child was indeed a monster, and having saved him, she would now have to kill him.

Great evil would he commit; and generations would speak of his savagery. And in his lust to gain power in the domains of faery, he would be the catalyst that signaled to humans that the final battle had begun—except that it would not occur solely between *Tuatha* and *Fomhóire*. The humans would join in . . . and the humans might very well prevail. As to whether the three races would survive such a cataclysm, she could not be certain. All that she knew was that Jack would start the war.

There was one chance to prevent that future . . . to destroy him now.

She got very drunk, and then she staggered down the cellar steps with a huge knife in her fists.

"Mother," he whispered from the shadows. "Mother, what are you doing? Why are you here?"

"To . . . to tell you that I love you," she stammered.

Her heart was breaking. The life of a wisewoman was very lonely; the other villagers feared her, and no man dared marry her. She had been doomed to a life apart, a life alone . . . until she had taken Thak into her heart, and into her home. As he was cursed, so was she, in a certain sense, and though he had been misshapen and unloved at his birth, she herself had grown to love him.

Mothers do not kill their children easily. Either they are mad to begin with, or go mad from the deed. She knew this. She feared this.

And yet, she knew what she must do.

"If you love me, why are you carrying a knife?" Thak asked her. His voice was filled with anxiety. As he shifted in the darkness, hidden even from her, she heard the clank of his chains. Light from the stairway flashed first on two large links, and then on her knife, as if the very metals spoke in secret code to one another. She did not know what they said. She only knew that she must not fail in her terrible task.

"To . . . to cut your hair and keep you handsome," she replied, her words slurring drunkenly. She staggered, catching herself against the banister, and felt her soul plummet to the hellfires of the *Tuatha* deathplace and back again.

He snorted. "If that is so, why are you weeping?" he asked her. "My darling mother, don't lie to me. You are not here to cut my hair."

She wept harder and said, "You know."

"Yes, I know. Of course I know. You have foreseen it, Mother. I am different. New. I am the only hope of the faery races to rid the earth of human beings."

"Thak, you are a halfling, that is all," she said to

him, her head spinning. Flung across the earthen wall, she saw his nightmarish shape, and her heart broke in pieces for him. Her misguided attempts to save him from the *Tuatha* had bedeviled his mind.

"I am a champion," he insisted. "A god!"

"You must . . . you must stay to the shadows," she said quickly. "Leave well enough alone. You were not born for large things."

"I was born to start a war," he whispered, his voice low and menacing. Without realizing, she took a step away, unnerved by the cold cunning of his words. "Mother, haven't you realized it yet? This halfling whom you bequeathed to the shadows is a new sort of creature. He is a god."

"Oh, my boy," she said urgently. "My boy. I'll bring you up to the sun. It was only to protect you that I kept you hidden away. But I do love you. I love you as if you were my own child."

"You kept me hidden under your heart." Thak began to laugh. The sound froze her blood, for she clearly heard insanity in it.

"Yes, yes, I did," she said eagerly, hoping to reason with him, to find a spark of light inside his restless mind and fan it. "I kept you hidden under my heart."

"Then I will let you keep it."

He sprang at her, pushing her to the ground. She screamed as he towered over her, and she realized that he had broken his chains. Bending over her, she smelled strawberries on his breath and was vaguely baffled—*It's winter now, and there are no strawberries*—and then he grabbed the knife.

"Oh, no," she whispered. She took a breath and awaited pain.

"I will not kill you, Mother. You gave me my life," he said simply.

Then he chained her leg and cuffed her across the face, sending her into temporary darkness while he made his escape.

When Thrial, his father, learned that Thak still lived, he went straight to the midwife's hovel and slew her. He cut off her head and threw it into the river. Downstream, her foster son found it, and lost what little was left of his mind.

There, a *Fomhóire* reconnaissance party discovered him while they were scouting the defenses of the *Tuatha*. Their first impulse was to kill him, but there was so much of their own race in his appearance that they decided to make a pet of him. Gradually they restored his mind as best they could with magicks and special herbs, and he was more than happy to tell them everything he knew about the ways of the *Tuatha* in return for the promise of a new life among the *Fomhóire*.

Then came what the Romans called the Last Battle, and the resultant exile of the *Fomhóire*. Thak was glad of it; it made him feel safer from the hatred of his father's people. Thrial hated Thak, and would slay him if ever he found him alive.

Perhaps it was a coincidence; perhaps it was destiny. But one moon-filled night, when Nemain, the *Fomhóire* Queen of the Gods, was brewing a potion for Balor, their king, the steam from her cauldron encircled Thak as he stood at the perimeter of their prison, staring into a scrying stone at the human lands. He was looking into an oak grove that was shrouded in a heavy fog. There, a ghostly band of Druid priests were busily sacrificing a young maiden. She was bound to a large stone on which were odd symbols.

At the foot of the stone a large dog howled in misery and terror, dodging the kick of one of the Druids.

The leader raised a beautiful curved knife and plunged it into her heart. And in that very moment, a bolt of lightning crashed from the human land through the barrier and scarred Thak through his heart. Some of the mist from Nemain's cauldron entered the wound and congealed with Thak's blood.

He cried out, stumbled forward . . . and tumbled into the oak grove, landing on top of the girl, whose body was convulsing in its death throes.

The Druids fled, screaming. Thak leaped to his feet, unable to find purchase on the slippery, bloody body, and the dog leaped at him, screaming like a human being—

—and both were returned to Thak's own dimension.

The dog became Thak's boon companion, and was found to be a magickal creature. They were inseparable. No one else would dare befriend the madman of the *Fomhóire,* though everyone made sure to be civil and respectful around him.

For hundreds of years, the *Fomhóire* worked on finding the magicks that would allow Thak to escape again.

What they did not realize was that they were assisted in their efforts, by amorphous beings called the First: evil without form, seeking form. Churning like the steam of Nemain's cauldron, roaming in search of hosts, and souls, things to feed on and things to inhabit . . .

They began to work on his filling his subconscious with their viciousness and their brutality.

Those he preyed upon began to write his story.

Some of it was true.

Chapter One

It was a bitter, wet night, and decent folk were escaping indoors, savoring the well-earned delights of hearth and family. Elegantly dressed husbands checked pocket watches as they returned home from their enterprises; wives and ladies' maids sailed in from their endless rounds of visiting and shopping. Aproned nannies supped with their charges, the well-scrubbed, apple-cheeked offspring of the upper classes. Knuckles were rapped, faces were cleaned, and then the heirs and heiresses of the Empire were presented to their parents, who accepted the little ones' dainty kisses. Then off to bed, in nightcaps and nightdresses, snug and smug and very, very safe.

But in Whitechapel, it was another matter.

In Whitechapel, there was no escape.

It was indecent to be poor, and Whitechapel was the poorest part of London. There was no safety here, no lovely homes filled with fancy food and snobby servants; only a vast relief that one had survived another day.

Night was on, fullforce, and it was busy. It was a drunk in an alley gesturing an equally drunk and bitter day laborer forward, taunting, "Come on, then, come on." It was a brute with patched clothes forcing a young girl into a darkened doorway.

It was a monster in a cape with long, sharp knives.

The indecent poor of Whitechapel faced a long, cold night where Death was everyone else on the prowl in the streets, and there was no escape from him—or her—except freezing stiff first and cheating the bastard of the hunt. In Whitechapel there were simply the poor, the victims of the world. Here there were very few wives and husbands—there being little reason to marry—and if anyone in the neighborhood knew someone so grand as an actual nanny, it was a rich relation who had somehow made it out of Whitechapel and got a new accent on, learned how to curtsy and also how to lie about her past.

It was indecent to be poor, and somehow one's own fault, and in one's blood and, therefore, impossible to be rid of. There was naught to be done for poverty save provide the filthy lot with workhouses and poorhouses and debtors' prisons. They could not be improved. Hadn't Christ reassured his fellows, "The poor are with you always"?

Wretched problem, the indecent poor. Maybe the

Butcher of Whitechapel had the right idea, scare them
into better behavior, make them go indoors and off the
streets of a night, or face a hideous demise . . . but
those were words best mumbled out of the side of
one's mouth after the ladies had been excused and the
gentlemen were enjoying their brandies and cards.

What the Butcher—the Ripper—did to the poor
was indecent, but after all . . . the lower classes did
need thinning. There were how many prostitutes in
London this night, perhaps twenty-five thousand?

Shocking.

Intolerable.

At least those unfortunates were all contained elsewhere, away from the feather beds and mobcaps and
nurseries that came from the blessings of good breeding and education.

Contained in hellholes such as Whitechapel, frenzied with Death.

On this December night, Whitechapel teemed with
activity as half-starved men and women struggled to
eke out enough pennies to survive another night.
Gaunt-faced men bartered with ill-tempered pub men
for the leavings of another's supper; boys begged for
scraps, for pennies, for rags to wrap around their
frozen feet. In doorways and alleyways, babes froze in
their mothers' arms.

There was gin everywhere, and the desperate pop-
ulace reeked of it; it stank in the sweat on the brows of
hopeless men half-mad with consumption and hunger.
It spilled on tabletops as men scuffled over cards and
imagined insults. It gave the unfortunate women of

Whitechapel Dutch courage as they strutted down the cobbled streets, beckoning like sirens to the lads, to the men, promising the same thing gin did.

Gin and sex; tears and flopsweat ran in rivulets down the filthy streets, and everything got lost in heavy fogs thick as blankets. Fog was the eiderdown of the lowest classes, the mob; fog was the curtain that shielded their degradation from aristocrats and royals, who also blamed the denizens of Whitechapel for their terrible lot in life. Fog was the wool pulled over the eyes of all Londoners as politicians blamed not the poor, but the Jews, for all the suffering and premature death.

And the poor blamed God.

Somewhere in the bitter night of eight December, 1888, fog was the cloak of a madman who lurked on every street corner, glided silently down every alleyway, knives and torture instruments at the ready. His name drifted like a wisp of nightmare, a twisted handkerchief soaked in blood.

Jack the Ripper.

He had gutted two women, and because they had been whores, the sister bangtails were sure the police would never find him—because the police would never look. They would take their fine, swaggering walks down the streets, accosting the beggar boys and winking at the landladies; then they'd make a few noises about "leads" and "information" and retire to their fine offices to smoke and ruminate . . . and another poor girl would be found in the morning, flies buzzing inside her petticoats, blood congealed beneath her like a mattress thrown in the middle of the street.

Lyin' down on the job: It was a coarse old joke in their line of work when you found a mate of yours had been murdered. It made her death less terrifying to sneer at her, say she got what she deserved, stupid whore. Piece of trash. Only stupid whores got killed. Smart ones got out somehow, got married, got a business going.

Just last night was long enough, and the nightmare that was this awful life would be over.

But not by dying.

No one gave prostitutes respect, not even other prostitutes. Any girl to give up her virtue was a Judas to her sex, no matter how hungry she got or how many starving brothers and sisters waited for the money she made. No one was tougher on a brand-new streetwalker than the older ones . . . because here was another fallen angel, another soiled dove, and it was more disgusting than any proper lady could stand. So them last bits of propriety hated the pretty new ones . . . and then once she got slagged-looking, lost some teeth, reeked of gin—in short, had lost her womanly virtues—then she was a bit of all right, one of the sisters of the streets.

It was the fault of the fog, all the butchering; if there hadn't been any fog last night, there wouldn't have been another murder. The streetwalker's name had been Mary Kelly. What a fool that chit had been, to wander about in the fog, hanging on to gentlemen and promising to do things their fine wives could not even imagine.

What a right fool.

"I 'eard she wasn't all there. In the 'ead," Barbara said. She leaned forward and tapped her skull, paper-thin lids fluttering from all the gin she'd had to drink that night. She still had all her teeth, which were white and fine. Her eyes had gone dead, though; it was the look that said that the streets had already claimed her, though she insisted she had just got to London three weeks before from the north country, and had launched herself in the profession only because her aunt, who was going to teach her how to embroider linen, had died of the influenza.

Elizabeth had known Barbara was lying from the first moment they met.

Elizabeth worked alongside Barbara these nights; explaining that she was too afraid to go on her own. Barbara was grateful for the company. The gentlemen didn't mind; they had no shame when it came to their needs, and the prospect of enjoying the pleasure of more than one doxy—or at least of having her look on—thrilled and excited them.

Still, trade was a little slow tonight, and there were fewer men of the higher classes strolling amongst the general heathenry. Jack had scared them off. Several of the other girls had announced that they were giving up for the evening, and planned to congregate at the Three Bells for as long as they could nurse a single glass of gin.

"We ought to go in, too," Barbara muttered, stamping her feet to warm them. The sad peacock feather in her bright red hair drooped in the wet weather. She had on a low-cut dress of dark pink and a shawl of puce; the ensemble did nothing for her ivory complexion, yet who was Elizabeth to say anything? She was wearing all black, like a widow.

"Can't go in yet," Elizabeth muttered back at her. "Jimmy would have my head on a platter if I came back with nothing but two coppers." She sighed heavily. "You're right not to have a man to answer to, Barbara. All they cause is trouble."

Barbara's smile was sour and mean. It made her look tired and old, and in their trade, that was not good.

"Men. Bleedin' barbarians. Look what they've driven fine girls like us to do. It would be better if we could make our own way in the world without them. All of us." She sniffed. "You're a fool, Elizabeth, to let your Jimmy boss you like 'e does."

"He takes care of me," Elizabeth said quietly. "He's good to me, in his way."

"What, he puts the bruises where the paying customers won't see them?" Barbara huffed and readjusted her shawl around her shoulders.

"No. It's not like that," Elizabeth replied. "You should come and meet him, Barbara. He'd take care of you, I guarantee it."

Barbara raised her chin and sniffed. "I'll never 'ave a man, my fine girl. Save my shillings for myself and someday, take a ship to America and leave this 'ellish place forever." She looked around in disgust . . . and there was much that was disgusting to see.

"America," Elizabeth said wistfully. It was a favorite topic between them, going to America. Elizabeth knew Barbara would never go there, but talking about it passed the time. *And both our days are numbered.* . . .

"I'll go to New York and I'll be a lady, and keep slaves like the Americans." Evidently she did not realize that the Americans weren't allowed to have slaves anymore. "I wants some'n, I'll snap my fingers."

Barbara demonstrated, then shrugged as if she was ashamed of wanting anything more than a doss and a slug of gin, and tucked her hands inside her armpits. "I'm catching my death, Lizzie-lass. Let's go in."

"One more hour," Elizabeth protested, glancing about, surveying the pickings. A few men sauntered along the opposite side of the street, but they appeared to be as poor as she and Barbara were. One had his elbows sticking out of his jacket. The other was covered with grime. Her stomach turned at the thought of his touching her.

She added, "Could be the rich men are still at the theater, that's why they're not about."

"They're not about because they don't want their bellies slit open." Barbara glanced up and down the street. "Cor, with this fog, we couldn't see Jack come up on us if he was ten feet away. It's too dangerous out here." She turned shining eyes to Elizabeth. "Let's go in, lamb. It's not a good night."

Elizabeth shrugged her halfhearted resistance. Then, a rat skittered down the street and she jerked, startled, though God knew she saw more rats in a day in Whitechapel than there were diamonds in Queen Victoria's jewels. Shadows danced in the darkness, making phantoms and nascent nightmares, and she thought about what had happened to the prostitute Mary Kelly last night. The girl had been very young and beautiful—new to the trade—and she'd been gutted like a fish.

It could happen to any girl in Whitechapel, in the dark, in the fog.

"Please, pet. I'm shaking with cold. See?" Barbara held out her hand. "Your Jimmy will understand if you go in. Better a whore who didn't make her lot tonight than a whore who'll never earn another penny."

"Oh, all right, then," Elizabeth said, sighing.

Elizabeth turned to the right toward the main street, where the Three Bells and its noise and warmth and gin waited like a half-drunk granny.

"Not that way," Barbara admonished, shaking her head. "There's a shorter way down this alley."

She smiled and gestured for Elizabeth to join her as she entered a low, narrow street with an overhanging second story like a Roman arch. The windows were all dark.

"One of my customers showed it to me the other night. We can be at the Three Bells inside of ten minutes and avoid them big carriages and all the horse dung."

"If you're sure, Barbara," Elizabeth said.

"I'd stake my life on it," Barbara replied.

"Makes no difference to me." Elizabeth looked around, taking note of how deserted the street was. The only sound was the echo of their shoes on the cobblestones. She glanced up at the darkened windows and frowned.

"But you know, Barbara, if the Ripper comes down this way, there'll be no one to hear us. No bobbies."

"They wouldn't come for us no matter if he attacked us inside St. Paul's," Barbara scoffed. "We're whores. And he'll not come here," she added, sounding unconvinced. "The pickins are too slim."

"He only needs one to do his devilry," Elizabeth answered uneasily.

The other bangtail drew Elizabeth into the narrow alley. A cat squalled and darted away, landing in a crate of rotten cabbage that stank to high heaven. Faint music sounded, an accordion, and Elizabeth thought of her father, who had been blinded in the war and had played a hurdy-gurdy on a street corner until he died seven years ago, when she had been all of nine.

Barbara shivered as she looked right and left. "He'll not come in the next ten minutes, anyway. And by then we'll be safe and sound inside the Three Bells."

Elizabeth demurred as Barbara took another step into the alley. "It doesn't feel right. It's not safe. It's too dark."

"Come on. Don't be such a baby." Barbara gritted her teeth. She grabbed Elizabeth's arm and gave it a tug. "You haven't any brass, Lizzie. That's been your trouble in life. Why you 'aven't made anything of yourself."

"And you have?" Elizabeth tossed back. "You're a bleeding duchess, yeah? With all your fine talk of America and your servants?"

"Oh, now you've done it. You've gone and vexed me," Barbara said in a low, dangerous voice.

Half-turning, she took a step away from Elizabeth. Her face was averted; Elizabeth cocked her head, watching the other woman, waiting to see what she was about.

She hadn't long to wait.

Barbara hissed, "You've vexed me indeed," and

showed Elizabeth a terrifying face, a nightmare image of monstrous evil. "Say you're sorry before I kill you."

"I . . ." Elizabeth stumbled backward, catching her balance against the grimy wall behind her. She wiped her hand on her skirt.

"Say it!" Barbara threatened, advancing on her.

Elizabeth's eyes widened. "I'm so sorry."

The monster smiled. "Apology accepted, me girl. And now . . ."

"But not sorry enough," Elizabeth continued, moving her hand into the hidden pocket and drawing out a finely carved wooden stake.

The vampire's eyes went wide. "Cor, it's you, ain't it! Oh, my stars, my stars, I thought you was a story!"

"Yes, I'm the Slayer," Elizabeth affirmed, gathering up her skirts with her free hand as Barbara slowly backed away. It was her turn to advance. Her training took hold as she assessed her surroundings: crates of garbage, made of wood; lights still out in all the windows; no footfalls, no sense of anything else to observe their mad, fatal dance.

"We was walking the streets together," Barbara lamented. "We was mates, you 'n' me."

"Yeah, you were walking so you could rip open some poor sod's throat," Elizabeth said coldly.

"And you, so you could turn me into a pile of dust." Barbara's glowing eyes darted left, right, as if she was seeking a way to escape. Elizabeth had already assured herself that there was nowhere for the vampire to go.

"I only take the bad ones," Barbara whined. "The

sick ones. Them that God's got his hooks into already, going to die soon, anyway."

Elizabeth said nothing, only prepared to strike. She put herself in the defensive posture her Watcher, Sir James—the "Jimmy" of their nightly conversations—had taught her, and took a moment to think of her mother, as she always did before facing death head-on.

The vampire, sensing that her end was near, nervously licked her lips and half-raised her hands in supplication. "No! Don't! Please, mistress! I . . . I can 'elp you," she said brightly. "I know who Jack the Ripper is, see—'e's one of us. A vampire." She kept her brows raised, her eyes innocent. On her vampiric face, it was almost comical to see.

Elizabeth laughed mirthlessly. It was as if Barbara had read her mind—or overheard her heated conversation with Sir James earlier in the day. He had forbidden Elizabeth any action against the Ripper, no matter how hard she argued that no human being could do the things he had done, and therefore, he must be a demon. There was no proof of that, and so, she could not declare war on him.

"I *wish* that Jack was a vampire," she now told Barbara. "Then I could have a chance at him. As it is, they say he's a human monster, and I can't touch him."

Despite her terrifying countenance, the vampire looked horribly dashed, as if she had actually expected her offer to save her life. "Well, don't take it out on me. It ain't me fault that he's not a vampire," she pleaded. "I'd have turned him right quick . . ." She thought the better of that. "That is to say, I'd have butchered him, Lizzie. I still can do it. I'll hunt him for you."

Elizabeth said nothing, only moved slowly forward, waiting for her chance to plunge the stake directly into Barbara's unbeating, vampiric heart.

This one is for my father, she thought. He'd been killed by a vampire, though of course Elizabeth had not known that at the time. Throat torn out, blood all gone . . . now she knew the signs. Sir James had assured her that the vampire who had savaged him had died, and that her father had not been transformed into one himself . . . but she knew better now than to believe much that he had told her. Horrible as it was to contemplate, her father might yet walk these streets as a vampire himself.

Barbara tried another tack, smiling sweetly and holding out her hands. "I been a bit of all right to walk with, eh? Ain't done nothing to try to harm you in the entire week we been together. I been a good friend to you, shared my gin with you, din't I?"

"You're nothing to me," Elizabeth replied coldly, "except something that I have to kill."

At that, Barbara turned tail and tried to run. But Elizabeth pushed off with her high-button shoes and launched herself at the vampire, grabbing her around the waist as the two dove straight for the pavement. Barbara landed with an ungainly thump; Elizabeth was on top of her and turning her over as fast as she could, grabbing her shoulder, pinning her, and raising her stake high over her head.

"'Elp!" Barbara shrieked to the walls, to the alley. "It's Jack! 'E's going to kill me!"

"No one is coming," Elizabeth assured her, although she listened for the clatter of footsteps, the bleat of a bobby's whistle. There were none. She was still alone with the vampire. "No one is going to save you."

"No, it is Jack! 'Tis! 'E's behind you! Mistress Lizzie, 'e's behind you!" Barbara screamed, her gaze darting from the pointed end of the stake to a place past Elizabeth's shoulder and back again. "I can save you from 'im, only let me up. *Please let me up!*"

Elizabeth ignored her and brought the stake down, pushing it into the dead flesh, ramming it home through the dead heart.

The vampire shrieked, and then she exploded into a shower of dust.

At the same instant, in case her warning had been true and the Ripper lurked behind her, Elizabeth leaped to her feet and whirled around, the stake held out like a sword.

There was no one in the alley . . . save the Slayer herself.

With no one to see her, Elizabeth crumpled back onto the rough, wet stones. She leaned her weight on her palms and retched violently. Bile and gin came up, and she was terribly sick to her stomach. Her forehead beaded with sweat. Then the tears came, harsh and wild. As she sobbed, she shook all over, head to toe, contorting so badly that one coming upon her might assume her to be palsied.

But she wasn't palsied. She was terrified.

Elizabeth the Vampire Slayer was sick to death . . . with fear.

Sir James would be so disgusted with me, she thought, and of course the thought brought no comfort. He had been her Watcher for an entire year, and he had no sympathy for her lamentable condition. Indeed, it was so unheard of for a Slayer to be a coward that there was nothing about it in the texts.

"Blood will out," she had once heard him say, when discussing the problem with another member of the esteemed Watchers Council. She'd burned with shame; her family had been very common. Indeed, the Watchers Council of Britain had declared themselves quite amazed that such a low-class chit had been called to be the Slayer. It wasn't at all what they'd been led to expect from their various readings and predictions.

"Well, Our Lord and Savior was a Jew, if one considers the matter," Lord Morchwood had declared. "And yet, He turned out to be quite a good sort."

Elizabeth was shocked, and yet not surprised. None of the men present had realized that she, Elizabeth, had followed Sir James to the Council Headquarters and was now spying on their privy council. There were thirteen of them at a long, rectangular table of deep wood set with candles and sharply cut crystal goblets, the Prime Minister William Gladstone at one end, and Sir James at the other.

At his words about Jesus and Jews, the others chuckled—a few somewhat uncomfortably, as Gladstone's predecessor, Benjamin Disraeli, had been a Jew, and one should not speak ill of the dead.

She wondered if the others knew, as she did, that Gladstone spent a great deal of time attempting to rehabilitate prostitutes—that he loved looking at them and speaking to them, but was so ashamed of his vice that he would whip himself before his meetings with them, and never actually employed them for their services. But he cloaked his desire with trying to "help" them, and all the ladies of the night knew what he was about.

Cheap bastard. Many a fallen woman she had met on her patrols had complained of being given a meal and a glass of wine, then made to listen to his theories about rehabilitation. His lectures centered on learning a trade that a thousand women could do better already, and were starving to death at it—making lace, running a flower stand—or marrying brutish men who would spend all their wages on gin and beat them when they got home.

One girl, Annette, had shocked the great man by declaring, "Sir Bill, I'd rather hang meself than do as you suggest. In fact, give me tuppence for the rope and I'll be off, thank you very much."

Elizabeth's musings were disturbed when one of the Council members whose identity she didn't know sympathetically patted Sir James on the shoulder.

"My condolences, James," the man drawled. "You've waited a long time for this opportunity. It was your turn to guide and mold a Slayer, and when the other died, I raised a glass to you, knowing your girl was Chosen. Who would have known she would turn out to be such a coward? Bad luck."

The others nodded, and Elizabeth flooded with shame.

"One can only hope she'll die soon, and we'll have another go at a brighter girl," Lord Morchwood put in as he sipped from his fancy goblet. "But, of course, your candle will have burned out as well, James. I've never heard of a Watcher who's had more than one Slayer to look after."

"Yes, well, there it is." James sighed deeply, looking very disappointed with his unfortunate lot in life. "Perhaps she'll buck up eventually. After all, she *is* British."

"One assumes, at any rate," Gladstone remarked.

Hidden in the shadows of the Council chamber, hot tears washed down Elizabeth's face and she had had to bite her fist to keep from crying aloud. She had never felt more alone.

When she'd been told that she was the Slayer, and had been presented to the handsome young aristocrat who was to look after her . . . well, she had counted herself a lucky girl. Alone, a penniless orphan and trying hard to help her mam keep the little ones from starving . . . it seemed like a novel by Charles Dickens—like *Oliver Twist*. Elizabeth had been given beautiful clothes and her own room; she had thought she'd gone to heaven.

Then her training had begun, and she'd had to face her very first vampire. It had all gone very badly, and Sir James had shouted at her, "I ought to have you whipped! Get out of my sight!"

She had thought of doing herself in. It was an agony to be judged such a horrid failure . . . and all because of her blasted cowardice . . . and then, to hear how ashamed he was of her . . . it was more than she could bear.

And so she had given it her all, tried hard to find courage deep within herself. But there was none. She was terrified of the vampires and demons that she was pledged to kill. She rarely slept without laudanum, and she never went out on patrol without first fortifying herself with a bit of drink. None of it helped. The one hundredth night of slaying had held every bit as much fear as the first.

Now, in the foul alley way, she looked around to see if anyone had seen her, then she awkwardly got to her feet and leaned against the wall of the nearest building. She was shaky and drained, but she knew she had to report to Sir James as soon as possible. He always wanted to hear about her evening patrols; she got the distinct feeling that he kept careful track of her successes, as if he had to prove to someone—either the Council or himself—that she was worth keeping around. Those were questions she could not answer. Nor was she certain that she really wanted to know the answers.

But she had done her best tonight, for Queen and country; in a filthy street in the worst part of London, she had destroyed a vampire she had walked beside for an entire week, and she had lived to tell the tale.

Is that not brave? Am I such a coward, then?

Still trembling with fear, the Slayer moved back into the teeming throngs of the indecent poor.

She walked unsteadily, and her breath came with difficulty. A man dressed in rags leered at her and made an indecent proposal. A woman carrying a pale infant perhaps a year old yanked at Elizabeth's sleeve and demanded money for milk.

"I haven't got any," the Slayer said truthfully as she glanced down pitifully at the child. It was wrapped in nothing but a dirty, tattered shawl. Its eyes were closed, its mouth slack. "I'm so sorry."

"Damn your eyes, you 'eartless strumpet," the woman hissed, and moved on. As Elizabeth watched them go, the child's arm slipped loose from the shawl and dangled limply in the frigid air. It was thin, and frail; a lump formed in her throat as she realized that it was quite probable that the babe would die in the night, from the cold and want of milk.

I'll go ask Sir James to give me some money, and then I'll find her, she thought. But that was utterly ridiculous. She would never see that woman again if she let her go.

"Wait!" she called to the mother, thinking that she would ask her to accompany her home, and demand that Sir James give her some money directly.

But the crowd on the street had already swallowed the woman up. Elizabeth could see her nowhere.

She ran in the direction she had last seen her, scanning the gaunt, gray faces, the eyes bright with fever and gin; and then she saw—

—monstrous—

—a flash of something on a man's passing face; something sinister and very evil. Her heart skipped a beat and she whirled around, her Slayer's reflexes propelling her to follow him. "Sir," she said, and grabbed his sleeve.

But when he turned around, nothing was there but a disinterested frown and a single raised eyebrow. Save for the red sheen of his cheeks, there was nothing remarkable about the man who looked at her as if he assumed she was a bangtail about to proposition him.

She let go of his sleeve and stumbled backward. Had she imagined the evil she'd seen there?

"What, are you mad?" he demanded, drawing his coat around himself and stomping away.

As she watched him go, a great swirl of fog rushed over the scene, as if hurrying to meet him. Apparently unaware, he stalked into it, and the thick blanket of white concealed him from Elizabeth's view.

The fog kept coming, mercilessly so, covering everyone like a shower of new-fallen snow. Elizabeth realized she would see neither the man nor the woman with the hungry baby in her arms, and felt unaccountably defeated.

Wearily, she slipped her hands under her armpits as the vampire Barbara had done, and headed for home, no less afraid, and dispirited to boot.

Sunnydale

Just like fashions, various types of the bad go in, go out. It's almost like the fashion show of evil. One year, it's lots of vampires; one year, it's those weird Knights and their obsession with Dawn. But through it all, Sunnydale stayed in the number one spot of Ten Most Inconveniently Evil Places in This Dimension.

Inconvenient, that was, if someone who happened to be tagged for Slayer duty actually wanted to have a life. . . .

Once known as *Boca del Infierno,* or "Mouth of

Hell," Sunnydale had been founded over two hundred years ago by some very unlucky Spaniards who'd had the foresight to name their town but not to move on and live somewhere else. The happier "Sunnydale" name came later.

Some early Sunnydalians had wondered why the founding *padres* opted to stay, once they had decided that the town they were building had anything to do with hell at all, but no matter. Any of the old-timers who had the brains to ponder that notion were ashes now, and beyond caring what evil crawled out of the hole in the ground beneath the ruins of Sunnydale High School.

Buffy had been a student at Sunnydale's old high school, and Willow and Xander, too. They were Class of 1999, end of an era in so many ways. Anya—formerly Anyanka, the vengeance demon— had started dating Xander and decided to resume doing so after he survived the apocalyptic battle with the Mayor. Buffy, Xander, Willow, and their class-mates had also prevailed, for the most part, and now, here they were . . . still in Sunnydale and still battling things that crawled out of the Hellmouth.

Oh, yeah, and Spike was back in Sunnydale, too, after a great run with Dru, taking over the Master's gig from the Anointed One. But he hadn't been able to stay out of trouble, and now he was fully chipped by Buffy's old boyfriend's secret government ops and unable to hurt humans.

Now Anya, Xander, Spike, and Tara were sitting on gravestones because the grass was too wet, and

Xander was humming an old folk song to himself to while away the hours.

"'And the something something something, just to keep her from the foggy, foggy dew.'"

"You shouldn't sing songs you don't know the words to," Anya said irritably. "It's a waste of time. Which is precious."

"Are we having another 'Oh, my God, I'm dying inch by inch, let me freak out' moment?" Spike asked, sounding even more irritable than Anya. "Because if that's the case, I'll pack up my old kit bag and head back to the crypt."

"Shut up, Spike," Anya snapped.

"It's a great old song," Xander pressed. "It's about some guy who has sex with a fair young maid in order to save her from the foggy, foggy dew. Y'know, just dew it. Dew wah, dew wah."

"*Please.* Forbear," Spike growled. "I'd like to keep down my supper."

"Rat goulash?" Xander sniped.

Spike drew himself up. "For your information, I—"

"—would rather not hear about it," Tara cut in. "All right?"

"All right. How about this? 'Take me out to the Hellmouth, take me out to the graves,'" Xander sang. "'Buy me some garlic and Cracker—'"

"Shut up, Xander," Anya and Spike chorused.

"Hey," Xander said. "I can sing if I—"

"No, mate, you can't." Spike rolled his eyes. "That's the point."

Buffy glared at the lot of them—or rather, at the

blurry shapes she could barely make out in the thick, gray fog. Since moving to Sunnydale, she could not recall such a dense fog as they had tonight. It made it far more interesting—*Slayerese for dangerous*—to hunt for the Congara demon that had been terrorizing the neighborhood surrounding Waverly Park. The cemetery was on the other side, and Buffy was hoping that tonight it would show, trying to eviscerate something, and wind up dead.

"Will *all* of you please shut up?" she demanded of the blurry shapes. They sort of kind of moved, shifting on their perches, and she had a flash of inspiration for something new at Disneyland that would be called the Haunted Tiki Room. "I need it quiet."

"We're not fishing at the old swimming hole, Buffy," Spike said archly. "Nothing to scare away, y'know? Congara demons are deaf."

"Then Congara demons are luckier than we are," Anya grumbled.

"Gee, Ahn," Xander said. "I was just singing." He sounded puzzled. "You usually like my singing."

As Buffy resumed her patrol along the perimeter, Anya said, "I'm sorry, Xander. Sitting here in the fog waiting for something that's got a bigger mouth than it has a body is making me irritable, and the discordant notes you're hitting are adding to the mix. Plus"—she took a breath, then lowered her voice—"there are wild bunnies in the park."

She gestured helplessly, her mouth a baby pout with the lower lip thrust forward. "They can get through the chain-link fence. I've seen it before."

"Ah. Understood," Xander said sympathetically. "Bunny jitters."

"Bunny jitters," she agreed. "I don't know what Spike's excuse is for being so cranky."

"There is no excuse for Spike," Xander said, and chuckled goofily.

Buffy allowed a quick grin to pass over her features before she got all serious face again. *My friends. I think I'll keep 'em. Even if they are kinda wacky.*

She took another few steps before she realized that yet more fog was rolling in, curling and falling like a phantom ocean as it headed straight toward her. She raised her brows and tucked in her chin, bracing herself for the first chilly wave, then snorted in derision— *it's only fog*—and met it head on, walking directly into it. And . . . it was only fog.

But more than bunnies could be hiding in it.

Her beloved crossbow was in her hands, and she had a quiver of bolts at the ready. Plus, a stake tucked into the belt of her stylin' black leather pants.

Which are clinging to me like ew, wet dead things, she thought. *Note to self: In fog, stick to wearing something that breathes. Not literally, of course. Because that would be very gross.*

Then, in the abundant blankets of white thickness, something brushed her hand. Something that was not a cute rabbit or other friendly graveyard mammal, but sharp and jagged, something that cut her fingers with a quick, mean slice and sent her into attack mode. Without a moment's hesitation, she let fly a crossbow bolt.

A high-pitched, inhuman wail pierced the night, and Buffy sprang into classic Slayer attack mode. She bounded forward toward the sound, executed a shoulder-high sidekick that made impact with a solid mass, and followed it with a back kick. The double action pushed the mass off its center of gravity. It wailed again and moved away.

Buffy pursued it, finding it again with the heel of her boot as she kicked it again, and again.

"Need help?" Xander called.

"Got it!" she grunted.

However, whatever it was, she couldn't see it, and that was freaking her out a little. Still, dead demon she couldn't see was better than living demon she could see. So she kicked it again for good measure. And again and again and again. She was a whirl of total againness.

Then it wasn't there again. Buffy shot forward, did a roundhouse, did a sidekick. She impacted with nothing. *Huh.*

Slayers had a spider-sense about creatures of the bad, and Buffy knew without a doubt that this one had checked out of her air space.

Still, just to be sure that she was right about that—*okay, with one small doubt for Slayer kind*—she hunkered down and scrabbled forward, aiming her crossbow low. There was nothing in her path. She zigzagged left and right, raising her crossbow like Riley on Initiative-style patrol. She was still finding no obstacle that would indicate she'd wounded it so badly, it had collapsed.

Maybe it flew away.

"Can it fly?" she shouted.

"No!" Spike bellowed back. "Not if it's a Congara."

Good.

"Then again, it could be something else. One of them zingy things from Australia, rips your head off in midflight," he added, half to himself. "Or an eye-plucker." He chuckled. "Haven't seen a good eye-plucker since Dru and me—"

"Can they dematerialize?" she cut in.

"Nope," he answered. "What's up? You lose the bloody thing?"

She scowled as she tried to scoop away the fog. No go; she couldn't cut a swathe through it, nor even thin it out well enough to see. She crept swaddled in it like a mummy. And a blind mummy at that.

"I didn't lose it," she retorted. "It left."

"Left," Spike echoed, snorting.

"Yes." Buffy straightened her shoulders. "Left. Took a hike. Vamoosed."

"Um, tonight's the sixth moon after the Horizon of Osiris," Tara piped up. "If it's a Congara, it's got to kill six living things tonight in order to survive for another thousand years."

"Well, we know it's killed at least one," Buffy muttered. Coming home from the Magic Box, Buffy had nearly stepped on—or in—one very savaged tiny baby possum in the middle of Revello Drive.

Little possum, but that was enough for Buffy to send Dawn home. That, and a massive math test Dawn was supposed to study for tonight. Dawn was not loving the order, but Willow had volunteered to go with her, and

Dawnie was much cheered by that. She adored Willow.

Satisfied that Dawn would be safe, Buffy had returned to the Magic Box to find Xander and Anya arguing about something. Upon hearing about the possum, Xander had eagerly offered to help Buffy patrol for its eviscerator.

"You're just trying to avoid the subject," Anya had flung at him.

"Subject?" Buffy had queried, curious.

Anya frowned in Buffy's general direction. "I'm not allowed to talk to anyone about it," she bit off.

"On our way out the door?" Xander begged Buffy.

"I'll go, too," Anya informed them. "There is nothing left to dust and I've counted the money twice." She sighed. "When I was a vengeance demon, I'd go torture some man horribly, in the mood I'm in."

"Yay?" Xander said weakly.

"Come on," Buffy told them. "If there's a trail, I don't want it to grow cold." Maybe they would kiss and make up. Maybe not.

"Is the possum still fresh?" Xander asked now.

"Why? Are you hungry?" Anya said darkly.

Buffy was sorry she'd invited them. They had been more with the bickering than the hunting and lurking. Then Spike had lumbered out of his crypt like a bear out of hibernation, announcing that he was bored—and up for killin' things, too.

Buffy wondered if Willow's magicks could help relocate this thing. So far, Tara hadn't been able to do much on her own. But there was the whole keeping-them-separated thing. Tara and Willow were still splitsville.

Buffy swept forward, then cut figure eights, then finally jogged the perimeter of the cemetery. The others had gotten quiet; all she heard were her own footfalls and her breathing. If anything else was out here, it was doing a good job of playing dead, squished possum.

As she trotted on, she stumbled over what was probably a chunk of broken gravestone, caught her balance, and continued on. She was getting bored, and her fingers hurt. She needed to clean them and slap some bandages on her cuts. And she was cold.

Somewhere behind her, Spike drawled, "That's it, then. Fun's over. I'm packing it in."

"Quitter," Xander flung at him. Then he whined, "Buffy, can we go, too? Maybe Tara can whip up a spell to track this puppy. But otherwise, seems to me you're gonna be spending all night running in circles. And my butt is wet."

"I have to agree with him, even though what he's saying is wimpy," Anya said. "My butt is wet, too, but *I* didn't complain or ask to leave," she added.

Buffy heard Spike chuckle.

"Anya, I'm not being wimpy," Xander insisted. "Just practical. We're going to get pneumonia out here."

"We are not, and you *are* being wimpy," Anya shot back.

"Hear, hear," Spike said. "Demon girl's got a point."

"Could we discuss this at home?" Xander asked his one true love-demon. "And could you please think about what you're saying in front of other people and . . . things?"

"Hey," Spike protested. "No need to get personal."

"You *are* a thing," Anya informed him. Then she said to Xander, "Every group needs the deadpan newbie who says what everyone else is thinking. I read it in your new issue of *Starlog*. In the bathroom. I'm your Seven of Nine, so to speak. Except for the enormous breasts. Well, my breasts aren't all that small, but—"

"Ahn," Xander begged.

Spike snorted.

"It is getting a little cold out here," Tara ventured. "Maybe we should go."

Trust Tara to try to smooth things over.

"As of course we're speaking of nippy," Spike drawled wickedly.

Trust Spike to try to rough them up again.

Buffy wasn't pleased at the prospect of giving up the hunt, but on the other hand, she wasn't sure there was anything left to hunt inside the Shady Hill Cemetery. *It could even have popped into another dimension,* she reminded herself. *This is Sunnydale, after all.*

"All right. Let's go home," she said.

No one moved. Then Anya cleared her throat.

"You must carry me, Xander," Anya announced. "In case there are . . . you-know-what's." She lowered her voice. "I promise I won't try to hurt you."

"Then, yay," Xander replied.

"The only good bunny is a dead bunny," Anya continued, to noises of lifting and arranging. Buffy assumed she was making herself comfortable in the arms of her boyfriend. This was the Anya-Xander version of making up if she had ever seen—or heard—it.

One mission accomplished, she thought happily.

"Take it indoors," Buffy suggested, knowing that she sounded cranky. But she did have some crankiness mixed in with the joy of her friends' makeup makeout session. For all she knew, the Congara demon had five more kills to make tonight.

Which will be a better score than me tonight. Congara Demon six . . . the Slayer a big fat zero.

The group bunched up and began to walk. Buffy turned on her flashlight, and the others followed suit. It was weird to see their faces disappear and reappear as they walked through the billows of fog. It was like a bad mummy movie. Shamble, shamble, shamble, eek, there's someone's face again.

Never got those movies, Buffy thought. *The Mummy could barely walk. How come he always caught up with people who were running for their lives? What was that all about, some kind of death metaphor?*

"Are you going home, too, Buffy?" Tara asked. "Because I—I'm not . . . I mean, I'll be going back to my place, and . . ." She trailed off, looking forlorn.

"We'll drive you home," Xander told her, giving her a brief smile. "Our car's at Buffy's house."

"Oh." Tara looked anxious.

"Way out at the curb, not even the driveway. We'll just leave," Xander promised her. "We won't go in."

"Th-thanks," Tara managed. She sighed. "I'm sorry."

"Nothing to be sorry about," Anya assured Tara. "Willow's using too much magick. You want her to stop. It's just like in Al-Anon." She shrugged. "I had a boyfriend with a problem."

"Yeah. Couldn't sing," Spike said. "Drove you to the bottle."

They walked along, and Buffy moved over close to Tara. She could practically feel the tension coming off the Wicca. Waves of it, the same as Willow whenever Tara's name was mentioned. They both missed each other terribly. It was such a sad situation.

"She's doing well," Buffy said softly, deciding not to add that Willow had used magicks in the cave earlier that evening. "You'd be . . . I'm . . . really proud of her."

"Good," Tara said mournfully. The corners of her mouth pulled up in a weak smile. "That's really good."

"Speakin' of twelve steps," Spike said.

"I'll make sure you guys get back okay. But then I'm coming back out." Buffy flushed hard, knowing that Spike was processing that information and making plans. *And God help me, so am I.* "Something's up tonight," she added defensively. "Slayer-sense still tingling."

From Spike's quarter came another wicked chuckle, and she flushed to her roots. But luckily no one could see her roots, on account of the fog.

And all she saw of Spike was his white hair and black duster as it moved through the thick blankets of muted gray. Focusing on his duster, she thought of another vampire who had worn one and how it had wafted behind him when he walked, when he fought beside her; a very different vampire, a different sort of addiction . . .

Tara nodded. "I feel it, too," she said, glancing around. "This fog is weird. It's so thick. I think it's been magickally created."

"We get fogs," Spike said, sounding bored. "We've always gotten fogs. We're near the coast. Hence, fogs. Pea soup."

"Not like this," Buffy gritted. "We're not in London, Toto."

"Hey," Spike protested. "No need to get snotty."

"The fog is hiding the bunnies," Anya muttered, turning the conversation back to more important things. She looked hard at Buffy. Her dark eyes were troubled. "You *will* protect us from the bunnies, won't you?"

Buffy crossed her heart. "Not for nothing am I called Buffy the Bunny Slayer," she quipped.

"Oh, I thought your *name* was Bunny," Xander returned. "Bunny the Vampire Slayer."

"It's my domain name," Buffy volleyed, remembering the good old days with Xander of riff, counter-riff, double-riff. Everything had been simpler back when he was an angry young man and she was oblivious to the fact that he had a crush on her and Willow ended up sobbing in the bathroom when he lost his virginity with Faith.

Okay, maybe not simpler.

While Anya processed their exchange, obviously trying to figure out if they were mocking her, Xander said, "We'll just give the evil rabbits to Spike. He looks thirsty."

"They're all evil," Anya said anxiously.

"Ha bloody ha," Spike glowered. "Taunt me all you want, Harris, but when I get this chip out of my head . . ."

"Taunting now," Xander announced. He smiled pleasantly at Spike.

If looks could kill . . . Spike's head would explode.

The creature—not at all a Congara, not at all—panted, then glanced up lovingly at its master. Jack stroked the fur of the Hound as the two stood on the rooftop of the Slayer's home, watching the progress of the small-boned, very lovely blonde as she and her band approached. She was loaded down with a weapons satchel and a number of well-meaning friends.

"Very good," Jack said, smiling.

The friends would help slow her down as he and she began the dance. Their presence would probably make it possible for him to kill her off very soon. On the other hand, Jack had learned not to miscalculate the strength of a Slayer. That last time, in London . . . he shrugged. Huge mistake.

That was then. This is now.

And I am back in the delicious and strange world of human beings.

It was true that he had once served the dark God Balor and his Goddess, Nemain, and of his people, the *Fomhóire,* who had taken such good care of him all those decades. True that the *Fomhóire* believed he still answered only to them.

But the fact was, now that he had drifted back into this world, he saw what astonishing changes had come about. The British Empire was dead. The Slayer was an American.

The people of the New World had many ways foreign to those who had come from the Aulde Sod.

The old Gods are . . . the old Gods. Outdated and useless. They cannot hope to lead in a world such as this one has become. But I . . .

. . . I was born to be the champion of the darkness, those whose forms can change with the years. Those who long to come over because their own dimensions are so excruciatingly unchanging and dull.

I brought terror to humans back in London a century ago. I shall do so again. And I shall lead this world into hell, smiling and singing my own processional hymn as my minions join me from more hell dimensions than there are in all philosophy.

Here, in this time and place, I am a god, as I told my old foster mother.

And I shall wipe these creatures from my lands.

Smiling to himself, he watched the tall, dark-haired boy. The one called Xander. *Muscular lad, that.* He'd be a fighter, maybe present a small challenge when the death-dealing came. And the shy blonde with the stammer. So very sweet. Had some magicks, had some power. She, too, might prove interesting.

Of course, in the end, they would both die.

He made kissing noises at the Hound, who slathered a combination of mucus and blood. "I need a nightcap. Let's go kill something."

As smoke drifted from its mad, vacant eyes, the Hound chuffed eagerly.

Jack closed his eyes and murmured a few words in the ancient tongue. The fog in the cemetery rushed up to them, like the ivory-limbed arms of lovesick women, stretching and extending to wrap lovingly around them, master and Hound. The fog clung to the two, enveloping them; thick waves and piles and blankets of the stuff. Fog such as Sunnydale had never seen.

But Sunnydale would see more of it. Much, much more. *And then, in the madness that it brings . . .*

Jack smiled in delicious anticipation.

The Hound chuffed again.

The fog increased, thickened, increased again. He remembered the Druids in the grove with a fondness he usually reserved for the dog, and sighed.

"I usher in the new millennium," Jack chuckled.

He raised his hands into the air.

And then the two were gone.

Chapter Two

London, 1888

Spike kept his hand over Dru's mouth during the murder of Barbara the vampire trollop. She struggled and wept, helpless to stop the slaughter of her newest darling. Waves of hatred and helplessness radiated from her.

Spike was incredibly aroused, and held her tight.

As soon as the damnable Slayer had flounced away, Barbara's vampire sire threw herself out of the darkened window overlooking the alley and landed, sobbing, in a shower of glass on top of the ashes that had been her lil' sweetling.

"Dru! No!" shouted her own grandsire, the exquisite Darla, who leaned out of the broken window and glared at the young, mad vampire.

Darla the vampire was dressed in a black off-the-shoulder ball gown, her blond hair swept off her milky white shoulders and impossibly long neck. Jet beads caressed her throat, and black feathers curled in her hair to kiss her cheek. Her white arms were swathed in long black gloves, and a black shawl spread across her bustle, which was decorated beneath its fullness with a satin red rose.

The white-haired Spike, the newest-made of the four; and Angelus, Darla's lover, whom she herself had changed joined her at the window. All had been witness to the killing. All had studied the Slayer's technique . . . and had seen the bizarre transformation that had come over her once Barbara had been dispatched.

She's terrified, Darla had thought, intrigued. Then she had grinned. *She's smarter than most of them. This will be fun.*

Angelus and Spike looked on, both dashing in evening clothes. The four vampires had been to the opera, to see Gounod's *Faust.* Drusilla had been all eyes and gasps, losing track of the fact that what they were watching was a mere entertainment, until Spike had had to physically restrain her from leaping onto the stage and biting the naughty tenor on the neck.

Now, as Drusilla emoted the tragic bel canto of grief, Angelus vamped. Smoldering with anger, he leaned out of the window and shouted, "Hush! Whsst with that noise!"

Spike chuckled and gave him a sidelong glance.

"Relax, Angelus," he said in his affected Cockney accent. Since his change, he enjoyed playing the rough-

and-tumble jape, but the truth was that the soul that had left him had been gentle, poetic, and far more middle-class than his current accent revealed. "It doesn't matter how loud she weeps. No one'll come runnin' to see what the fuss is all about. This is Whitechapel, after all. Besides which, my Dru can take on a proper mob and come out of it the victor. You seen her do it."

Darla pulled her fan from her reticule, swept it open, and laid it against her bodice as she smiled up at the dark-haired, brooding vampire. Seeing the light gleam in Angelus's glowing eyes, she leaned her head against his chest and looked up lustily at him. "Angelus isn't worried about that, are you, my boy? About the noise. Or a mob. His anger is for the Slayer."

"I hate her." Angelus gritted out, balling his fists. "I hate this one. I want to take her down."

"You hate them all," Darla said adoringly.

"This one in particular," Angelus bit off. "She's killing our new ones left and right."

"She 'as been thinning our ranks," Spike considered, as the three continued to watch Drusilla's paroxysm of grief. She was howling now, like a sad little puppy, and it was quite a pitiful sound. Anyone who heard it would pay it no mind; litters by the dozens howled so in Whitechapel, starving of a cold winter's night. No one had the resources to waste a moment of sympathy—or a bit of a meat bone—on a mere mongrel.

"Drusilla's been making too many new ones as it is," Darla said. "It's been more difficult for us to hunt. People are frightened."

"That's because of the Ripper, not Dru," Spike put

in. "More folks stayin' indoors of a night, scared of their own shadows." He shook his head. "They had any brains, they'd send the Slayer after him."

"She can't," Darla reminded him. "The Ripper is a human being. She's not allowed to kill her own kind."

Darla put Angelus's arms around herself and snuggled against him. "Angelus is doubly unhappy because his harem is being decimated, aren't you, my love? All those pretty young things Dru makes for you, staked into ash." She sighed. "I shall find you someone beautiful to devour, Angelus."

"Then the Slayer will take her down," Angelus grunted.

"Only if you let her," Darla challenged. "I can't believe a mere girl can stand between you and anything you want."

"No girl can," he said brusquely.

Dru was still weeping. Spike crawled onto the windowsill, crunching glass beneath his fine evening shoes, and dropped down beside her.

"Barbara! You're scattering her!" Dru shrieked, pummeling him.

"Oh, dear, she's so mad," Darla drawled languidly.

"As I am for you," Angelus whispered into her ear. He nipped her earlobe; her drop earring cast a shiver of light against the gloomy, dark wall to their right. The fog had dissipated enough to cast moonlight against the two lovers as Darla turned in his arms and met his hungry kiss.

"Angelus, Angelus," she gasped, and he drew her down toward the floor. As she sank onto her knees, she threw back her head; he bit her hard, and she cried out from the sheer pleasure of it. Like two wild animals, they ripped and tore, losing themselves, lying down on the floor of the abandoned room, mindless of the dirt and dust, rolling and taking and being taken.

"Ah, lass," Angelus moaned, his Irish lilt thickening as he began to undress her. "'Tis a magickal thing you are, and I am bewitched."

"Good," Darla breathed, climbing on top of him. "That's very good."

Their moment was broken by a shout, this one of delight, and emanating from neither of them.

"It's Jack! Come for the game!" Spike called. "Jack the Ripper!"

"Ah, me, what a choice of entertainment I have to make," Darla murmured, smiling into Angelus's eyes. "You, or a butcher who's still breathing."

"Let's see him, though," Angelus urged. "He's a famous devil."

"No devil, so I hear. Just a man. And men can be killed." Darla's creamy skin appeared to grow rosy at the thought.

"Let's kill him right, then." Angelus smiled and eased her away. "It'll make for fun."

"As you wish," she assented. "We always have good times after we've had fun, eh?"

"Always."

She nimbly stood, smoothing her dress, and glanced through the broken window, fondly watching their young ones cavorting in the alley. Angelus followed soon after, fastening his trousers.

In the alley below, Drusilla, in her scarlet evening gown, and Spike, rather dashing in his silk opera cloak, had cornered a man similarly attired. He seemed ordinary enough, rather shorter than Spike, and beneath his top hat, long brown hair tumbled down his back in curls. He was wielding a cane with a blade on the end—not an uncommon sort of weapon in these lawless days—and Angelus found himself intrigued by the confident aggression evident in the man's posture. He was clearly unafraid of the two vampires, who had dropped their human masks and were hissing and advancing on him. Spike came at him from the left and Dru from the right.

"Why don't they simply rush him?" Darla asked, observing with interest but not yet poised to join in.

"Perhaps he's got something with him," Angelus suggested. "Some holy water or a cross. Something we can't see."

Sure enough, as Dru took another step toward him, a silver cross in the man's left hand glittered in the moonlight.

"Why do Spike and Drusilla assume he's Jack the Ripper?" Darla asked Angelus. "Unless he handed them his card, he looks like any other gentleman we're about to devour."

Angelus grinned at her as he helped her onto the windowsill. Darla was stronger even than he was, but in her ball gown and corset it would be difficult for her to step down from a carriage, much less climb out of a window. He might be dead, but chivalry was not.

"She's Dru," he said. "Do you need to ask how she

knows?" He was referring, of course, to the fact that
his get had the Sight. Drusilla saw things, knew things,
that no one else did. Angelus had driven her mad when
she'd been alive, convincing her that her gift had been
a present from the Devil himself . . . and that she was
surely damned for all eternity because of it.

"Well, I'll soon find out for myself who he is,"
Darla said, and stepped daintily from the sill. With no
care at all, she plummeted toward the street.

He hopped up and jumped down after her, landing with ease on his feet like a cat. He had been disappointed to learn that many of the popular notions
about vampires were myths, including the fact that
they were supposed to be able to transform into animals or mists. Just about now, it would be entertaining to frighten this monster of a man . . . and to make
him drop the cross he was holding.

"He knows about our kind," Angelus said.

"Look at his face, Angelus," Darla said as the two
were greeted by lupine smiles from Spike and Drusilla,
each of whom flanked the man, and who wagged the
cross at each of them in turn. "It's positively demonic."

It was true; his sinister leer spread so wide across
his face, one would have thought his mouth would
crack in two. His eyes spun crazily, and were dark
throughout; there was no color to them at all. If he was
a man, he was a madman.

"Smells 'uman, though," Spike said to the group.
"Or, at least, not like a vampire."

"He doesn't smell human, either," Darla commented. She sniffed the air. "Angelus?"

"Strawberries," he said, intrigued. "He smells like strawberries."

"So fresh, and so tasty," Dru cooed. "Strawberry gent reeks of greening patches and dead dollies. 'Run and catch, run and catch. The lamb is caught 'n the strawb'ry patch.'" She swayed to her own music, and that of the spheres. "Your mum was the monster, eh? The ugly one, gave you powers and magicks?"

She waved her fingers at him like silken veils, undulating back and forth like a harem dancer. The effect on many of her victims was intoxicating to watch; it distracted them, made them forget their wills. Then she would blithely slash their throats.

"I disemboweled my mother when I was born," he said, keeping his cross about his person but smiling pleasantly at her, as if not at all put off by her rude questioning. "But yes, she gave me much. As did my father."

"Ah." She moaned with pleasure. "You are a knight in shining armor. A warrior in the cause of the Great Battle."

He lowered his head.

She swept a deep curtsy, dropped to her knees, lifted up his opera cloak, and kissed it.

"'O, strange new world, that hath such creatures in it,'" Darla said, misquoting Shakespeare.

Then Dru grabbed the cloak in her teeth and smiled up at the stranger, all wanton smiles and lustful invitations for him.

Angelus loved her in that moment, recalling how earnest and prim she had been when kneeling in the confessional and pouring out her terror. Masquerading as a priest himself, Angelus had assured her that, yes, she was indeed cursed, and ought to surrender to Satan as soon as possible. There was no hope whatsoever that God would ever want her.

"Put it down, put it down," Drusilla whispered at the man. "Put down the cross and walk into my teeth, you great, devouring beast."

"Do you fancy me, then?" the man asked, chuckling. "But not my cross?"

"Oh yes, oh yes," Drusilla said joyfully. "I don't like your cross at all." She ran her tongue around her mouth. "But you, you would give me such pleasure. I can tell."

"'Ey, now," Spike protested.

"Your man is threatened," observed Jack—if Jack the Ripper he was. He was highly amused.

"Oh, he's no man," Darla cooed. "As well you know."

"Too bloody right," Spike put in, drawing himself up.

"He's Irish," Darla commented. "Like you, Angelus." She held out a hand to her love. Angelus gathered her fingers between both his hands and bent over her wrist, a courtly lover.

"Oh no, not Irish like himself," the man said, chuckling again. "Not at all."

His voice seemed to come from somewhere other than his mouth. It possessed a hypnotic, echoing quality. Darla heard it, too, and gave Angelus a questioning look.

"Oh, I do fancy you, in your elegant clothes," Drusilla cooed at him, "you flesh-eater. You don't break hearts, you tear them out of their bodies." She smiled brilliantly at him. "Mine's not beating, but you may have it."

"Dru," Spike growled, shooting her a glare.

"He is a wolf," Dru continued, "grabbing up the strawberries and ripping out their guts." She made an appropriate gesture, then flicked her hands as if shaking off gore only she could see. She cooed to herself a while, licking her lips, sucking nothing off her fingers. Still on her knees, she swayed in a circle, lifting her arms above her head. She closed her eyes.

"And then you bow and scrape to your lord and lady, and it maddens you because they don't appreciate you. But there is all that fog, and then . . ." She shivered. "I want to come with you and see the faery. They will kill us, easily. Easily. Ooooh." She began to weep. "Oooh, bad dog!"

Angelus ticked a glance her way. "What are you seeing, Dru?"

"He's Irish, like you," she said. "You know all the stories, Angelus." She rolled her eyes. "All the tales of faery are true. He is one of them."

Darla raised her brows. "Really? A man of the faery race?"

"There are many," Drusilla told Darla anxiously. "There are baddies and boogies and things that go slash in the night. And he is a bad boogey. Oooh, very bad. He will slash us!"

"I shall slash *you*," the man promised her. "Lovely charmer."

The man posed, and in that moment, Spike rushed

him, declaring, "Any slashing done here will be done by me!"

Then Spike was a blur of fists and fangs, attacking the faery man, who dropped the cross and began swinging the blade of his cane at Spike. Spike laughed with delight—the vampire was always a good one for a skirmish—and backed his rival up against a brick wall encrusted with mold.

Dru came at Jack the Ripper from the other side, springing at him like a wolf herself, burying her fangs into the back of his neck.

The man shrieked in frenzied agony. Darla swept into Angelus's embrace, and the two elders watched their offspring proudly.

Jack crumpled to his knees. Spike opened his mouth and prepared to strike—

—and then, as if from nowhere, fog tumbled from the sky like a sudden, astonishing torrent of foamy rain. There were buckets of it, loads; a glowering storm of it that immediately smothered all sound and sight.

Angelus shouted, "What's this, then?" but not even he could hear his own voice. All he had was his sense of touch; he couldn't even smell Darla, though she was clinging to him, clearly frightened.

He took her hand, and together they darted forward. He swept the space in front of him as they moved, in mocking imitation of the old blind man he had murdered some years ago. The codger had played the hurdy-gurdy, and he had almost driven Angelus insane with his noise and his "music." The old man had used a shepherd's crook to maneuver through the crowded filthy streets to the corner where he played, and the tap-tap-tapping and the incessant grinding had finally put Angelus off his feed one night.

It was a simple thing, to kill a blind man.

Now, as he moved forward, he was blind himself. The fog was as dense as a solid object; he couldn't even feel the soles of his evening shoes against the uneven cobbles. It was the closest thing to being in the Catholic version of limbo he could imagine; and for a fleeting instant he was terribly afraid that he had just died the second, true death. If limbo did exist, then hell did, too. He wouldn't mind being damned, but he didn't want to writhe in pain for all eternity. That was more the sort of thing Drusilla longed for, not he.

Then slowly he realized that he had not shuffled off his nigh-immortal coil. Relieved, he shook off his anxiety, but not before he realized that he had lost track of his beloved. "Darla?" he called, but he couldn't even hear his own voice.

He flexed his hands, then felt pressure against the fingers of his right hand. *It must be Darla.*

He squeezed back, unsure if she could feel it, and then he *knew* he was touching the faery man, and not his vampire lover. A pervasive sense of corruption and evil seeped through him; a frisson of shock skittered up his spine; and he instinctively moved his left hand in front of his chest just in time to block the sweeping movement of a wooden stake aimed directly at his unbeating heart.

With his vampire strength, he kept his hand wrapped around the stake and pushed it away from himself. A heavy weight followed, and then he heard Darla shout, "Angelus!"

He could make out a shape about a foot from him in the fog, and what he saw was bizarre: It was Jack the Ripper, only not. The man's body shook from head to toe and, as Angelus looked on, it shifted and bulged, the bones of his face and chest rotating, and all the other bones following suit. For a split second, Angelus was looking at the back of the man's head, and the right eye popped out on a stalk and glared at him.

Then the figure whirled back around, and his left eye was a giant red blister on his cheek. His mouth gaped all the way back to his ears, a scarlet wound so huge, Angelus could see down his throat. His hair stood up on his head, and blood dripped from it.

Angelus was startled for a fraction of a moment; then he rushed the creature with all his force . . . and the fog closed once more over Jack.

Angelus grabbed empty air.

As suddenly as it had tumbled into the street, it dissipated, leaving the four vampires in various poses of battle, blinking at one another.

The strawberry scent pervaded everything, like a coat of fresh wax on a tabletop. It was so thick, Angelus could taste it in his mouth, like jam.

No one spoke for a few moments, and then Spike said, "All right, then. What just 'appened?"

"Oh, he was beautiful, beautiful," Dru murmured, swirling in a circle and raising her arms upward. "A god. A god, and the chariot of the night swept him away." She giggled. "The vapors trail after him like the bulls."

Then, hearing music only Dru could hear—like most of the music Dru heard—the dark-haired vampire clapped her hands over her head and snapped her fingers in fierce staccato rhythm. "Let's go to Spain. I adore the bulls."

Stomping her feet, she grinned at Spike and posed for him like a Spanish Gypsy, arms above her head and slightly pulled back, chin high, torso arched like a bow.

"There are lots of bulls in Spain," she finished. "Perhaps that is where we'll find him next." She threw her arms over Spike's shoulders. "Take me to Spain, my darling."

"Shut up," Spike snapped at her. "I hate Spain," he added, although as far as Angelus knew, Spike had never been there. "And as for ever seeing him again . . ."

He trailed off helplessly as she completely ignored him, wandering over to a large shard of glass, dipping low, picking it up, and making cuts at the wisps of fog that churned from the ground.

"His mouth, so big and wide, to gobble them up," she sang. "His mouth eats time. Minotaur. Minotaur creature of the Whitechapel maze!" She cradled the shard as if it were a nursing infant, unaware of the large slice she cut in her white chest. Blood sluiced down the bodice of her gown.

"Drusilla, don't get so messy," Darla groused at her. "You go through clothes faster than an infant."

"Yes, Grandmother. I am so sorry. I will take care." Dru dipped a curtsy and Darla shifted her weight, clearly irritated with her. Still in her curtsy, the mad girl wiped her own blood on her hands began to lick it off her fingers, sliding a coquettish glance Spike's way. "Spike, fancy a taste?"

He smiled, pleased to be the object of her resumed flirtation, and walked to her, slipping her forefinger suggestively into his mouth. He began to suck. Their eyes locked, and they communed in their own private world.

Darla turned to Angelus and said, "What was it? I have never heard of true faery. They're a myth, are they not?" She inhaled delicately. "I smell his scent even now. He is not human. He must be a demon."

"Aye, demon, 'twould appear," Angelus returned. "Viking Berserker of some sort?"

Darla turned her head toward Drusilla as if waiting for confirmation of his guess, exposing her exquisite throat to Angelus. He felt a nearly insensate thrill of longing, and could barely keep his attention on what she was saying. "What was it Dru said? 'He eats time.' Y'know, Darla, she's mad as a hatter, but her visions are usually true. If one can decipher them."

"Can one?" Darla queried, watching Drusilla and Spike. The white-haired lad had shifted his attention to Dru's bleeding chest, and he was lapping hungrily at the delicacy with his vampire tongue. "Can you decipher, Angelus? She's your daughter. Do you understand her?"

When Angelus didn't reply, she glanced at him over her shoulder. Her right brow raised and her mouth curled in the whisper of a smile. He, too, was watching the young lovers. The sight of their appetite had stirred him. His eyes were gleaming and he had transformed again, his vampire face well etched and finely honed.

I made him, she thought proudly. *He's such a perfect monster.*

He stirred, and gazed at her. His eyes burned her. She shivered with delight and anticipation.

"What are you thinking?" she asked huskily.

"You know what I'm thinking." His gaze smoldered, and he held out a hand. "Let's find a soft bed."

"Who needs a bed?" Darla replied, gliding into his arms. She let her head fall backward. "Who needs to lie down?"

"Ah, me darlin'," he whispered hotly in her ear, nipping the lobe. "Me own girl."

"I'm no girl," she gasped. She threw her arms around his neck. "As well you know."

Distantly Angelus heard Drusilla singing, "People and time, he eats them. People and time. He serves them up. And he's 'ungry, Spike."

"So am I, Dru," Spike said. "Very hungry."

Dru's laughter trilled, and then there was silence in the street. Angelus swore he could hear his own heart pounding, the blood rushing hot and thick through his body; but he knew that was only an illusion. He was dead, and his heart could not beat.

Not even for Darla.

The Slayer Elizabeth came to the crescent of marble homes where she lived with Sir James. She didn't like the place; it was gloomy and forbidding, all the furniture oversized and very dark. Sir James obviously relished his position as Watcher in a world other than that of the daylight; there were stone gargoyles hanging over every doorway, and he kept a small private museum of monstrosities, some of which he had ordered Elizabeth to procure for him.

The most intriguing, in Elizabeth's opinion, was a lock of hair cut from the head of a man who had been hanged, been pronounced dead, and then revived to curse the judge who had sentenced him. Then he apparently "died" again. One of the onlookers had chopped off a lank when the body had been loaded into a plain wooden coffin, destined for unholy ground. The observer had sold the bit of hair to Sir James the same day the man had been buried.

"Knowin' Your Lordship's interest in things of the otherworldly," the man had said. For indeed, though Sir James's identity as a Watcher was not publicly known, his fondness for "otherworldly" things was known all over London.

It was Elizabeth's and Sir James's opinion that the man who had been hung had not been a man at all, but a vampire who had had the lucky fortune to have been hung in the shadow of the Tower of London. The gloomy day and the shadows of the great fortress had prevented him from bursting into flames, and the hanging had done nothing to him. He had merely feigned death in order to escape—like the Count of Monte Cristo, the hero of a French novel that Sir James had read to her to inspire her to bravery.

The hair was dark, soft, and wavy, and though she didn't like to touch it, the weight of it in her hand would remind her of all the things that she, as the Slayer, would never know—the caress of a man's hand on her own hair, children tugging at her locks, her hair growing gray.

She wondered, of a lonely, moonless night, if the lock of hair belonged to the same vampire who had murdered her poor, blind father.

A fortnight later, the judge had died from a vampire bite. Sir James had been delighted by this connection with "their" world, as he liked to call it, emphasizing the words "our world" when speaking of it, like someone referring to their own class—"our sort, our station"—that sort of thing. To Sir James, his connection with the occult was indicative that he was a very special, very important person.

She knew that to him, she was only a means to an end, rather like a locomotive tramping from London to wherever he might send her. She was a machine, and a defective one at that, known to sputter and balk when terror overwhelmed her.

Wearily, she put hand to door knocker; though she lived in the house, she was not allowed to enter it without first asking.

He'll be proud of me, she thought with hope. *I killed someone tonight.*

The very thought of it made her head swim; she was once again overcome by fear and panic.

Then the door swung open with a stately air, and Mrs. Mead, the housekeeper, stood in the threshold.

"Good evening, miss." The thin, black-haired housekeeper touched the locket at the throat of her dour black dress; she couldn't quite suppress the grimace that crossed her face as she glanced down at Elizabeth's "strumpet costume," as she had termed it. But she was a proper British housekeeper, and kept her opinions to herself—if not off her features.

"Thank you," Elizabeth said, as she pulled off her shawl and handed it to the housekeeper, who obviously did not want to so much as touch it.

"Shall I make tea?" the housekeeper asked.

"That would be lovely, thank you," Elizabeth murmured. "I didn't realize how cold I was. I don't know how those unfortunate women manage it, night after night."

"With gin," said a voice on the stair. "And sin."

The two women looked up at Sir James, who was smiling faintly at his own bad poetry. He was wearing his burgundy satin smoking jacket and he carried a pipe in his left hand. He reminded Elizabeth of the creation of Sir Arthur Conan Doyle, a fictitious detective named Sherlock Holmes. Sir James had read those stories to her as well. Like Holmes, Sir James had dark hair, an aquiline nose, and heavy brows over deep-set brown eyes. He was really quite handsome, and his smile could be winsome and kind.

Firmly she reminded herself that he was not her friend—and he would be shocked that she had ever thought of him in any way but as her superior in the battle against evil.

"Sir James, good evening," she said, and curtsied.

He inclined his head. "I'll join you momentarily in the parlor," he announced. He looked at the housekeeper. "Some port, if you don't mind, Mrs. Mead."

"At once, sir." She said to Elizabeth, "I'll put on the kettle for you."

Queen of the household, the housekeeper swept off to do her duties. Sir James had assured the Slayer that the pinched old woman had no notion of their "peculiar relationship"—that is, that he was her Watcher and she, the Vampire Slayer. According to Sir James, Mrs. Mead believed the two were in the employ of the government as spies.

Elizabeth could never tell if the housekeeper truly believed that, or if she was humoring her employer, who was known to be eccentric. Whatever the case, it was obvious that she didn't approve of his having a young girl in the house to whom he was not related by blood or by marriage. And since Mrs. Mead couldn't properly communicate her displeasure to her superior and hope to keep her job, she took it out on Elizabeth.

Aware that she was now alone with her Watcher and feeling acutely uncomfortable, Elizabeth hesitated and gestured to her filthy clothing. With a blush she said, "Sir, if you don't mind, I should like to bathe straight away," she requested. "We could speak after—"

"That won't do," Sir James declared, shaking his head. "I have a very busy schedule. And the Council is awaiting my report."

I could sponge off in five minutes, she thought resentfully, but said nothing. It was ever thus; like Mrs. Mead, she was little more than a servant of the house, and Sir James held authority over her. Her position in the order of things had been made quite clear to her when she had been called to serve as the Chosen One.

"In fact, this elevates you in social standing," Sir

James had informed her. "Your family are quite . . . a lowborn lot, are they not?"

Lowborn or not, my mother and father birthed a Slayer, she thought fiercely. *And I risked my life tonight for Crown and country.*

Without replying, she stomped across the black-and-white marble foyer.

I'll show him. Wait until he hears of my catch.

"Is there something wrong, Elizabeth?" Sir James called after her, his voice clipped and challenging. He was quite aware that he had insulted her. And she was quite aware that he didn't care. In fact, he enjoyed it, believing that it spurred her on despite her weak character.

The problem is . . . it does. He is right to do it. No matter how he angers me, he is wiser in these matters than I am. . . .

"No, sir," she managed. "Nothing is wrong."

She kept her balled fists at her sides. Despite her frustration, her shame got the better of her. If left to her own devices, she would never go out on patrol, never stake vampires or fight demons. It was his prodding that kept her on her course.

The Gothic arch hanging over the parlor had been taken from a French cathedral said to have sheltered a coven of witches masquerading as nuns. Propped to the right of a burgundy velvet sofa was an old mummy case, and beside that, some dusty books on necromancy written in Aramaic. In her temper, Elizabeth resisted the temptation to "accidentally" knock some or all of it over, and stationed herself before the fire, her back to the other garish and gruesome objects in the room.

As she warmed herself, the stench of her clothes repelled her, and she grew even angrier at being forced to give Sir James an accounting of her evening in her filthy state. Then, as she stood waiting for him, the memory of her battle with Barbara took hold. She felt sick to her stomach as fear washed over her, as strong and fresh as if she were in the midst of it. Death leaped on her, pummeling her; every shadow in the room was a harlequin specter of pain and failure, and she began to pant.

The room spun wildly, tilting and rocking. Her heart was beating too fast, and she lost track of her direction. With a crash she fell against the mummy case; it fell over, the books sliding after it. Blinded with fresh terror, she heard the crack of wood, and then a shout.

"Hello! What's going on?"

Sir James loomed over her like one of the massive suits of armor, his features a mask of displeasure. There was not a trace of concern for her anywhere on his face.

She looked up through tears and knew she had to lie to him.

"Ill," she managed. "Something . . . in the fog tonight. A . . . a strange vapor."

"Vapor, you say?" he asked sharply, eyeing her. Elizabeth looked away.

"Oh, sweet Virgin Mother," Mrs. Mead said, rushing up behind Sir James. Her face was drawn and pale with horror as she crossed herself, keeping her distance from Elizabeth. "She has the plague."

He squatted down and put his hand to her forehead. "Dry and cool," he said accusingly. He narrowed his eyes, speaking to the housekeeper while he stared at the Slayer. "She's not got the plague, Mrs. Mead. Do you, Elizabeth?"

There was silence. Elizabeth heard her heart pounding and tasted the bile in her mouth. "I-I . . . no, sir," she said dispiritedly. "I don't."

"Mrs. Mead, Miss Elizabeth needs refreshment. Go and fetch her a bowl of soup. And *two* glasses of port," he added with a self-important air, the aristocrat bestowing largesse. He would not have thought to offer her anything if she had not been in such acute distress. A night of patrolling, and she would have stood before him with her hands folded like a schoolgirl, hungry, thirsty, and tired, reciting her sums while he sipped his port.

"Two glasses," Mrs. Mead replied, like the navigator on an oceangoing vessel. "And the tea?"

"She shall have her tea later."

"Yes, sir." She ticked her glance at Elizabeth, her disgust evident.

Elizabeth hesitated. Her widowed mother had brought her up as a poor but good girl. Spirits were not to be touched by such as she. But she was too cowed to refuse, and only hung her head and silently wept as Mrs. Mead's ebony skirts rustled and she went away to do as her gentleman requested.

As soon as they were alone, Sir James leaned back

on his heels, rose, and glowered down at Elizabeth. Reluctantly he extended his hand.

"Get up, now. We both know what this is about, do we not? The same thing as always. Your fear. Your lack of heart."

"But sir, it was . . . she . . . ," she stammered. Then she swallowed and announced, "Tonight . . . I made a kill!"

He raised a brow. She bobbed her head, accepting his statement, and put her hand in his. She didn't like to touch him, and he made no secret of his distaste for her. Even when training, they kept their distance from each other.

"Sit there," he said, indicating the stonework that extended from the fireplace. He didn't want her filthy clothes on his fine furniture.

Abased, disheartened, she did as she was told. She hunched forward until she realized that her scandalous bodice revealed far more than ought to be exposed, and she leaned back against the mantel. Tears streamed down her face.

"Oh, for God's sake, do control yourself!" Sir James snapped. He stomped to the bell pull and yanked hard on it. "Mrs. Mead! Where are you?"

In the kitchen, Marietta Mead jerked up her head. One hand gripped the bottle of port her master had requested. The other rested against the doorknob of the opened door of the servants' entrance.

On the other side of the door stood a young woman with black hair and eyes set against skin the color of alabaster. Truly that; skin whiter than one saw in the Grecian friezes in the British Museum.

The girl wore red, the color of strumpets, and her fingernails were brilliant crimson, as if she had dipped them into . . . something. They appeared to be lacquered, and very wet.

"Let us in," the dark-eyed young woman urged her. "Dear sweet lady, let us in, let us in. I am so hungry."

Her lips parted. Mrs. Mead blinked, and the whiteness of them, the sparkle. Her gaze fastened on the girl's fingertips as she waved them at her. She found herself thinking of the tentacles of an octopus.

Then a young man moved from the shadows, and she was reminded of a silver-white wolf. He was pale, and his hair was a luminous, pale silver-gold; his eyes were catlike and cunning. His smile was lazy as he slid his arm around the waist of the girl, draping himself over her shoulder and smiling at Marietta in a thoroughly indecent manner.

Though shocked, the housekeeper could not look away. The girl giggled, rubbing herself against his torso; her sensuality frightened Marietta out of her wits. She had never seen a man and woman behave so; she herself had never tasted the pleasures of such a union, and she was both repulsed as they entwined themselves around each other, and drawn toward them as they smiled welcomingly at her.

The girl gestured with her fingers. "We want to come in," she said in a low, eager voice. "You have dollies we want. Dollies to blind! Pluck out their eyes and have them with our tea!" She made stabbing motions with her fingers.

The housekeeper swayed. She clutched the bottle to her chest.

"Mrs. *Mead!*" a man's voice bellowed.

"The port," Mrs. Mead said. She looked down at the bottle in her hand as if it were a foreign object. Then she looked back up at the pair, so strikingly beautiful, so alluring.

"Dru wants into the palace," the girl said with urgency. "Wants to dance with the princess. Birdies brought us here. Sparrows with black wings, mmm . . . mmmm." She swept her free arm up and down, up and down. "Over rooftops like skeleton heads! Chimneys belching stink."

A bell sounded impatiently.

In a daze, Mrs. Mead turned around and headed for the parlor.

"Damn her," Spike said as the two vampires watched the retreating figure. "Dru, you've lost your touch."

"She is the guardian," Dru said to him. "She is the one keeping little dolly's eyes in her head. Dragon queen!" She made whooshing noises. "Hear her wings flapping, whum, whum, whum! Let's make her our mum. Let's start her over, click, clack, she's a broken dolly, her eyes all gone. All she sees is gargoyles." Her laughter seemed to echo against the brick.

"Don't tell," Dru called softly. "Don't tell, Dragon Guardian!"

"Hush, then," Spike growled at her. "We're out in public, Drusilla."

"I want to follow after her," she told Spike, raising up on her tiptoes as she pressed her fingers together. "Savage them all before they can blink." Bouncing up and down on the tips of her shoes, she grinned maniacally at him, evilness and madness glinting in her eyes like the stars she claimed so often to hear. "See that Slayer with my own eyes. And then pop hers out of their sockets, like grapes."

Spike kissed her. "I want the Slayer as well, Dru. Only you know how badly I want to slash that chit's throat."

"Angelus already has killed Slayers," she cooed. And he'll kill this one for me, too. He is so powerful, so brave. Our very own . . . daddy."

"He's older'n me," he retorted, stung. "Over a century older. My turn now." He flared with fury at the thought of Angelus killing this Slayer, too, and how impressed Drusilla would be if Angelus did it. How she'd throw herself at him, preen and flounce . . . "I'll kill this one."

"No. I have a better idea. If we can, let's turn 'er," she said, grinning back at him. "A vampire Slayer become a vampire," Dru enthused. "I'd let you have her, Spike. Good, then evil, she'd be all yours." She kissed him on the cheek. "As much as you wanted."

He vamped and grabbed her shoulder. "You are not one to give me permission to do anything. You may have sired me, Dru, but you are not my master. Never forget that."

"Oh!" Her eyes glittered. "You are a big lion, aren't you? Grrrr." Her laughter was a crescendo of high, melodic notes. He wasn't certain if she was laughing at him or simply enjoying his show of strength and manly virtue. He was about to ask her, then realized that would show weakness, so he clamped his mouth shut and glowered at her. Her response was to become more animated, more adoring.

Aha. I'm learning, he thought smugly. *Women really do like the rough and tumble.*

"I hear voices," she added.

"You usually do," he whispered, growing more amorous. "Lord knows you're never alone."

"Sh. Listen." Grinning, she pointed at the kitchen door. "They're coming."

Vampires had excellent hearing—if there was really anything to hear. At Drusilla's prodding, Spike focused; there really were voices, and the words they spoke drifted into the kitchen.

"The Ripper is not a demon," the man was saying. "He is a human being, however much a monster his actions declare him. I have it on the Council's authority. And I repeat, that as such, he is off limits to the likes of you."

"Yes, sir," said a female voice. She sounded defeated, and yet Spike noted a tremble of defiance in her tone. He felt oddly proud of her.

"That's the *Slayer,*" Drusilla whispered, her eyes widening. She made flapping motions with her arms and raised her chin, staring at the midnight sky with such a look of ecstasy on her face that Spike had to restrain himself from pulling her to the porch floor and ravishing her. "She really is here!"

"Yes, Dru," he said slowly. "I thought that was the point."

She batted his chest. "Oh, Spike! Don't you see? The man might be her Watcher! Perhaps they live together! Naughty kittens! We shall turn them together! We'll turn them both! We shall become world renowned for our cleverness." Her eyes gleamed. She licked her lips languorously and sighed with eagerness.

"That's a risky proposition," Spike observed.

"*Angelus* could do it," she taunted. "He would do it."

There were footsteps. Then a tall, dark-haired man sauntered into the kitchen. Spike and Dru moved away from the door, keeping to the shadows of the night.

"Mrs. Mead, you're getting old," The man grumbled, and shut the door. "No wonder it's so cold in the parlor."

Like two naughty children on the verge of discovery, the vampires pressed themselves against the brick wall, losing themselves in the ivy, barely able to suppress their giggles. Dru gripped Spike's arm, digging her fingers into the flesh until he began to bleed. He grinned at her, and she at him.

"We'll turn 'em both," he promised her. "If that's what Drusilla wants, that's what she'll get."

"That's what I want," she told him, clapping her hands together, then grabbing up Spike's icy fingers and sucking on them one by one. Her eyes blazed as she smiled up at him. "That's exactly what I want."

"Then I'll get it for you," he promised, feeling ever so much the man.

"My Spike," she said lasciviously. "Flap your wings. Bite them with dragon teeth! Take their jeweled eyes and make a crown of stars. Royal jewels in the dungeon! My Spike."

"If you wish."

"I wish."

They kissed.

First.

Chapter Three

Sunnydale

When it rains, it pours. But when the Hellmouth seethes, it's a Krakatoa of the bad.

The Sunnydale Hellmouth was a deceptively innocuous-looking fissure in the earth, located directly beneath what used to be the library of Sunnydale High. From time to time it emitted noxious fumes, and the poisonous vapors drew demons from all over the world.

On occasion, the Hellmouth disgorged them as well.

The thing that crawled out of the fissure was vaguely human-shaped, his battle armor made of leather and bone. His name was Milak, and he was a blood brother of Thak the Shapeshifter.

Milak was covered from the top of his flat, enormous skull to the tips of his taloned feet with thick, bristly hair, and his eyes bulged like a fish's. In the world of the *Fomhóire,* Milak was considered to be exquisitely handsome. His courage was renowned. His willingness to die for the *Fomhóire* cause had garnered him accolades and honors that made his sacrifice worthwhile . . . at least for those of his clan who would survive him.

He was dying already. He could feel it. The only one of his kind who could move into this dimension and live through it unscathed was Thak. Milak would not be so lucky. He had only a little time to complete his mission.

In his right hand, Milak carried an enormous battle-ax, and in the other, a crude map to a place called Shady Hill Cemetery. There he would meet with "Jack," and hand over the precious object that he had needed back in England, and which had eluded him since then: the Sacred Fog of Nemain.

The fog had been distilled at last, and once Jack released it into the air of this human place and murmured the incantations only he knew, the vast army of *Fomhóire* would burst through the Hellmouth and destroy the human race forever. Thus empowered, it would turn its attention to the *Tuatha,* and annihilate them as well.

Milak couldn't think much past those few facts; his brain had been badly damaged by his arrival into this dimension.

Soon, all that would be of the past, and his people would cry his name at their victory celebrations.

"Slayer?" Milak muttered softly, hefting the ax and surveying his surroundings. He stood in battle posture for quite some time. Then, assuring himself that he was alone, he lowered the ax.

In terrible pain, he made his way through the debris of the ruined Sunnydale High library, stumbling and falling any number of times. There was some manner of leathery sustenance on the floor; sniffing, he picked up a handful and took a bite. The desiccated meat was good; he took another bite.

Then he shambled on, fear gripping him as his mind began to crumble. Milak was loaded to the entrails with magickal energy, imbued with unbelievable strength, precision reflexes—everything his leaders could impart to him so that he could defend his precious cargo.

Certain that he was alone, he dropped his battle armor to the floor. Then he squatted and pulled a short black dress from a pouch that had dangled from his waistcoat.

"Good-bye, my self," he whispered.

The pouch was a sacred object of the *Fomhóire*. Made of the skin of a *Tuatha* king from centuries past, it was a precious reminder that at one time, the *Fomhóire* had entertained reasonable hopes of reigning supreme in the world of faery.

But what it contained was even more precious . . . the secret weapon of the *Fomhóire,* newly created: the Sacred Fog from the Cauldron of the *Fomhóire* Goddess of Panic, called Nemain. The fog had at last been successfully distilled from the mist of Goddess Panic's cauldron, and now it gurgled and boiled inside a beautiful vial carved of leprechaun rainbow and studded with jewels, some said from the Crown of Bran himself. It was intended for Thak. He had gone a little ahead into the human world, assessing their defenses. The stars were aligned, and the time was right for conquest. It would be the *Fomhóire*'s finest hour.

A diluted vial of the same Sacred Fog had been prepared for the demon messenger. Now Milak held up this second, plainer-looking vial. With a bit of trembling, he yanked the cork stopper off.

Strawberry scent invaded the cavern.

He bade farewell to memory, to love and to life, and drank the potion down.

With a shout, Milak fell to the floor. The fog gripped him, sending him reeling in confusion and agony as the liquid worked its way through his brain. The firelike pain was unimaginable, and as he suffered and writhed, the stalwart soldier reminded himself that once the transformation had occurred, he would not remember this torture. He would not remember anything. Life as he had known it would no longer exist.

And yet . . . the pain was so horrible. Milak cried out, then bit into his fists to keep himself from alerting the Slayer or any other human with his screams.

It grew worse, and worse still. It was beyond description.

And then . . . the Fog worked its magicks. The ethers dissolved Milak's memory and congealed; dreamy, false memories flooded Milak's bleeding brain; the Sacred

Fog altered his very bones and skin and muscle, and Milak the Powerful was gone . . . forever.

Caught in the throes of terrible rebirthing, he writhed on the floor, vomiting and groaning, until he passed out.

When Milak awoke, she was a young human woman named Maeve. She didn't remember why she was there, but that happened to Maeve a lot. She drank; she used. She was not a happy child.

Sighing with resignation that she'd had another blackout, Maeve put on her black dress, pulled on and tied her boots, and arranged her long, black hair down her back. She touched the beautiful cylinder, resting her gaze on it for quite a long time as she struggled to put her confused mind together.

My name is Maeve, and I need to find . . . Jack and give this stuff to him.

This stuff . . . has something to do with me, she thought as she moved the battle armor and the ax behind a pile of rubble and arranged a few pieces of wood on top. Then she flexed her index finger, closed her eyes, and touched the wood.

Smoke rose. Heat from her flesh seared the wood; as she lifted her finger away, the whorls of her fingerprint branded the plank. The lines were in the shape of the great maze through which all souls must race, pursued by the Hound and his master, the Jester. In the Tarot, he was the Fool; on playing cards, the Jack.

And I gotta find him, Maeve thought. *I'm his . . . I'm his drug connection. Yeah, that's right. I'm bringing him this stuff from . . . my dealer.*

As she began to rise, a rat scampered from the pile

of debris and skittered over her shoe. With lightning-fast reflexes, she grabbed it up, wrung its neck, and flung it so hard across the cavernous space that it was a rat no longer when it landed.

Huh. That's weird, she thought. *I must be stronger than I thought. And I must be having a really, really bad day.*

Then she got up and began to walk.

Xander, Anya, and Tara drove slowly away from the house, as Spike followed Buffy inside. She said to him, "Don't make yourself comfortable," and went upstairs. She heard Spike humming to himself, heard the *fwwwip* of a match.

"No smoking!" she shouted.

There was no answer.

In the bathroom, Dawn was brushing her teeth.

"Hey," Buffy said.

Dawn brightened. "Bff!" Dawn said, then pulled out her toothbrush. "Hey!"

Buffy gave her a hug. "How are you?"

"This fog is so freaky, Buffy," Dawn replied earnestly. "I don't think those guys should be driving in it."

"Good point, but they're already gone." Buffy shrugged. "And I have to go back out, too," she added.

Dawn's crestfallen face was another whack on the dinged hood of her sisterly self-esteem. Buffy went for a peace offering; the Summers sisters' legal tender was sugar. "Hot chocolate later?"

"Sure." Dawn looked down at her toothbrush. "If

you come back soon enough, my chocolate will have a nice Cresty taste."

"You got the little marshmallows?" Spike called from downstairs.

Buffy rolled her eyes and smiled uncomfortably at Dawn, who said, "I didn't know Spike was here. Is he going with you?"

"No," Buffy said quickly, then quietly cleared her throat and kept her gaze wide and honest. "I mean, yes, yes he is. Because of the fog. Patrolling with a patrol buddy. Except he's just a buddy. Well, not buddy, because, Spike." She laughed her dorky laugh of not good at lying. But Dawn didn't seem to notice.

"Good." Dawn nodded. "Because you never know what's coming in fog like this." She picked up her water glass and took a sip, rinsed, spat. "Not that I've ever seen fog like this before."

"Me, neither. But I'll be careful." She pointed at Dawn's toothbrush. "Be sure to floss. We can't afford dental bills."

"Okay." Dawn held up her toothbrush as if she were taking an oath.

"Willow will be in all night," Buffy said firmly, because Willow had better stay put or there would be worse than hell to pay, there would be the Slayer. "Do what she tells you to do. Unless it involves staying up all night."

Dawn made a show of snapping her fingers. "Darn. That was the plan."

Just then, Willow plodded down the hall with two pillows in her arms and said loudly and on purpose,

"Meet you downstairs after they leave for the all-night movie marathon."

"Ha." Dawn smiled anxiously at her sister. "Ha. Funny joke, Willow."

"It's okay, Dawnie," Buffy said. "You can stay up late." She narrowed her eyes at Willow. "But not all night."

"Hey. D'you have a bloody all-you-can-rent card at the video shop?" Spike called from downstairs. Buffy heard the clatter of plastic video containers. "Bloody hell. How many films has Meg Ryan made, anyway? More to the point, is she naked in any of them?"

Buffy scrunched her face in parental disapproval. "How many videos did you rent, Will?"

"It's Saturday night," Willow reminded her. "No school for Dawn tomorrow, unlike me in my younger days, when I had computer club. We always met bright and early on the weekends because we never had anywhere to be on Friday nights." She smiled winsomely.

"That's so sad," Dawn murmured. Then she flushed and said, "Hey, wait a minute. I don't have anywhere to be, either. That's even sadder."

"You're too young to date, anyway," Buffy said.

"And you're here with me," Willow said warmly. "Which, okay, I'm practically your aunt, but there's Cherry Garcia ice cream."

There was a moment. That had been Joyce Summers's favorite flavor.

Buffy broke the spell. "So, Spike and I will have a

quickie . . . that is, take a quick tour around town . . . which shouldn't take long, since we live in Sunnydale. And we'll come back here for massive amounts of ice cream and hot chocolate," she announced. "I mean, I will. Because Spike will want to get home to his uncomfortable crypt and be alone."

"No date, either," Dawn said.

"I'll stay for the marshmallows," Spike called.

"As if," Buffy muttered.

"I can't believe you said that," Dawn chirped. "'As if.' That is *so* passé!"

"You're dating yourself, big sis," Willow drawled.

"That's because no one else will date her," Dawn teased, then grinned to show she was kidding. Then stopped grinning when Buffy gave her The Look.

"Before you go," Willow continued. "I did a little more research on this Moon of Osiris thing. There's about two dozen different versions of what it is. None of them are happy."

"That figures," Buffy grumbled. "Give me the gist."

"Fog. Death." Willow raised a red eyebrow. "And did I mention the death? Plus I have a bad feeling. Actually, I think you should stay here with us. Skip patrolling."

"Yeah." Dawn nodded eagerly. "Good idea. Best idea. Skip the whole deal and watch Meg Ryan. Hey, Spike could stay, too."

Downstairs, the clatter of plastic ceased and desisted. Buffy knew Spike was listening carefully for her reply. A thrill of erotic tension centered at the base of her spine and fanned upward, and she wondered if it showed on her face. She knew he wanted her to insist on patrolling. And she knew why.

It was incredible to her that she could sneak away night after night, making love with him, with Spike of all people—*or things*—and no one so much as suspected. She remembered the night of her seventeenth birthday. It had been her first time, and it had been with Angel. It was wonderful.

The next morning had not been wonderful at all. She had awakened alone, and she was certain that her mother had known that she had done the deed. But Joyce had chattered on about her special day, and Buffy had scooted away upstairs . . . wondering where Angel was, her emotions a jumble of joy and a strange sadness she had not anticipated, having gleaned most of her what-sex-is-like data from magazines designed to make her yearn for cosmetics.

Angel had been so long ago . . . a lifetime ago, literally. She drooped inside, wishing for it to be Angel who was downstairs, even after all this time. They were two old soldiers now, knew the score, knew it wasn't on their side of the tally sheet. If life was a bowling tournament, their being together was a gutterball.

But it was so wrong that she couldn't be with him, couldn't have him, while Spike was always available, always willing and waiting. *Spike.* The loser vampire of all time.

Flushing, she thought of Spike's hands on her . . . his touch, his lips, his hunger, and passion; the frenzy, the way he made her feel something, feel anything . . .

. . . and realized that Willow and Dawn were gazing at her, waiting for her answer to a question she hadn't heard them ask. "Um," she said tentatively.

"Please, Buffy," Dawn said quietly. "It's all crazy-weird out there. You could get hurt."

Buffy cleared her throat, wishing she could give in to her sister's wishes. Knowing she couldn't. "Really, I-I can't," she told them both. She gave her head a nod. "This fog gives the bad guys a lot of cover, and they know it. They'll probably be real cocky tonight. I mean, really cocksure. Swaggery." She laughed nervously. "Out to do harm. Which means, Buffy goes on patrol."

"But you won't be able to *see* the bad guys," Dawn persisted anxiously. "They might creep up on you and . . ." She slumped. "You already died once."

"Twice," Spike called up helpfully.

"Shut up," Buffy sang back.

"Dawn has a point," Willow cut in.

"Will. Dawn." Buffy cocked her head. "Nights like this are why there's a Slayer. Not to worry. I'm double-oh Buffy, with a license to kill demony things. I'll use Spike as a decoy," she added too brightly, as if she had to justify his accompanying her. "Every demon in Sunnydale wants to kill him. Right, Spike?" she called.

He didn't answer. Her stomach flipped.

Did he storm out when I told him to shut up? But I always tell him to shut up. It's what we do.

That, and a lot of other things.

"Well, I'm right," Buffy assured her. "They do. Spike is totally hated by his own kind. Which, yay for our side. Because when they come out of the fog to kill him, I'll whup their butts."

Dawn didn't look convinced as Buffy smiled at her.

"You're right. I'm just being silly, worrying about you dying. Because, hey," Dawn murmured in a totally defeated tone of voice, "no big."

Buffy saw her abject fear in the slump of her shoulders and she said, "I'll patrol quickly, Dawn. Then I'll come home." *I will,* Buffy promised herself. *No stopping at Spike's. Or stopping with Spike. Not tonight. No way.*

Dawn nodded sullenly, and this time Buffy was the one who felt defeated. *It's like I'm a single mom trying to date,* she thought.

Yeah, trying to date a serial killer . . .

"Ooh, wait," Willow announced. "I've got something for you." She said to Dawn, "It'll help keep her safe."

She loped down the hall, leaving the two sisters to stand together in an uncomfortable silence. Then she returned shortly with a small clump of braided rope. She handed it to Buffy, who examined it, had no idea what it was, and looked questioningly at the Wicca.

Willow took it from her, turned it over, and showed it to them both. "It's to protect the wearer from blood and fog," she said. "An old sailor's knot, actually. Because they might slip on the deck and hurt themselves." She flashed Buffy her signature half-smile. "Actually, because they might slip on the deck and impale themselves on a harpoon, contract gangrene, and get tossed overboard."

"Oh. How cheery and useful." Buffy put it in her pocket. "Thanks, Willow."

"It works on land, too," Willow added, gesturing to Buffy's pocket. "They were very common in the Victorian era. People used to make them from the hair of dead relatives."

"Cooler still," Buffy riposted, looking pained.

"Only, this one is rope."

"Bummer," Buffy drawled. That actually elicited a giggle from Dawn.

Willow kept going. "So, if things get . . . dicey, pull it out and press it against your forehead, okay? It'll open your third eye and allow you to see trouble brewing. Plus help you keep your balance."

"Okay." Buffy leaned forward and gave Willow a peck on the cheek. "Thanks. You're a blessed being."

"My bonnie Dawnie," Willow said fondly, she clapped the younger girl's shoulder. "What say we look for the Ben + Jerry's? Ice cream a starboard, me hardy?"

"Good idea," Buffy said. "Save some for me. Save lots." She wagged the braided rope at her sister. "I'm gonna stick this on my forehead to make sure you're behaving."

"There's nothing else to do but behave," Dawn grumped.

"That's as it should be." Buffy nodded her approval. "Casting off now."

"Smooth sailing," Willow said.

Dawn's eyes glistened. She looked too young and too fragile for Buffy to leave alone, even if it was with a powerful witch who would rather die than let anything happen to her. Buffy felt terrible. Their mother's death had been so hard on Dawn, and then Giles's abrupt leaving. No wonder she was messing up in school.

I've really got to spend more time with her, Buffy thought guiltily. *And less time with Spike . . . oh, God, no time at all with Spike. Tonight I'll tell him it's over. That we're over.*

If he's still here, I'll tell him right now.

She turned on her heel and went down the stairs, pocketing the braided rope and nervously hooking her hair behind her ears.

When she saw Spike in front of the door, her heart skipped a beat. She forced herself to behave naturally as he gave her a dismissive glance. He had lit up another cigarette; the smoke seemed to caress the sharp angles of his silhouette, and she took a moment to look at him, really look at him.

He's evil.

I want him.

Buffy glared at him and said, "Spike, you know my home is a no-smoking zone."

"Uh-huh." He inhaled the smoke, held it, and exhaled.

"My sister breathes this air."

"Right." Inhale, exhale.

"Spike." She stormed toward him and tried to grab the cigarette out of his hands. He held it above his head and smiled lazily down at her. His eyes, how they twinkled; his dimples, how scornful.

"Rules are made to be broken, love. You know that."

There wasn't much more she could do to him

without frightening Willow and Dawn, so she pushed him roughly out of her way. She reached for the door-knob. His hand clamped over hers as she turned the knob, his fingers as cold as the grave.

And yet . . . she burned for him.

"Don't you tell me what I can and cannot do," he said with dead calm. His voice had lowered an octave, and she knew he meant it.

She stared at his fingers, his hands. The flesh on them was dead, and yet they were the only things in this world that made her feel alive.

"Shut up. Just shut up," she flung at him, supremely frustrated and ashamed.

His answering chuckle was smug, assured. "We're done with that, Slayer. The you-telling-me-what-to-do part. I'm not your whipping boy anymore."

She glared up at him; he grabbed her by the elbow and pulled her against his body. He wanted her, and he wanted her to know it.

She lowered her gaze, not willing to let him see how his desire affected her. Because she wanted him, too.

His deft fingertips caressed the tendrils of hair around her temples. Tears of shame sprang to her eyes as her skin sang when he touched it.

"I know where you live, Buffy. And it's not where I jump at the sound of my mistress's voice and do her bidding."

"Spike . . ." *I'll stop this now. I'll tell him to go away, now.*

Footsteps on the stairs alerted her that Dawn and

Willow were coming; she set her jaw and said under her breath, "I'm opening the door now."

He narrowed his eyes, taking her measure, and made a grand show of opening the door for her. Then he stood aside, sweeping wide his arm, gesturing for her to make her exit.

She was aware of his eyes on her as she walked past him and into the thick blankets of fog.

Then he was on the porch beside her, his cold breath on the back of her neck. "God, I wish I could bite you," he murmured.

She tingled everywhere.

God help her, she tingled.

I wish I could kill you. I wish that someone else would do it for me. Do you have any idea how much I loathe you? How much I loathe myself for being with you?

"We are going to patrol," she said crisply. "Patrol *only*."

His answer was a deep-throated laugh.

And Buffy knew, in a cloud of misery and deep despair, that she was lying only to herself. Spike knew the score better than she did.

Far, far better than she did.

" . . . because we really do need to discuss the you-know-what," Anya was saying as she chattered beside Xander in his car. Tara was on the other side of her, staring out the window, apparently lost in thought.

I wish I was lost in thought, Xander thought as he stared straight ahead at the fog. *Which . . . does thinking that mean I am lost in thought? Then stop me before I think again. Because the wedding . . . too much thinking there.*

"You're not listening to me!" Anya protested.

"I am. I am." He moved his head but not his eyes. The road was nowhere to be seen, but he could still make out the occasional red flare of brake lights ahead of them. *We should have stayed over at Buffy's house. The fog is unbelievable.* "You said that some of your demon girlfriends have gone vegan. Which I'm saying, good for them, this is a small planet and nice of them to save the higher-order calories for those of us who appreciate them."

"Yes, and so they can't have any of the entrees that caterer suggested. No chicken, no dove—"

Tara stirred. "Dove?" she said anxiously, looking at Anya. "I'm sorry, what are you talking about?"

"Not eatin' it, either," Xander said. "Because, eww." He flashed his beloved a hopeful smile. "Hey, how about those vegetable lasagnas in the friendly freezer section of our local Stater Brothers? We could zap a few of those and, *voilà,* vegetarian yumminess that even my uncle Rory would eat. Well, not that he's all that picky, as long as it's something he can pick the cigarette butts out of. There's also some microwavable schwarma in the deli case and—"

"No, no, no!" Anya half-shouted.

"Easy there, sweetie," Xander said, as if he were trying to calm down a rabid dog.

"I am not serving frozen food at my wedding reception!"

"Well, yeah, you probably are, 'cause catering,

well, they do that sort of thing," Xander said slowly, knowing that he really, really should shut up, but somehow not able to make it so. It used to be like this when he was dating Cordelia. He would know he should shut up, but he couldn't do it. Not when there might be points to be scored off her incrediby superficiality and her superior 'tude in the dissing contests he and she used to indulge in.

When am I going to learn? He didn't know if he was overtired and overnervous or what, but being distracted by a food fight, verbal or otherwise, was not a good idea.

"They do not do that sort of thing," Anya insisted. "My fellow vengeance demons have attended hundreds—okay, thousands—of wedding receptions, and I know my cocktail weenies, Xander."

"Sock you for fresh, stick you with defrosted." He nodded sagely. "Worked for a caterer for a brief time. Well, actually not. The bartender at the college and I created a few ravishing Chex Party Mix trays for the students, charged 'em for—"

"You're not making any sense," Anya interrupted. "And you're not taking this seriously." Her eyes welled. "Xander, this is our *wedding* reception."

He opened his mouth to speak, realized he was way past the better part of stupidity, and clamped it shut again. There was no way he was going to win this. Hell, there was no way he was going to break even.

And speaking of brakes . . . there they are again, the brake lights. Xander gingerly lifted his foot off the gas pedal to put more distance between his car and the stop-'n'-go fan ahead of him.

We should have stayed at Buffy's. I cannot afford to get into an accident, not with my insurance rate already jacked up so high. It's expensive being a Scoob. And now that I'm getting married . . .

. . . oh, my God, I'm getting married!

The other guy's brake lights went off. Xander slowed down even more, trying to let the other get a little farther ahead of him.

"You don't care," Anya said again.

Xander was beginning to lose his patience. He had enough to deal with, trying to make sure they didn't have an accident.

Then the brake lights flashed back on.

"What is the matter with this guy?" he grumbled.

"Huh?" Tara asked, shifting her attention from the conversation between him and his beloved intended to the windshield. She frowned slightly. "What's going on?"

Xander gestured. "I know the fog is scary, but he keeps putting his foot on the brake. On, off, on, off. I'm afraid I'm going to smack into him."

Anya laid her head back against the seat and raised her gaze toward the car's ceiling. "Sounds like our wedding. Not the smacking," she added. "But that's starting to sound like a good idea."

"Hey, we agreed," Xander said, wagging a finger at her as he kept his gaze on the road. "We don't go to bed mad. Or with broken bones. And that sounds so dysfunctional." He smiled uneasily at Tara. "Ha ha. We don't go in for that sort of stuff. The hitting and the breaking. We're a kinder, gentler engaged couple."

"Unless it's my heart," Anya said. "Breaking that is just fine for some people." She sniffled.

"Ahn." Xander kept his frustrated sigh to himself. "Hey, lighten up a little, okay? It's food." He heard himself. "It's food. Hey, how about little bags of Doritos at each place setting? Krispy Kremes for dessert, and we could—"

"Xander!"

Anya looked about ready to throttle him; he thought to himself, *Why do I do this? When will I resist the urge to do the riffing thing and learn to say, "Yes, dear"?*

"Maybe w-we should pull over," Tara said. "Let the other car go on ahead."

"I would, if I had any idea where the curb was," Xander replied. He gestured to the twin set of lights ahead of them. "I am so not loving this guy and his little red brake lights."

Only, hey, not little red brake lights. Fog's a little thinner; getting a better look at them now—

"Xander . . . ," Tara gasped. "Look."

The erstwhile brake lights were actually glowing red eyes. They were huge, maybe a car wheel across, almond-shaped, and fire burned within them. They grew larger as Xander stared numbly at them. How he could ever have mistaken them for brake lights, he had no idea. Because they were throbbing, living things; they were things that were drifting toward them in the fog. "Anyone you know?" he shouted to Anya.

"What?" She lifted her head from the seat and looked through the windshield.

The crash came next, and as Xander's head slammed against the steering wheel, he found himself thinking, *Me. It's what's for dinner.*

Then something was yanking the driver side door off its hinges and Anya was screaming and Xander was going somewhere where no thinking was allowed.

None at all.

Bath, England

"No!" Giles shouted, bolting upright in his wrought-iron bed.

Beside him, Olivia blinked awake. She sat up, too, blinking and staring at him. For one split second, he felt as if he had awakened beside a stranger. Then, calming a little, he found his center in her beautiful, troubled face. Her black hair ringleted softly around her temples and jawline, and her deep brown eyes were wide and startled.

"Rupert, what's the matter?" she asked, touching his shoulder and scrutinizing his features.

Giles's heart pounded. His forehead was covered in sweat. As he began to pull himself together, he patted her forearm. She took her hand and pressed it against his chest. His heart was beating fast.

"I don't know," he told her honestly. "I suppose I had a bad dream."

He wiped his forehead, reaching across her to fetch his glasses from the nightstand. He looked around at his flat, eyes adjusting to the bright sunlight that was streaming through the lacy curtains. All was as it should be. There was his messy desk, his revised résumé atop a few letters of application for various jobs. There was his photograph of Buffy and the others in a macaroni-encrusted frame Dawn had made for him.

There was the lovely bottle of wine Olivia had brought with her last night, and on a silver tray, some bits of cheese and a few grapes. There were her panties. . . .

"But it was only a dream," Olivia pressed. There was a catch in her voice, and she knew she was not so much looking to reassure him as she was looking for reassurance from him. Giles knew that his return to England summoned up all kinds of questions for her about their future together. She was hoping he had left all the terrifying truths of his life back in Sunnydale with his former charge, the Slayer. He also knew that it was quite possible that Olivia would leave him forever if that didn't prove to be the case.

"It was only a dream," he promised her. When she didn't relax, he touched her lovely cheek with his fingers. "Honestly. It had something to do with guitars and extremely gorgeous women in bikinis."

She smiled wryly. "My own private Austin Powers."

"Mick Jagger, *please,*" he returned, thrusting out his chest in self-mocking. "My band almost opened for the Stones once. Actually, someone once asked me if I was Roger Daltry." He chuckled with some measure of discreet pride.

Olivia chuckled back. She posed. "Do you know, the other day someone asked me if I'm Halle Berry?"

"Incredible." He sighed and shook his head at the lunacy of the general population. "You're far more beautiful than she could ever hope to be."

"Good answer," she murmured. "The best answer."

They kissed, the gesture a closure to the previous conversation and a most definite change of topic. The night terror had passed.

Languidly, Giles pushed the duvet down and stretched, then happened to glance at the antique clock he'd found in a jumble sale in the nearby town of Salisbury, home of the Cathedral and the plain where Stonehenge reached for the moon. "Christ, it's nearly nine o'clock."

"It doesn't matter." She lay back against the pillows, her dark skin beautiful against the creamy satin bed linens that she favored. "We've got nothing in particular to do today."

"Oh?" He tilted his head. Then he traced the curve of her temple and let his fingertips trail down her cheek, to rest on her lips. "Nothing?"

"*Oh.*" She settled in, stretching like a sleek cat, glancing down at him and smiling at what she saw. "Perhaps I was in error. Seems we've plenty to do."

"Indeed."

He bent to kiss her again, grateful that he had his own life to lead now—a life that included nightmares, yes, but of the dreaming time. They signified nothing. They were not worthy of daytime notice.

I'm no longer a Watcher, he thought wonderingly. *I'm the one doing things now, not sitting on the sidelines.*

And yet . . . I wonder how Buffy's been sleeping these days.

"Rupert," Olivia said reprovingly.

"Sorry." He smiled at her, and kissed her. "I'm here."

In the Sidhé

Beneath the streets of the human world of Sunnydale, the center of the *Tuatha* kingdom pulsated like a beating heart. This was the land of the *Sidhé* of Irish folklore, though back in Ireland the faery folk lived in hollow hills. Like so much else of the Old World, things had changed significantly with the move to the New World—which had occurred because Buffy Summers, the reigning Slayer, lived here.

Banshee, king of the *Tuatha,* clenched his fists so hard that his blood—which was a pale, crystalline blue—wafted from the centers of his palms and drifted toward the root-encrusted cavern that was his throne room. The grand chair he sat upon was made of the bones of his enemies, most of them human, and any king worthy of the name had many enemies. Sets of femurs bound together made the throne's legs, and each leg rested on the bones of a human foot. The seat and back were shaped to fit the king from clavicles from which sinewy flesh still hung like spiderwebs. The throne was upholstered in dried skins, then woven together with the frayed, clotted hair of the corpses of witches that had been discovered in the walls and ceiling of the cavern. For *Sidhé* was located beneath a graveyard, one of a dozen in the Sunnydale city limits—and this particular one was the last home of at least thirteen witches, by the king's own count.

Leaning forward, steam rising from his head, he watched the world above with two withered human eyes floating in front of his own watery blue ones. They were magickal eyes, handed down from father to son back in the old country, and said to have been the reason the witch Maggie Wall had been burned on a pyre of coal doused with tar back in Scotland in 1657. According to tradition, they had popped out of her skull when she had burned, and a raven had caught them and dropped them into Eire. He had no reason to doubt the story, for at least once every thirteen moons all he saw were flames, and he heard screaming echoing distantly in his ears.

With those eyes, King Banshee could cast his vision into the world above. Sunnydale attracted the bad dead and the undead as well as living monstrosities. The Hellmouth called to them, and the Hellmouth disgorged them.

And the Slayer tried to kill them all. But she was only one young woman, and those who shunned the light were legion.

Now, as he watched the place almost directly above his head, his rage ignited. Swathed in suspicious fog, a dark-haired girl in a black dress had flung herself at a passing car, yanked off the door, and was dragging out the occupants. They were friends of the Slayer—Xander Harris, his consort Anya, and Tara, a witch.

The girl might look innocent and frail, but Banshee saw her true shape: She was a warrior of the *Fomhóire*.

They've escaped from exile, he realized. *And what she has on her person is the means for moving into this dimension via the Hellmouth.*

For what he smelled on the disguised warrior—what the foot soldier was carrying—made his heart scream. The creature carried what the *Fomhóire* had searched for for centuries—the distilled mist from the cauldron of the evil Nemain, their goddess, and consort of their foul god, Balor.

When she had first cooked despair and disorientation in her cauldron, this mist was said to be the result. Her deed was the basis for the ancient Greek myth of Pandora, who was said to have released the evils of the world upon itself. It had been Nemain who had actually done it. Her name in the old language was Panic, and this vial was cause for panic indeed.

There could only be one creature for whom that potion was intended: Hell would reign on earth if the vial was opened and consumed by Jack, the shapeshifting favorite of the *Fomhóire* and traitor to the *Tuatha Dé Danann* half of his heritage. Jack was the only one of the *Fomhóire* who had been able to escape their prison and walk among humans. By spying on him, Banshee had learned that Jack sought this very mist. If he understood properly, once Jack drank the mist, the walls to the limbo place where the *Fomhóire* had been imprisoned for lo these millennia would simply melt, becoming mists themselves. And the *Fomhóire* would be able to cross through, as Jack himself could do.

The fogs that had fallen into Sunnydale of late had alarmed Banshee—he suspected that Jack had summoned them, and that soon they would begin to work their magick on the inhabitants, demon and human both. For these fogs were a diluted version of the potion in the vial; and after they had circulated in the atmosphere for an indeterminate amount of time, panic and disorientation took over living things.

It had been that way back in London, over a century ago. That was the second time Jack had managed to slip into the human realm. The first, he had tumbled into a Druid grove. Reveling in the human sacrifice he had inadvertently happened onto, he had re-created it himself the next time he was there, and made a name for himself in the annals of history—Jack the Ripper. He had brought hell to earth that time, and human beings had never been the same.

Not even the Vampire Slayer, whose name had been Elizabeth, had managed to stop him. A story of total defeat, that. A tale that Banshee hoped the current Slayer knew well, so that she would not repeat the fate of Elizabeth, whom Banshee had been unable to help.

I tried. We all tried. We failed to save her, and we did nothing to thwart Jack. The only reason he was unable to succeed was that he didn't have the potion back then.

But he does now. Or will, soon. If we don't stop him.

He turned to his captain, MacNair, who, like Banshee, was pure *Tuatha*. He was sapphire-eyed, his hair nearly white, his skin a milky blue resembling human death. In their day, his people had been considered quite fair; nowadays, when they were seen by modern folk, the humans fled, assuming them to be the walking dead. The fact that their entry place into Sunnydale was through a crypt in one of the dozen cemeteries within the city limits did nothing to dispel that image. As a result, and having no need to walk among the humans, Banshee had forbidden any of his people to venture into Sunnydale.

But King Banshee knew his order was disobeyed by the younger faery. The young ones had no memory of how faery had been persecuted and destroyed whenever they were discovered. Even the Sunnydale Slayer had mistaken a number of them for vampires, and slaughtered them almost before they'd exited the crypt that was their passageway.

As if the danger was some kind of extra added attraction, they had begun daring each other to sneak out into the upperworld, grab some kind of proof that they'd made the run, and come back with full bragging rights. Street creds, they called it, just like the human children.

But that was all to the good, he realized now. He could send a band of foolhardy *Tuatha* after the *Fomhóire* warrior, steal the vial, and bring it back here before the *Fomhóire* knew what was happening. Then Banshee would destroy it.

He would have to do it right, and he would have to do it quickly. Else Jack would do something to counterattack—of that, Balor was sure. *Maybe call on demonic allies. Of course the* Fomhóire *have forged alliances in their exile. The last time they attempted to take over, they appealed to the vampires of London.*

If they do that again, we will have our Last Battle on the streets of Sunnydale, he thought with grim satisfaction. The same icy ambition ran through his veins as through the veins of the young ones who were willing to risk death for the glory of surviving an attack by the Slayer. If he could be the king who destroyed the *Fomhóire* once and for all . . . the glory that would be his would survive his death!

Contrary to belief and folktale, neither *Tuatha Dé Danann* nor *Fomhóire* were immortal. Left alone, they would live hundreds of years, even thousands. But they could be killed. Contrary to the lust for life vampires clung to, *Tuatha,* at least, were more philosophical about letting go of it at last. Maybe it was an artifact of having lived in a country where poetry was revered as a living thing, but to a *Tuatha,* being sung about and remembered in verse was nearly the same as immortality.

It underscored the importance *Tuatha* placed on actions, deeds. To their way of thinking, being exiled to a dimension where they could do nothing but bide their time was a fate worse than death for the *Fomhóire.* The barbaric *Fomhóire* didn't seem to agree with that; for them, survival was the key factor. Better to live in shame and degradation than to die the most honorable and noble of deaths.

In the street talk of today, Banshee thought, *dying is for wimps.*

MacNair was still waiting for his king to speak. Banshee said, "There is a *Fomhóire* aboveground disguised as a young human girl. She's carrying the Sacred Fog of Nemain."

MacNair's lips parted in shock.

"Jack the shapeshifter has come," Banshee continued. "At least, I assume he has. The city of Sunnydale is filled with fogs, the way London was that time he arrived in the human realm. And you remember what happened back then."

The other *Tuatha* nodded thoughtfully. "I was awfully young during London. I don't remember much, except all the blood." He paused, remembering. "There was so much of it that it seeped through the ground and dripped onto my face while I was in my cradle."

"It tasted good, didn't it?" the king asked him, smiling faintly. *Tuatha* as a race didn't prey on humans for their blood, but they liked the taste very much. "The streets ran with it for days. I'll never understand how that was kept out of the retellings. So many details about Jack the Ripper were obliterated. And yet, the bare bones—if you will—of the story remain intact."

MacNair gestured upward with his long, ice-blue fingers. "The humans have always been that way. Short lives and shorter memories. Look at all the things that happen in Sunnydale, and not one of them wants to admit the truth of them. They blame gangs for vampiric attacks. Mutilated bodies wash up on their shore and they talk about bad luck deep-sea fishing. It's so absurd."

"It's the power of story," Banshee asserted. "It's not the tale, it's he who tells it." He grinned. "A fine bard of their own said that. Stephen King.

"Assemble a raiding party," Banshee ordered.

"Hell, take an army. Take them aboveground and get the vial from the demon without delay. By the looks of 'her,' the mind is beginning to disintegrate." He smiled at MacNair. "It's luck for us that the *Fomhóire* appear to have alliances with demons who have almost as much trouble traveling to this dimension as they do."

MacNair smiled back; then his smile fell, and he said, "But if they get the vial to Jack, he can bring them through . . ."

"If they get the vial, they will have no trouble at all traveling here themselves," Banshee agreed.

"Then my army is on its way to stop him," Mac-Nair assured him. With a slight bow, the tall, thin *Tuatha* turned on his heel and hurried away, shouting, "Bram! Cethis! We're going above!"

Banshee sighed. He wanted to go, too. But in case something should go wrong, the *Tuatha* needed to prepare for, at the least, a reprisal, and at the most, a full-out war. His wisdom and battle skills would be needed.

And we'll need to talk to the Slayer, he thought, hating the idea. He had no idea how she felt about his race—did she classify *Tuatha* faery as demonic? He hoped that warning her about the effect the fogs would have on her own people would reassure her that he had good intentions—although, truth be told, he didn't care if all the humans on the planet died. But that was not the same as actively killing them himself.

This Slayer appeared to be a practical sort of woman. Long-lived for a Slayer. And she was the love slave of one of Banshee's strongest aboveground allies: the white-haired Spike.

Ah, we have such a history, we two, Banshee thought, smiling grimly. *What ballads our exploits would make. I wonder if he's told her about Jack and Elizabeth. I wonder if she knows what lies in store if I don't get that vial.*

It's all shifting around in the mists the same as it did the first time. When that fog cleared, there was a dead Slayer.

And blood.

So very, very much blood.

His smile vanished. He was an old warrior, and he savored the prospect of battle as much as the next soldier king. But he was also the protector of his people, and he had evolved with the centuries. Might and right aside, if there were other ways to ensure the survival of the *Tuatha,* it would do well to discover them.

He clapped his hands three times. From the shadows, a misshapen dwarf popped into view, bowing and scraping. His head was shaggy with brilliant red hair, and he wore the skin of a small cat that he had trapped down by the Sunnydale docks. His feet were bare, and they were nothing but a mottle of carbuncles and calluses, rather like the hull of a sunken ship. Leprechauns were not at all the "By gosh and begorrah" little imps depicted in human stories. They were vicious, cruel, and amoral.

As such, quite useful.

"Your Majesty," the leprechaun said with a silken tone. "What may I do for you, sir?"

Banshee so despised the leprechauns that he had trouble remembering their names and their places in their hierarchy. But this one he knew. This one had been his confidant for more centuries than Banshee cared to count. His name was Flinn.

"I want you to hide something so that it can never be found again," Banshee announced.

Flinn raised his chin with pride. "Our gold can never be found."

"That is pure blarney, leprechaun," Banshee said sternly. "You often give it away of your own free will. Usually in return for human favors. Wives, for instance," he drawled.

Flinn laughed heartily. "That is so, King Banshee. The men of my race have a softness for human wives."

"I'll give you a favor in return," Banshee said. "We'll have a bargain, you and I." He held out his hand. In the center of his palm lay the wizened eyes of the witch Maggie Wells. "Look upon Sunnydale, and tell me a thing you want. And you shall have it, if you swear in advance to hide what I have you hide."

"Hmm. What is it?"

"I will not tell you," Banshee informed him, "until you agree to the bargain."

The leprechaun was intrigued. "An interesting proposition, that. Very well."

Banshee waved his hand over the eyes. They rose into the air; Flinn positioned himself behind them and looked into the upperworld.

At a murmur from Banshee, Flinn's perspective changed again and again. He saw the streets of Sunnydale—Main Street, with its quaint shops, including the Magic Box, the Sun Cinema, and his favorite, the jewelry store.

"Nothing there that I cannot claim for meself," Flinn said, feigning disinterest. He moved his head away from the floating eyes of Maggie Wells and yawned.

"Wait. Watch."

King Banshee moved his hand before the eyes. Flinn looked back through them, and his view became that of a flying bird, winging its way over the cursed little town. On he flew, and then he saw a two-story house; the eyes took him to a large window in the center of the ground floor.

"The Slayer has a sister," King Banshee told him. "And others have wanted her."

"Hmm." Flinn grinned eagerly as the eyes moved his view through the window and into the room. And there she sat with another female . . . the woman of his dreams. A beauty beyond comparing. She was so lovely that he could say nothing more coherent than "Ah!"

Banshee nodded. "Is she not fair?"

"Aye, King Banshee." Flinn clicked his teeth eagerly. "What a woman. Skin so fair, and hair . . . the color . . ." He groped for the proper way to describe it.

"Like chestnuts," Banshee ventured, having spent some hours peering through the windows of the Slayer's home himself.

"Chestnuts? No, indeed," Flinn protested. "Like . . . fire. Beautiful fire."

Banshee laughed. "Ah. You're looking at the friend. The Wicca. No, small man. She'll have nothing to do with you. It's women she prefers."

"She's a Wicca?" Flinn echoed, staring at the red-headed woman who was seated beside a young girl.

The two were watching television. "Even better!"

"She does not care for men," Banshee repeated.

"I'm no man," Flinn said carelessly. He rubbed his hands together. "I want her. I want the Wicca."

Banshee sighed, amused. Leprechauns were such odd wee folk. Thoroughly contemptible, but their antics could be quite entertaining. *Rather like ferrets.*

"You've never seen Willow Rosenberg before?" King Banshee asked. "I'm surprised. She is the best friend of the Slayer."

"Her name is Willow? Even better!" Flinn said. He tore his gaze away from the witchy eyes of Maggie Wells. "It's she I'm wanting."

"And her you shall have. So our bargain is made."

"With whiskey," the leprechaun insisted.

"Very well."

The faery king clapped his hands. At once, a serving girl appeared and he told her that he wanted the finest of hard drink in all the *Sidhé.* She curtsied, left, and returned with an old-fashioned flask and two crystalline goblets.

King Banshee poured two full measures for the leprechaun and only one for himself. His raiding party was even now racing to intercept the enemy. Their leader must keep his wits about himself at all times.

They drank, Flinn comically smacking his lips. King Banshee rubbed his hands together as he poured the little man another round. "Now I'll tell you," he said. "You will be hiding the Sacred Fog."

Flinn paled. "No, milord. We can't do such a thing. Even if it existed—"

"Oh, it does," Banshee assured him. "And we are about to steal it from the *Fomhóire* warrior who hopes to deliver it to Jack."

"The Ripper? He's in Sunnydale?" Flinn backed away. "I can't do this. If he ever heard that I had hidden it . . ."

"You drank on it." Banshee poured him another. "Your bride-to-be is a magick-user," he reminded Flinn. "She can use magicks to protect you."

Flinn frowned. "I can't, King Banshee. It would be the end of me life."

Banshee gazed levelly at the leprechaun. Then he reached beneath his throne and pulled out a long, heavy sword. The hilt had been carved from what was, quite clearly, the skull of a leprechaun.

"Your life could end here, tonight," the monarch drawled.

Flinn was outraged. "We have always worked for you with honor!"

Banshee sighed. "Those days are over, little man. I'm fighting for the life of my people now. Your life seems so . . . insignificant by comparison."

He caught up the floating eyes and cupped them in his hand, like a man about to play dice.

"She is a beautiful girl. I'm sure that you both will be very happy."

Flinn's smile was philosophical. "Well, then, Banshee, I'll save the world and be a happy imp at the end of day."

"Well said." The king of the *Tuatha* replaced his sword beneath his throne. "Very well said."

* * *

Sprawled on the couch beneath her old Tigger throw, Dawn half-knew that she was almost asleep. She could hear the droning of the TV. Beneath the throw, Dawn realized she was shivering really, really hard. Her hands were clenched, and her teeth were chattering.

My God, I'm freezing. My feet are like ice.

She tried to open her eyes, but they were too heavy. She tried to move her body but she felt paralyzed.

My heart . . .

. . . it hurts . . .

Throbbing inside her chest, her heart ached like a very sore muscle. Which it was, muscle, but no reason for it to be sore. As she groaned softly, she tried to shift away from the pain in her chest; it was almost as if someone were squeezing his hand around it, compressing it, squeezing the blood out of it. She could do nothing but feel the pain, which was increasing.

My heart isn't beating. . . .

Help me, Willow. Where are you?

"Dawn?" Willow asked aloud.

And Dawn opened her eyes. She blinked at Willow, laying her hand over her heart, and then gazed all around them. "Willow?" she cried.

The sofa on which they had both fallen asleep was surrounded by dense fog. It was so thick Dawn couldn't see the carpet. She couldn't even see the TV, or the walls. The only thing that she could see was Willow.

"What's going on?" she shouted, scrabbling over to Willow's side and burying herself inside the Wicca's embrace.

Willow opened her hand and murmured something in what sounded like Latin. At once, the fog noticeably thinned. She said it again, and a hole formed in the dense, wet mist.

Then she stood up. Dawn kept hold of her, pleading, "Don't move!"

"Stay there," Willow ordered her.

"Willow, please!"

Dawn stretched out her arms as Willow moved into the fog. It drifted behind her, shielding her from Dawn's sight. There was a moment of blind terror, and then suddenly, Willow's voice rang out.

The fog vanished.

Willow was at the door; she leaned against it and ran her hands through her short red hair. "Maybe Buffy didn't shut the door all the way," she said. "And the fog drifted in."

Dawn tried to swallow around the lump in her throat. "I had a bad dream," she told Willow. "Or something. My heart." She touched her chest. Her heart felt fine. "I guess it was a dream," she said uncertainly.

Willow returned to the couch and sat cross-legged facing Dawn. "Tell me," she urged. "Tell me about the dream."

Dawn thought a moment. "I don't remember it anymore. It was . . ." She was puzzled. "I think it was about Meg Ryan."

"Well, if I was in love with a guy . . . hello, lesbian, but if I was," Willow said, "I wouldn't just do the happy dance when I found out he put me out of business." She wrinkled her nose. "I think this movie is just whacked."

Dawn giggled. It felt good. "Me too. That was what I was thinking in my dream, actually. I remember it now. And I had this ache. . . ." She touched her chest. "It really hurt."

"No wonder, the position you fell asleep in," Willow said. "Let's get you upstairs and in your bed before your big sis comes home and busts us both."

Outside, thunder rumbled. Dawn shrieked and grabbed hold of Willow. A jag of lightning jittered across the front window, and then the sky cracked open. It began to rain.

The two stood together for a moment. The rain rapidly shifted into a downpour, cascades of water smacking the windows. Another jag of lightning flashed, and thunder made the windows shudder. Tree branches scratched the walls of the house.

Lightning crackled again, and then two more times in rapid succession. The accompanying roars of thunder were enough to shake the house.

Dawn whimpered and held on to Willow.

"Easy," Willow soothed her, smoothing her hair. "It's just a storm." Her voice was a little tight. "Just a plain old ordinary storm. Hey, it'll probably clear away all the fog."

"You must think I'm a big baby," Dawn said, sniffling. "Scared of my own shadow."

"No. I don't." Willow regarded the Slayer's little sister with sad affection. "There's a lot to be afraid of in Sunnydale."

"It's not all pop quizzes and compositions about the Constitution and the Bill of Rights," Dawn agreed wearily.

"Nope." Willow gave her a hug. "Let's go on upstairs. Cuddle up in my room until Buffy gets back." She glanced anxiously at the windows. "It shouldn't be long. She won't stay out in this."

"She's never home," Dawn said softly. "Sometimes I almost forget what she looks like." At Willow's skeptical glance, she said, "Okay, not. But I do miss her."

"She has a lot on her plate," Willow reminded her, shepherding her toward the stairs. "Slayage, worrying about bills. I know it's not easy being the sister of the Slayer."

"True. But it's also kinda cool." Dawn smiled shyly at Willow. "It's kinda cool having you around, too."

"Thanks."

Willow took the stairs first, Dawn following behind. They'd left all the lights on, which, waste of electricity and Buffy would probably say something about it when she got home. But Dawn liked the light. Not so keen on shadows and darkness.

They went into Willow's room. Dawn noted a cardboard box beside the door labeled TARA and felt a pang. Tara and Willow were like her two aunts; it was like having another divorce in the family.

Except that when my parents got divorced, I didn't exist. My memories of that time are created, planted to make me and Buffy assume I'm real.

Which I am now, she reminded herself firmly.

Willow reached the bed and pulled back the covers.

Then she said, "Hey, how about something warm? I'll make us some tea. We'll save the chocolate for when Buffy gets back."

"Okay," Dawn said, before she realized that that meant Willow was going to leave her alone and go back downstairs.

She was too embarrassed to take it back, so she kept smiling as Willow gestured to the bed and said, "Get in and get snuggly. You want some chamomile?"

"Sure." Dawn crawled over to Tara's side and made a show of pulling up the quilts and sheets and being all okay. She said, "You have any good trashy magazines?"

"Well, I have schoolbooks," Willow offered.

"Mmm, no thanks. There's a *Seventeen* in the kitchen."

"I'll get it. Be right back."

"Sure thing." Dawn pulled her knees up and rested her hands on them. "I'll be here."

Willow turned and walked as steadily as she could out of the room. *Oh my God, oh, my God,* she thought. Her hands were trembling wildly. *I need something. I need some magick. . . .*

In the hall, she flexed her hands and then put them under her arms, acutely self-conscious, wanting to do nothing to betray her condition. When she reached the stairs she went slowly, clinging to the banister, afraid she was going to throw up.

The kitchen seemed impossibly far away. She moved through the living room, switching off the TV—

the credits for *You've Got Mail* were still rolling—then made it into the kitchen.

When the phone rang, Willow nearly leaped through the ceiling. She grabbed it up. "Buffy?" she queried.

"No, mi darlin'," said a voice she didn't recognize. "Just a friend. But a friend with something that you need, I'm thinking."

"Hello?" She frowned. "Who is this?"

"My name is Flinn. I'm . . . I've seen you here and there. We share . . . we have much in common."

Willow closed her eyes. "I saw you at that rave, didn't I?" she asked, embarrassed. "The one with the magicks from India." She dimly recalled giving some guy her phone number if he ever got any more of the potent herbs he had shared with her at the festival. It was hard to remember many details; she had been high on magick at the time.

"Yes," he said quickly. "I've got some now." He lowered his voice. "Thought you might want to come and have some."

"I . . . I can't," she whispered. "I can't leave right now." She took a breath. "Is there any way you can send me some of it magickally? Because, well . . ." She felt itchy, embarrassed. She didn't know this person at all. Didn't even remember his name. But the thought of having something to take the edge off was very tempting.

"I could meet you a few blocks from your house," he told her.

"I don't know you."

"Flinn."

"Almost like Riley," she murmured.

"It's good, what I have," he pressed. "You'd like it."

Licking her lips, she glanced again toward the stairs and picked up the kettle from the stove top. She carried it to the sink and turned on the faucet as she cradled the phone against her ear.

She closed her eyes, horribly tempted. She was feeling worse and worse; her hands were shaking so badly that she set the kettle on the counter and turned off the water. Balling her hand, she grimaced and let a wave of nausea wash over her.

Then inspiration hit: *I could put something in Dawn's tea, make her fall asleep. I could meet this guy, get a little something, and sneak back. It wouldn't take any time at all.*

She stared at the kettle. *I could do it and no one would ever know. It would be my secret and no one would get hurt.*

You don't know that, her conscience whispered. *Plenty of people could get hurt.*

Guilt rose as she remembered how Tara had clenched the dried flowers, the tangible evidence of the forgetting spell Willow had cast. That one had backfired very badly. And the one with the crystal. Nearly everyone had been killed.

But this would be just a simple sleeping potion. That's practically foolproof.

"I . . . I can't right now," she blurted aloud into the phone. "I . . . I can't leave."

"Ah, mi darlin', I don't have a car." His voice was soft and honey sweet, and Willow closed her eyes, swaying as if to music.

"Willow? Pretty Willow, I'll be outside the Bronze, all right? I'll be there for another hour, if you change your mind."

I'll get just enough to make the nausea and the dizziness go away.

Then she heard footsteps outside the window. The hair on the back of her neck stood on end; she hung up and dashed back to the phone cradle on the wall; she set the receiver into it and jumped away, grabbing up the kettle and putting it under the running water.

The kitchen door opened, and Buffy walked in. Her hair was a mess.

"Jeez, Buffy," Willow said by way of greeting.

"Yeah." Buffy smoothed back her hair with her right hand and made a good effort to smile, but she didn't manage it. Instead, she pulled out a kitchen chair and plopped into it, groaning under her breath.

"Hey," Willow said, "you okay? I mean, okay in terms of you?"

Buffy nodded, slumping forward and burying her face in both her hands. "Rough night."

"Even with the fog, huh? Creepies found you?" Willow asked, concerned, as Buffy nodded wearily. "Did you see any more trolls?"

"Any more . . . ? Oh. No." Buffy shook her head. "No trolls."

"Hmm. Well, given how gross they are, that's good."

"You find out anything else?"

Willow set the kettle on the stove, turned on the heat, and thought about the potion she had planned to slip into the tea. *What was I thinking? What if Buffy*

*had come home and found Dawn all alone again? She
would have been furious with me.*

*What if she had figured out that I'd drugged her
little sister?*

*God, how could I even think of drugging Dawnie?
What is wrong with me? Have I gone completely insane?*

"We were watching *You've Got Mail!* and the fog
just got in the house somehow," Willow told her. "We . . .
it was like we panicked or something."

"The fog scared you?" Buffy looked around. "Did
someone leave a window open or something?"

"I don't know. I never found anything. I just
came down to make tea." She gestured to the kettle.
"Chamomile. Would you like some? Actually, we
were going to hold off on the hot chocolate until you
came home."

"That's sweet," Buffy said distractedly. "I'll say hi
to Dawn and then"—the Slayer rose very slowly and
painfully—"take a hot bath."

Willow nodded. "I guess you stayed out of the storm."

"Huh?" Buffy looked puzzled.

"The rain. I guess it's stopped." Willow gestured to
Buffy's hair, which, while matted and tangled, was
dry. "You managed to stay out of it."

"Oh. Yeah." Buffy touched her hair again. "And
the fog's gone, too."

Willow looked out the window. Sure enough, the
night was its own regular self. The streetlamps were
shining and there were lights on in some of the other
houses on Revello. She knew from experience that their
fellow Sunnydalians firmly ignored all the weirdness

that went on. Everyone explained everything away with extremely lame reasoning: broken gas lines, gangs on PCP, the bad economy, the Republicans. It was always something else, never anything supernatural or evil.

Well, maybe except for the Republicans.

"I'll do more research tomorrow," Willow promised. "Dawn kind of needed someone tonight."

"Oh, that's okay. Of course. I'm glad you were here." Buffy sighed. "God knows *I'm* never here when she needs me."

"You're busy," Willow said loyally, realizing that she had been about to betray Buffy in the worst way possible: leaving her sister all alone on a scary night of the unliving bad. "Y'know, saving the world and all." *Unlike me. I just want to leave your sister alone so I can explore strange new worlds of wonder.*

"Yeah. Saving the world." Buffy looked down at the kitchen floor. "Well, I'm going on up."

"Good," Willow said. "Tell Dawn the tea's almost ready."

"Sure." She paused. "Make me some, too? We three can . . . hang."

"Absolutely," Willow said brightly. "We'll have a tea party, only not like in Boston. Here, we drink our tea." She didn't feel bright. She felt nauseated.

Buffy gave her a little nod and trudged slowly past. Willow was anxious. Was the Slayer losing her edge? She was older now than most Slayers ever got. Did her powers get used up at some point?

If that's the case, will she get to retire and live to a ripe old age?

Those were questions Willow couldn't answer. Nor could she answer the question that was foremost in her mind:

When will Buffy fall asleep, so I can meet that Flinn guy? 'Cause now she's home, and Dawn will be safe, and I can worry about my own problem.

Well, not problem. I don't have a problem. I'm just lonely, since Tara left.

She paced while the water warmed, checking to make sure the whistle on the kettle was properly positioned and would sound when the water had boiled. It seemed to be taking so long. The clock ticking on the wall made her edgy.

Did I put enough water in the kettle for three cups? she wondered. *Because I don't want to have to heat up more. Maybe the microwave will do it faster. But hey, almost boiling. So why doesn't the blasted thing whistle?*

Her skin was itchy. She scratched, looked down, and saw that she was tracking red lines into the soft skin of her inner forearm. Blood was beading up, and her own skin was under her fingernails.

I feel like there are ants under my skin.

She scratched, watching herself scratch. Her head began to pound, and she broke into a sweat.

She kept pacing, acutely aware of every noise in the house. Her own footsteps sounded like the bass line of a Darling Violetta cello-driven cross between Smashing Pumpkins and the Beatles. She heard the creaking of Buffy's footsteps in the hallway above her. the opening of the upstairs bathroom door, the sound of the filling tub.

When the teakettle whistled, she nearly jumped out of her skin.

Dawn's probably asleep, she told herself, but she went through the motions, anyway, snagging a couple of mugs from the cabinet and draping chamomile tea bags in them. She grabbed the sugar bowl and paused, seeing behind it a small vase that Joyce had brought home from her art gallery. Black with an elongated gazelle enameled in green, it was from Nairobi, and Willow had always liked it. Joyce had told her that one day she would give it to her. Buffy didn't know that, and Willow hadn't mentioned it. So she supposed it still officially belonged to the Summers sisters.

Joyce kind of belonged to me, too. To all of us. Our mom away from Mom. She was the only one who knew all of it—everything supernatural that was going on in Sunnydale. My parents sure didn't know . . .

But Joyce knew. And she would be so disappointed in me, she thought wretchedly.

Then she pushed the thought from her mind, setting her jaw and placing the sugar bowl on the counter. It didn't matter; Buffy's mom was dead. Besides, she would have appreciated all the pressures Willow was under.

Joyce took sleeping pills when she was stressed out. And sometimes she drank a glass of wine or that really fruity schnapps she kept in the freezer. This is just the witchy equivalent of doing something like that. I'm getting through a hard time, that's all.

I'll taper off and quit. But first I'll meet that guy.

Resolutely she got a third mug, poured in the

boiling water, dipped the tea bags, added sugar, and picked two of them up. Her hands were shaking so badly that the boiling water splashed onto her right wrist; she cried out and dropped both mugs. They crashed to the floor, one of them shattering. Willow jumped back awkwardly, slamming her elbow against the counter and knocking over the little African vase. It rolled into the sink and broke.

"Damn it!" Willow shouted.

She started to go to the pantry for the broom, then realized she needed to pick up the pieces of broken ceramic first. She bent down. Her head swam; she fell forward and put her hand over one of the shards. It cut deep.

She set her jaw and forced herself back on her haunches.

"What's wrong?" Buffy asked from the doorway. She had a towel wrapped around her head and she was wearing her moon-and-stars bathrobe. Water dripped from her bare feet.

"Dropped 'em," Willow said tightly. "It's okay. No big deal." She took in Buffy's appearance. It seemed that Buffy had just left the kitchen. Time was moving strangely for Willow. "Dawn asleep?" she asked.

"Yes. You're bleeding." Buffy crossed to her, helping her up and examining her wounded hand. She looked alarmed. The cut was deep, and Willow was bleeding profusely. "Willow, I think you might need stitches. We need to take you to the emergency room."

"No!" Willow cried, then lowered her voice. "No, it's okay. Look." She made a gesture over her hand and murmured words of healing. The blood flow slowed. It didn't stop, but she had deliberately framed the spell so that it wouldn't. *It looks better that way,* she thought. *Not so . . . magicky.*

"Buffy?" That was Dawn now. "Buffy, what's wrong?"

"Nothing, Dawn. It's okay," Buffy called.

Willow made a moue of apology and tried to pull her hand away, as if hiding the evidence might distract Buffy. "I woke her up. Sorry."

Buffy shook her head. "Sorry for getting hurt? Don't be silly."

"I'm fine," Willow insisted, wrapping a kitchen towel around her injury and putting her hand behind her back. "Go back to her. She was really scared. She'll be glad you're home."

"Okay." Buffy unwrapped her towel and sweetly handed it to Willow. "But if it doesn't stop bleeding, come and get me, okay?"

"Yeah," Willow said hoarsely. She took the towel from Buffy. As soon as the Slayer's back was turned, she draped the towel over a kitchen chair and got some paper napkins from the holder on the table. She wrapped them around her hand and watched the blood soak through.

She upgraded the healing spell with a few extra syllables. The room wobbled; she became incredibly disoriented; she only stopped herself from falling over by grabbing on to a chair leg with her hurt hand. Blood smeared from her hand onto the wooden leg.

Grimly she helped herself to a standing position. Then she stumbled to the counter and unrolled a wad of paper towels. Taking a deep breath, she slowly bent forward and began picking up the shattered mug. Oddly enough, the other mug had landed bottom-first onto the floor, and most of the tea had remained inside it; its tea bag was still immersed, still dispensing chamomile, whose curative properties included settling the stomach and calming the nerves.

"Thank you, Goddess," Willow breathed. She picked it up and took a small sip. The warmth suffused throughout her body, and she closed her eyes and took another sip.

After a few more swallows, she set the cup down on the table and set to cleaning up the mess. She found some comfort in the sense of ordinary routine. After she deposited the wet towels in the trash, she cleaned the blood off the chair and, as was a witch's habit, carried the bloody paper towels to the fireplace and lit them. She didn't currently have any enemies that she knew of, but no witch worth her salt left her own blood, fingernail clippings, or strands of hair anywhere where someone who could work magicks could find them.

As she watched the towels go up, she finished her tea. Then she trudged to the stairs and went very slowly to the second floor. She felt as if she weighed five hundred pounds.

As she had expected, Dawn was asleep. Bonus: Buffy was curled up beside her sister, completely out.

Willow was, for all intents and purposes, alone.

She stood staring at the Slayer and the former Key; for one instant—just one heartbeat—she thought about waking Buffy up and asking her to watch TV with her.

Then she tiptoed into the room and grabbed her coat and a knitted cap Tara had given her.

She touched the cardboard box containing Tara's belongings as if for luck—or maybe for forgiveness—and minced back into the hall.

She descended the stairway like a thief, having committed the crime and now looking only for escape.

The front door opened easily. The night was surprisingly cold, smacking Willow with its frosty sharpness. She put on her cap and closed the door very quietly behind herself, making certain it was locked. The porch light was still on; she snapped her fingers and it winked out.

She didn't want any witnesses, no one to see her stealing away to get a magickal fix.

But as she loped down the drive and started to blend into the shadows, her guilt and anxiety began to wash away, replaced by anticipation. It was going to feel good, so good.

She did a little dance step, then giggled and covered her mouth in case anyone saw her.

What the hell do I care? she asked herself. *I'm a witch!*

Willow grinned to herself in the night, feeling adventurous now, and nothing beyond naughty. Hey, she had her own life, and she wasn't hurting anybody. She was a responsible person—she kept up with her studies, took good care of Dawn. She was handling it all.

I can handle it all. I just have the flu or something,

*or did. That's why I don't feel very well. I was over-
compensating, worrying about going through withdrawal or whatever. But I'm not addicted to magick,
like Tara said. Hell, I'm fine. I feel great.*

She held out her hands. They were steady as rocks.

It's going to be such a great night, she thought.

Sweat pouring down her face, legs bent like an old
woman with rickets, the most powerful Wicca in Sunnydale hurried down the street.

The creature who was calling itself Maeve continued to stare down at the three unconscious human bodies it had yanked out of the car. *Not Jack. None of
them.*

She didn't remember about pain, and she didn't
understand dying; all she could process was these were
not he whom she sought. The false persona that was
Maeve did not know that her mind was already halfway
past total disintergration, and there would not be much
more thime before it would decompose inside her skull.
She also did not know that once that happened, her
body would transform back into its original form, and
then it would travel back to her own dimension.

And be dead.

The human with the short, dark hair was the most
gravely wounded. One of his arms was bent the wrong
way, and his eyes were half-open. If Maeve had
remembered injury, she would understand that he was
in shock.

The female whom Maeve had dragged out after
him from their vehicle had demon blood in her. Maeve

considered devouring her but dimly understood that time was critical to the success of her mission. Then she thought about ripping off some flesh to save for later.

She grabbed the female's leg and began to yank. Then the other female groaned, which caught Maeve's attention. Magick emanated from her. Lots of it, and very fine.

Without using conscious thought, Maeve understood that taking this magick could prolong her own life.

She had to live long enough to get the vial to Jack. That's all she knew, and all she understood. Survival was key.

Chapter Four

London, 1888

The Slayer did not leave the flat that night, nor her Watcher. Spike and Drusilla reluctantly returned to their lair. Once the secret hideaway of a minor Royal and his mistress, an opera singer. The place was splendid, furnished with Louis XIV divans and a massive baroque bed, milady's private dressing room, and one for His Majesty. Darla had found the place and Angelus had butchered the two inhabitants, as well as their retinue of servants.

Then Spike and Drusilla had shattered all the mirrors.

Now they stood like two disobedient children, enduring the lecture of their elders. Dressed in a fine linen nightdress and, over that, a peignoir of scarlet Chinese silk, Darla chastised them for staying out till nearly dawn. In the dead nobleman's embroidered smoking jacket and Arabian pantaloons, Angelus joined in, mocking Spike for a useless renegade who had no disregard for the safety of Drusilla.

Spike chafed at the paternal tone Angelus took with him, pouting and scowling until Angelus backhanded him, sending him sprawling on the red velvet settee directly before the fireplace, where a cheery fire warmed beautiful golden goblets brimming with fresh human blood.

After Angelus was finished, it was Darla's turn again. While Drusilla, having grown bored with the situation, blindfolded several new dolls she had stolen from a child's nursery the night before, the doyenne of their little band said harshly, "What neither of you knows is that more of your little girls were murdered tonight, Drusilla. Yes, your vampire daughters, all slaughtered. Six of them. They were tortured before they were dusted. That could have happened to you."

"Oh, Grandmother!" Drusilla stared at her, horrified. Her lovely dolly dropped to the floor and shattered. "What are you saying? Was Bettine among them?"

"Don't call me that," Darla snapped. She hated Drusilla calling her Grandmother, could not abide thinking of herself as old enough to be a grandmother, though she was hundreds of years old.

"Was she?" Drusilla pleaded. Bettine was Drusilla's newest creation, a young lady of some refinement who, upon her transformation, had become a licentious, ravening monster—and hence, Drusilla's present favorite.

"Yes, she was," Darla said, with obvious satisfaction.

Drusilla grabbed another doll from the heap, punched out the glass eyes, and clasped the puppet to her breast, moaning with grief. In her anxiety, she sank to the floor. "Who done it?"

"That demon in the fog," Spike grumbled, "That's what I'm bettin'."

Angelus nodded grimly, folding his arms across his chest like a pasha. "Aye. It was himself."

"Oh, we have to stop him!" Drusilla wailed. She fell onto her palms and began to crawl on all fours like a crazed mother cat sniffing out her kittens. Her knee caught on her hem and ripped the skirt away from the waist. She didn't even notice. "He's poking out their hearts. My dollies are all shrieking!"

"And Angelus's harem," Darla drawled, putting her arms around her lover. "All those lovely young vampires, disemboweled. It's horrible."

Her eyes belied her words; the thought actually excited her. She flashed a little smile at Angelus and turned to the mad vampire, who bowed backward, folding herself into a V shape on account of her large bustle, and was sobbing as if her unbeating heart would break.

Spike sat on the settee before the fire and pulled off his boots nonchalantly. Flexing his toes, he said, "He needs killing, that one."

"No. He's too dangerous," Darla insisted. "Steer clear of him, both of you."

"But . . ." Dru wiped her eyes and turned her gaze on Spike. She moved on her knees to him, placing her hands on his thighs and tilting her head as she stared up at him. Tears rolled down her cheeks. "However shall I bear it? I am alone, and the moon is singing." She cupped her ears. "'Go to the one, run to him, run.' I hear the batwings flapping, and the moon burns me, Spike. It burns my tears to blood."

He cupped the side of her face. She was so fragile, so beautiful. Her huge eyes were luminous in her milky skin. Her long neck, her exquisite décolletage . . . he stirred, wanting her.

"I should be ever so grateful if you popped his heart out," she whispered, then tucked in her chin and gazed up at him through her lashes. "I would give you kisses, Spike, up and down, up and down. Your blood will boil."

Her tone made him boil inside. It was a caress down the length of his body; it was a kiss in all the secret places no decent lady would have ever kissed him, had he lived a normal life.

"If either of you attempts to take him on, you will be very sorry," Darla announced. "Now, both of you, go to sleep. I'm exhausted."

She took Angelus's arm, and he led her out of the parlor and into the bedroom, where the two shared the fantastic bed. Drusilla and Spike slept everywhere else, testing all the flat surfaces in the den of wanton pleasure and illicit romance.

After the two elders were gone, Drusilla threw herself into Spike's arms and began to cry fresh tears. He held her, wanting her, and began to kiss and stroke her as she sobbed.

"He must be made to pay, naughty demon," she begged. "But oh, he was so terrifying, Spike." She smiled wickedly at him. "Was he not? Did he not yank the rotting flesh from your bones?"

Then she raised on tiptoes and kissed him hard. "How shall we do it?" she whispered. "Pop out his heart?"

Spike thought about how enraged Angelus would be if he, Spike, not only disobeyed him but succeeded in killing the demon interloper. That would add to his own credit and detract from Angelus. And that was a fine thing indeed. Drusilla looked far too fondly on her sire, and the blackguard had no qualms about claiming her affections in front of Spike. In fact, the Irishman rather enjoyed making Spike seethe with jealousy.

What better way to diminish him in her eyes? he thought. "Let's sleep on it," he said, grinning at her.

"No." She pulled herself away from him. Thrusting forward her lower lip, she made a fist like a petulant child. "I want you to promise me that you will kill him."

"Come 'ere," he ordered Dru, grabbing her wrists. He rose, pulling her to a standing position, and began to kiss her. "Tell me what you'll give me if I do it."

"Oh. Oh," she gasped, enjoying his hard love bites. She writhed in his grasp. "Things you can't imagine, my Spike. Things no one else has ever given you."

"Things you've never given *him*," he growled.

"Yes, yes!" she panted. "Daisies and tea parties. Dollies from the shops and the convents. And hearts. Lined up in rows."

"All right, then."

"Oh, Spike!" She thrust herself against him, her arms around his neck.

With a flare of excitement over the thrill of the dangers to come, he bit savagely into her neck and drank.

Sunnydale

Buffy started. She looked around, realizing she had fallen asleep beside Dawn in Willow's room, and yawned.

Willow must have slept elsewhere instead of waking us up, she thought, slowly getting up.

She shuffled, yawning some more, flipping on the light as she had a million times before as she crossed into the bathroom. She picked up her toothbrush, giving her face a quick glance in the mirror. Bruises. In her trade, coming home with bruises was the norm.

In my trade. No one has to know about the . . . the rough trade I do with him.

It all came spilling back—tonight's session with Spike, the handcuffs, the pain. The hurting and the writhing and the begging. And he loved it. He loved all of it, while she *needed* it. The way she clung to him, pleading, whispering, and moaning about how she had to have him or she wouldn't . . . she wouldn't be anything. . . .

"Oh, God," she moaned, and leaned forward, about to be sick to her stomach. She set down her toothbrush and splashed cold water on her face. It stung, and she was glad. She wished it hurt more.

But she had been hurt enough for one night. That was the only thing that could cut through her indifference: the pain.

It's like the fog. I live in a fog just like this, every day. I can hardly see anything, or hear anything. God, I hate being here.

She looked down at her trembling hands and fought back tears. *What's the old joke? What's the worst thing you can do to a . . . to a masochist?*

Nothing.

I'm sick. I'm so sick.

What does he keep telling me? I came back wrong.

She wiped her face with the back of her hand and took deep breaths. Resolutely she finished brushing her teeth and dabbed her face dry with a soft towel her mom had bought. As she refolded it, she noticed it was beginning to fray at the hem. No more luxurious Egyptian cotton towels from Bed Bath & Beyond for the Summers girls. From here on out it was thrift shop chic and making do, making things last.

She hung it back on the towel rack and glided quietly down the hall to get her pajamas. She crept into her room. The moon glowed through the fog like a watery flashlight beam, liquid, pale yellow light spilling over Buffy's made-up bed. Willow wasn't there.

Buffy changed back into her patrol outfit, then poked her head into Dawn's room to see if Willow was still awake. But she wasn't in Dawn's room, either. "Will?" she called softly.

There was no answer.

The Slayer went back downstairs to see if Willow had resumed her TV marathon, maybe with the sound off, but there was no Willow on the sofa.

She went into the kitchen. The pieces of broken mug were in the trash, and the kitchen had been tidied up. But there was no Willow—and no note.

She went back into the living room, scanning uneasily for signs of a struggle—old Slayer habit.

Buffy's eyes widened. The front door was unlocked. So not a good thing when one's zip code was Sunnydale-on-the-Hellmouth, California. "Willow?" she called, her voice rising.

She crossed the living room and carefully opened the door.

The fog was back. The cold, wet mist bobbed and wove in front of her, and she batted it away from her face, impatient to get a view of her surroundings. Then something tickled the base of her spine and—

She leaped back into the house, slamming the door shut. Her heart beat a few extra times. Her knees got weak, and she leaned against the door, fluttery and out of balance.

I'm not just startled. I'm afraid.

"This is dumb," she muttered.

She whirled around, curled her hand around the knob, and threw open the door again.

The fog still hung there like a thick net. She swallowed hard. The fear returned immediately, as if that net had been cast over her head.

"Will, you out here?" she called, her voice a bit wobbly. Taking a step over the threshold and peering into the night, she took a quick temperature reading of herself. Increased unease. Wigginess.

Had Willow done some kind of spell that left residue behind?

She waved her hands in front of herself to fan away more of the fog, creating a momentary hole in it to reveal . . . yet more fog. The streetlights were blobs of golden sheen; the rest of the street was cauled with the rolling blankets of white. Buffy shivered again, irrationally afraid.

Back inside she shut the door and leaned against it, her heart thundering.

Something's wrong. With me.

Lifting her wounded hand to her face, she unpeeled the bandages and examined the cuts that had been dealt her by the creature in the graveyard. Had she been infected with some kind of evil fear germs? According to Spike, wounds inflicted by Congara demons didn't do anything special. Okay, pain, but again . . . old topic.

Yet she couldn't deny that she was frightened. Suddenly and unaccountably so.

And Willow's missing.

She glanced toward the stairs. As the Slayer, she should go investigate. But as a sister, she wasn't going to leave Dawn, no way.

Then there was a soft tap on the door. She clamped her mouth shut against crying out and glanced over her shoulder. The triple windows cut a familiar shape into three equal parts . . . *and speaking of parts* . . .

. . . she opened the door, and Spike said, "Slayer," in a tone that spoke of business, not pleasure.

He walked in. He had on his black leather trousers, his boots, and his duster. That was all. He had rushed over to her house shirtless. Her nail marks were visible across his chest.

"Something's going down. Something big," he said. "Lot of ruckus in the cemetery. Woke me up, it did."

"And you came here instead of following this ruckus because . . . ?"

He glared at her. "First of all, you're the Slayer, not me. And second, I couldn't see anything in the bloody fog. I can't follow it if I can't see it."

"Could you smell it?" she demanded, and then she stopped, shocked by the look in his eyes. She had never seen it before . . . except for once, during one of the many times she had told him she was not coming back to him, not again.

Although so far she always had.

But now, the dilated pupils, the narrowed lids . . .

"You're afraid," she said wonderingly. "You came here to get me because you didn't want to face whatever it was."

"Bollocks," he gritted, then sighed and rounded his shoulders. "Yeah, I'm afraid. But I came to get you because I didn't want to face it alone, is all. I'm going back out there—I hope with you. If not, I'll go alone."

"Don't feel too bad," she said. "Abject terror happens to all of us sometimes."

"Oh, now don't go all high and mighty . . . ," he began, then cocked his head at her. She nodded. "You're afraid, too."

"I stuck my head out there . . . in the fog." She gestured. "Instant wig city."

They shared a look.

"It's bewitched us somehow. Given us the nerves." He craned his head toward the stairway. "Let's go wake up Madame Mim and ask her to—"

"Willow's not here," Buffy cut in.

"She left Dawn alone again?" Spike exploded. "Oh, my God, when I find her—"

Touched, Buffy put her hand against his chest. "She waited until I got home. Or she was taken away, or something."

Spike looked frustrated. "We can't both go out if no one's home with Dawn." He gave her a wave. "It should be me who goes. Right, then."

"No," she replied, putting her hand on his biceps. "You stay with Dawn. I'll go on patrol." She reached for a jacket and slipped on the sneakers she'd left by the door.

"Sorry? *No,*" he insisted. He pushed her toward the stairs. "She's your sister."

"I'm the Slayer."

"Dawn and I are mates," he shot back. "We get along." He grinned and pursed his lips together in imitation of a big, sloppy kiss. "Not as good as you 'n' me,"

"Is that all you can think of?" Buffy asked heatedly.

"No." A beat, and then, "I also think about stomping things and then killing them. Hey, vampire?" He leaned forward. "Bloodthirsty killer? Murderer?"

"Neutered," she drawled, then flushed as he chuckled. "What I mean is"—she reached for the door and pushed past him—"stay here with Dawn, no matter what."

"Buffy!" he called after her.

She went down the front steps and gave him a wave, making with a confidence she did not feel.

When the door slammed indignantly behind her, she lowered her arm and put herself on full alert.

Then she walked on into the fog. It was so thick, she couldn't even hear her own footsteps. She couldn't hear her breath. Could barely hear herself, say, "Okay. This is weird."

With no landmarks to guide her, she walked down Revello purely on instinct and memory; after all, she'd lived on this block for six years. She stepped off the curb at just the right time, crossed the street, wondering if any cars could possibly be on the road, and felt a tiny stab of satisfaction when she lifted her foot up to the sidewalk on the other side at precisely the right moment.

But what she mostly felt was an increasing fear. It was seeping into her, making her wilt inside like a scared teenager on her way home in the dark from the library. Like the girl she might have become, had she not been chosen to be the Slayer. She felt jittery, as if she had had too much caffeine, and shaky, as if she hadn't had enough to eat.

And afraid.

I'm okay. Nothing has happened to me, she told herself. But her blurred senses and mounting anxiety reminded her that something *had* happened to her— she had felt pretty much like this when she had been raised from the dead. *Or not raised . . .*

She remembered her terror when she'd realized she'd awakened imprisoned in her coffin, with little air and mounds of dirt above her. The animalistic frenzy to get out, get out, get out . . .

Buffy picked up her pace, walking faster, faster still. She was loping; she began to run. Perspiration beaded on her forehead. She ran faster.

I might run into something, she told herself. But she couldn't stop running. Faster.

Faster.

She was disoriented. She had no idea where she was. She tried to make herself stop running, but she couldn't. Her body was on automatic pilot. Every single cell was racing for survival.

Away from what?

Toward what?

"Nothing has happened to me," she said aloud. "I'm okay."

But no part of her believed that.

She picked up the pace, flying through the fog, panting now, and whimpering; her legs flew faster than she could keep up, and she was hurtling herself down a flat surface she hoped was a sidewalk. She thought about streetlamps and phone booths and newspaper dispensers and fire hydrants and shopping carts and dozens of other potential obstacles; she thought about ramming into something and breaking her legs or her ribs or her neck; she thought about falling so hard, she knocked herself out, and a car driving over her. She thought about all those things, but she couldn't make herself slow down.

The Slayer ran and ran, faster, faster. Her body was completely out of control. She couldn't keep up with herself. Her heart was beating too hard; her lungs couldn't get enough oxygen. Yet incredibly, she kept running, as if her "on" switch were stuck. She was going to run herself to death.

Then she heard screams, and she was glad she was running.

She shifted direction, mentally praying that her path was clear, and flew off the sidewalk at last. She landed wrong on her right foot, heard her ankle crack, and collapsed in a heap on the rough blacktop road. "No," she moaned, grabbing her ankle.

The screams grew louder.

It was Willow, and someone else.

She started to shout, "Hang on!" then realized that the fog would keep her hidden from view while at the same time prevent her from sizing up the situation. There was nothing to be gained from announcing her presence, except maybe calming Willow down a little, and from the sound of things, Willow had no reason to be calm.

Slowly, painfully, she got to her feet. The fear was gripping her again, and she shook her head hard, as if to shake off the all-encompassing sensation.

She took a step forward and began to buckle. Gritting her teeth, she took another step, and another. The pain was awful; the fear was worse. Nothing in her wanted to run to Willow's aid—except for whatever lived deep inside her, that Slayer spark of energy that made her what she was: a champion of the light.

She lurched forward, trying to remind herself that the adrenaline rush of her fear would soon coat her pain receptors and she would stop hurting. Only it wasn't happening; each step was a horrible stab in her leg, and moving forward was a monumental effort. She took a step forward, then dragged her injured foot behind herself. Another step, drag.

Hysterical laughter welled up inside her. *I'm walking like an Egyptian. An Egyptian mummy. Like those movies.*

Willow was shrieking uncontrollably. Buffy screwed up her face and forced herself to walk more naturally on her throbbing foot. She picked up her pace; each time she lifted her foot or set it down, she could feel the ends of her bones scraping together. The pain was unbelievable.

But not unbearable. Somehow, she bore it.

She moved on, guided by the screams.

The thing about being the Slayer was that she couldn't do her best. She had to do better than her best. She had to do whatever had to be done, or die trying. That was the mission statement. That was the way she had to live each day.

This might be that time, she thought. *That time I die again.*

Will I get to go back to where I was? Or will I get sent somewhere else, somewhere not as . . . amazingly wonderful . . . because I failed in my duty?

Buffy picked up more speed; then she sensed a thickness in the fog and made a fist. She called, "Willow?" Then she hauled off with an uppercut.

Her fist disappeared into something frozen; there was some kind of icy liquid all around her knuckles and the back of her hand, so cold that it shot needles through her skin and up her arm.

When she withdrew her fist to pummel the object with a sharp jab, it had gone completely numb. Buffy noted it but did nothing about it, simply threw her weight into the punch for added effect.

This time her arm penetrated the frigid thickness up to her elbow, and it stung with a cold so intense, it burned.

Then something grabbed her around the neck. She felt ice crystals forming up the back of her neck; felt frost sizzling in her hair. Her cheeks went numb. Her eyes teared and stung.

She dropped to a squat at the same time that she flung herself. Her assailant was thrown completely off-balance; whatever it was, it released her and stumbled with her momentum, tumbling in the identical trajectory as the Slayer.

It hit the street with a groan. Buffy pushed herself toward it, balancing on her left palm as she executed a perfect snapkick forward. The rest of her weight was on her injured left foot, and she gave out a grunt of agony.

But her right foot connected with nothing.

Whatever she had attacked, it had dissolved into the fog.

She pushed off from her left hand onto her right, managing to rise to a standing position, though she was half-frozen and in terrible pain. Then she heard a scuffle directly in front of her, put out a hand, and touched warm human flesh. She grabbed at it, got her hand around someone's forearm, and yanked, hard.

She hoped it was Willow; she threw her to one side and rammed her fist forward. Again with the frozenness, again with the pain.

This time, a voice whispered to her in weirdo language, and then the viscous chilly stuff she was touching became a liquid that ran all over her hand, burning it with cold, and then . . . it wasn't there anymore.

The voice whispered at her again, more softly this time; again, and this time it was an echo.

"I heard that," she shot back, though she had no idea what the words meant. She tried to memorize them for later playback, preferably to someone who knew how to do the research, but the syllables dissolved just like the fog.

A huge sound thundered so loudly, it shook the sky so that the fog became veils or curtains and fluttered with the vibration. It was like the largest sonic boom Buffy had ever heard. With the second occurrence, she was thrown to the ground.

Skyquake, she thought wonderingly. *Usually means interdimensional travel. Portals opening, closing. God, I hope it's not the Hellmouth. What if it's an army of demons? What if it's something I can't fight?*

She was back to panicking. It was a wonder she could fight as well as she did; she was so terribly afraid. Fear swept through her, making her sick to her stomach, turning her legs and arms to lead, and she began to make wide, awkward punches. She was hyperventilating, growing increasingly dizzy and disoriented.

If she hadn't had someone to save, she would have curled into a fetal position and wept, she was so afraid. Everything seemed to be rushing at her, in on her; she couldn't handle it anymore. It was crashing down on her, big gushing waterfalls of fear; she was drowning and she couldn't catch her breath. Fear was a pair of hands at the bottom of a very deep, very cold lake, wrapped around her ankles and holding her fast.

This time she leaped off her good foot into the air, executing a three-sixty and then a smashkick to the side. She hit another something, and this one toppled backward. She pressed her advantage, gasping when she hopped onto her broken ankle and thrusted forward with her other leg. She hit another target.

How many of them are there?

She was grabbed from behind, squeezed, while someone else smashed her in the face with what felt like a hammer dipped in liquid nitrogen. Her face froze up; she could almost hear it cracking and shattering apart.

Then suddenly the fog around her condensed and shrank, and she saw that the creature in front of her was tall, skeletal, and pale white-blue. It was a male, with white-blond hair and creepy crystalline eyes.

Flames shot past her shoulder, and the thing evaporated.

She turned her head.

Giving her a right good grin, Spike stood beside

her, legs spread and body angled tripod style, armed with a flame thrower.

"Hello, luv," he said, then pushed the lever. Flame shot forward just like in the movies, and the orange glow lit up Spike's cheekbones in a very flattering way. He had the love for the ultraviolence splashed across his face as he moved the thrower in a steady half-circle.

The blue guys sputtered into view as the fog evaporated. They were creepy, but yay, going away.

She didn't see Willow yet. Spike wasn't done.

"Where's Dawn?" she demanded, throwing a punch as she glared at him.

He cocked one eyebrow and looked a little put out. "The lovebirds are on their way over there," he said. "I phoned Anya and Xander."

She stopped fighting and stared at him. *"So you left my sister alone?"*

Spike clenched his jaw and spewed flame. "You were gonna die," he bellowed back. "I . . . I was worried, all right?"

"Buffy?" Willow's voice sounded shaky. Buffy could just make out the shape of the Wiccan getting Willow to her feet.

"Hey, Will. Glad you're all right." Buffy didn't look at her. She was too busy glaring at Spike. "Alone."

"Buffy, those things . . ." She looked around, staggering backward as she tried to catch her breath. "Oh, my God, those things. They came out of nowhere."

"Why are you out here?" Buffy demanded, swiveling her attention to the Wicca. "Why did you leave the house?"

"Gee, Buffy." Willow swallowed and frowned, her gaze lowered to the ground. "I . . . I had to get out. Had to take a walk. I'm . . . I don't feel well."

"Witch is right. Looks terrible," Spike ventured. "Well . . ." Suddenly the attackers were gone. He shut off the sputtering flame of the weapon and lowered the barrel to the ground. "Don't thank me now, girls. All in the line of duty. Which, not. Vampire.

"Thank you," Willow said sincerely. She swayed. Buffy reached out a hand and caught her forearm. Guilt caught up with every other emotion she had been feeling. Willow really was sick. And she had just been through a lot.

"What did they want?"

"They asked me about a viola or something," Willow said unhappily. "I don't know, Buffy. I wasn't taking very good notes." She shrugged. "Trying to live through it and all."

"Tends to distract one," Spike agreed, but his voice was strained. He looked . . . odd. Odder than usual. "Seems the ice cubes have melted away. Shall we go back and check on Lil' Bit?"

I told you to stay there!" Buffy poked him in the chest.

He dodged out of her way, not particularly troubled. "I am not your lapdog!" he thundered.

"Guys?" Willow said. "Alive?"

* * *

Flinn was furious. And he told King Banshee all about it. "I was about to collect my prize!" he shouted. "And your men attacked us!"

Banshee looked worried. He said, "They were confused. They lost their minds. It had to be a magick spell."

That was when MacNair, the king's second-in-command, strode forward to the throne and dropped to his knees. "We were bewitched," he agreed. "Confused."

"Afraid," Flinn accused. He pointed at MacNair. "He panicked. Attacked the wrong girl. Thought my Willow was the one with the vial."

"Is this true?" Banshee demanded. MacNair hung his head in shame.

"Then we must move even faster," the king said. "It's the fogs Jack brings with him. They're beginning to work. Soon the people of Sunnydale will go berserk. It's my guess that the *Fomhóire* will attempt to cross over in that time."

"*If* Jack has the vial," MacNair said.

The three—Flinn and the two *Tuatha*—looked hard at one another.

"If's not a word I like to use," Banshee said.

"Yes, Your Majesty," MacNair replied.

"In the meantime, keep your men off my bride-to-be," Flinn said. Then, with as much dignity as he could muster, he quit the throne room of the *Sidhé* of the *Tuatha Dé Danann*. In the earthen walls, the skeletons of dead witches quivered as if with fear.

He averted his gaze, and thought that perhaps no

redheaded lass and no bargain was worth risking his own life.

Flinn the leprechaun began to wonder if he was putting his efforts into the wrong cause.

Maeve was drawn to the bright lights swirling inside the fog. She lurched slowly toward them. A throng of people milled around buildings and configurations of glowing rods; tonal rhythms throbbed.

"Hey," said a human male. "How ya doin'?"

She stared at him, saying nothing. Her brain was trying to conserve its higher functions for the task of finding Jack. She glanced down at her map and held it out to the boy.

"Shady Hill Cemetery." He looked excited. "You going to a rave or something? Sweet. Can I come?" he asked, falling into step with her.

They walked on together.

She's weird, but she's hot, the guy thought. He turned to her and said, "Fog's weird, huh?"

"Jack's coming," she said to him. "We all are."

Her voice was like someone walking in a gravel pit. He decided he liked it. He said to her, "You a Goth?"

She cocked her head and said nothing. That intrigued him all the more. Most chicks couldn't stop talking.

Fog swirled around their ankles. Then suddenly the guy felt a wave of fear wash up and down his body, like someone dowsing him with ice water. He shouted and whirled around, wigging, and glommed onto the girl. Embarrassed, he made as if he was trying to hold her hand.

She looked idly at him. He grinned at her and said, "I guess someone walked over my grave. Do you know that saying? My grandmother says it all the time." He realized he was the one who couldn't stop talking.

The fear mounted, crawling up his shins and grabbing hold of his knees, shaking them. Making all of him shake. "Whoa," he muttered. He darted his gaze left, right, then said to her, "Let's get the hell out of here."

He took her hand and began to run. He couldn't help it. He was suddenly terrified.

So were other people. As the fog gathered and thickened, he could hear girls screaming and crying. Guys were beginning to yell at one another.

Then he heard a sharp crack. Someone had fired a gun.

Ahead, in the street, a warm red glow flickered. It took him a moment to realize that someone had set a car on fire. *This sucks,* he thought. *Didn't we just have one of these . . . riots in September? I'm going home.*

"Hey," he said to the girl, and then he realized something else: He was lost. In the fog, he had lost all sense of direction, and he had no idea which way to go.

"Hey!" he cried. His voice rose and cracked; he sounded twelve again, and he no longer cared if he was humiliating himself. He was scared, and he had had enough.

"Let's go to my house," he begged, as if somehow she would miraculously know the way.

"I have to get to Jack," she informed him.

That was when some strange . . . *things* rushed toward them in the fog. The guy was so startled, he fell to his knees, narrowly avoiding the first one to reach him and the girl. Whatever they were, they were icy cold, and tall, and kind of blue.

The chick said, "Take this," and she pressed something into his hand. "Run."

He didn't have to be asked twice.

Man, did he run.

Willow was in terrible shape by the time she, Spike, and Buffy got back to Buffy's house.

Xander and Anya had not shown up.

"You are so lucky you are already dead," Buffy hissed at Spike as she unlocked the front door. "Did you actually speak to them when you called Xander?"

"Uh . . . Lil' Bit?" Spike bellowed.

There was no answer. Buffy pushed past everyone and took the stairs two at a time. Just watching her made Willow nauseated.

Despite her own concern about Dawn, Willow excused herself and went into the downstairs bathroom to throw up. But as she knelt in front of the toilet, nothing happened except a few dry heaves. She shook from head to toe, her forehead dropping forward so that it would have smacked against the front of the toilet if she hadn't grabbed the sides first and held her head upright.

Oh, my God, did I just have a seizure?

She waited for the moment to pass; then she rose and splashed water on her face. After she collected herself, she went back out, joining Spike on the couch in the living room. Spike was hunched forward, hands jammed in his duster pockets. He didn't have on a shirt, which confused Willow.

Buffy came back down the stairs. "She's still asleep," she announced.

"Through that?" Willow asked.

Buffy looked sad. "She's used to sleeping through a lot of noise. First me being the Slayer, and then Mom . . . when Mom was sick. . . ."

"It's okay, Buffy," Willow soothed.

"It's not. It's so not." Buffy ran her hands through her hair and said, "Okay. We need to run down this thing."

"I'll drive," Spike offered. Then, as Buffy stared at him, he said, "What?"

"Is that a joke?" Buffy half-yelled at him.

"You asked me to drive." Spike frowned at her.

"I meant, have a debriefing. Are you brain-dead in addition to being dead-dead?"

"Hey," Spike said, glaring, "back off, Pink Ranger."

Ignoring him Buffy looked at Willow. "Maybe Xander and Anya didn't make it home."

"We . . . you should call Tara," Willow ventured.
Oh, my God, was my baby in a car accident?

"Xander and Anya were probably just shaggong and didn't bother with answering the phone," Spike said, but there was an edge of uncertainty to his voice.

Buffy crossed to the phone book and flipped it open, finding Tara's new number and dialing.

There was no answer there, either.

She looked at Willow, who said, "I want to go look for them."

Buffy hesitated. Spike stood this time raising his hand. "Hello? Predatory animal?" he said. "I'll go. You stay with your sister. And you"—he shook his head as he took in Willow's appearance—"you look like hell. You should stay home, too."

Buffy nodded. "I . . ." She trailed off, realizing she was torn. Her friends might be there somewhere, maybe hurt, maybe dead, but her sister was here, in their house. And froces were obviously marshalling out there.

Buffy looked hard at Spike and Willow. "Something's going on. You said so yourself, Spike. When we went out into the fog to look for Willow, we got scared." She held up her hands. "That is not a normal state of affairs when I go patrolling. I don't get scared."

"Well, um, you died," Willow said, half-raising her hand. "Now you know you can die. So you're more afraid . . . of dying," she concluded, looking regretful.

"False deductive reasoning," Spike supplied. "She died before. Before she died. With the Mooter. And she was still way ball's-out after that." He looked at the two women. "No offense."

"So. We were scared in the fog," Buffy said. "I mean, really scared."

"I wasn't," Spike asserted. Then he crossed his

arms over his chest and began to pace. "All right, then. I was. Which definitely means that something is going on. Something's wrong, and not with me."

"And I was just walking around, being sick, and all those weird guys attacked me," Willow said, raising her brows. "I mean, hello, not doing anything."

"They were, like, freeze-o demons or something. Really cold."

"I said a spell to ward them off," Willow added, nodding. "I made some fireballs and lobbed them at them. It helped a little."

"Was my weapon did 'em in," Spike said.

"I think those guys brought the fog with them, or made it happen," Buffy said. "Tara . . ." She paused as Willow blanched and looked down at her hands. "Tara said it was near the Moon of Osiris. Or just past it or something."

"She doesn't know about Osiris," Willow mumbled. "She has no idea about Osiris." To Buffy, she said, "This isn't about the Moon of Osiris and a Congara demon. It's something else. I don't know what it is, but I'll do more research. I'll find out."

Buffy smiled gently at her friend. "I know you will. You always do."

The phone rang. Buffy glanced at the others with big hope, then crossed into the kitchen to grab the portable off the wall.

"Buffy?" It was Giles.

"Hey. Everything okay?" she blurted.

"I'm not sure," Giles told her. "I had a most disturbing dream, and so I did a bit of research. It's the

Moon of Osiris, and I was wondering . . . is everything all right?"

"Giles, it's so weird that you're calling," Buffy said. "Things are happening."

"What sort of things, Buffy?"

"This fog and . . . cold, weird, tall guys and . . . fog." She rubbed the back of her neck.

"Indeed. Fog."

Giles's voice was a little distorted, probably due to the long-distance thing and all the satellites. Buffy had never totally gotten all that, but she figured it didn't matter as long as the phone company did. And since they seemed to be able to keep track of every single millisecond she used her phone—and charged her accordingly—she figured they had the ability to keep the lines of communication open without her help. Or understanding.

"There's blue guys. Not dark blue like those Blue Men you liked, which, go figure, but they're really cold, Giles. Like Mr. Freeze in *Batman*."

"I'm going to do a bit of reading, see if there's anything about it in the Watchers' diaries at Council headquarters," Giles said.

Buffy cheered up. *Giles, doing some research. My life is normal again.*

Spike sauntered into the kitchen, pulling a pack of cigarettes from the pocket of his duster. His chest was still exposed.

"Go smoke outside," she snipped at him.

"Not bloody likely," he said, pulling out some matches.

"And cover up your chest. You've got . . ." She trailed off as he looked down, grinned, and gave her a wink.

"I gather you're not addressing these remarks to me," Giles said.

"Sorry. No," Buffy replied into the phone.

"Dawn. She's all right?"

"Yes. She's fine."

"Then I'll research. Sorry for the lateness of the hour," he said, so polite and British that she wished she could just hug him. "With the time difference . . ."

"No problem. We're all up. The grown-ups, I mean. Been out fighting the bad guys." She tried to keep her voice light. "Just like the old days."

"And . . . positively horrible days they were," Giles finished.

"Oh, yeah," Buffy agreed.

They disconnected. She said to Spike, "Let's go look for Xander and the girls."

Willow watched them disappear back into the fog. Then she made her way up the stairs, feeling so very not well.

As she started down the hall, Dawn stepped from her room. Her eyes were enormous. "Willow?"

"Hey, Dawnie." Then Willow burst into tears. "I'm scared, Dawn. I'm really scared," she said.

"Me too." Dawn held her tight. "Buffy will make it all better," she said, but it was obvious she wasn't convinced.

* * *

Buffy and Spike shuffled through the fog. Buffy said to him, "Do you feel it? The panic? Is it rising inside you?"

He shrugged. He had become very quiet, and Buffy was trying to figure out what was up with him. Then, as if sensing that she was waiting for him to speak, he said, "Buffy, you know that I'm evil. Chip in the head, yes but deep down, I run with the bad dogs." He sighed. "Or ran, shall we say."

"Yeah. Now it's the kitten-betting poker set," she drawled. Then she grew serious, because she knew he was right and she knew that she tried to forget that because sex with evil things was not such a good idea.

I should have learned that lesson from being with Parker, she thought unhappily.

"It shouldn't exactly surprise you to know . . . that I've known some loathsome . . . things in my day."

"Spike, are you getting religion or something?" she asked. "Confession good for the soul you don't have?"

"I'm not confessing." He hesitated. "Well yeah, maybe I am."

He looked her full on. "This fog is rather familiar to me. Even though it's been over a hundred years since I've been in it."

She stopped walking. "What are you saying? What are trying to tell me?"

"Do you know what happened in eighteen eighty-eight?" he asked her. He looked deadly serious—no pun intended.

"Bad with history," she said brusquely. "Get to the point."

"There were terrible riots," he told her. "The inhabitants went wild with fear. It was an ugly noise that the government has denied to this day."

"The government . . ." she said slowly. "Of Sunnydale?"

"Of England. The *Crown*," he replied, looking slightly impatient with her. He lowered his chin and regarded her through his long lashes. "Whitechapel. They butchered one another. And lots of us." He gestured. "Us, by accident. We weren't who they were after."

"They, who? And they were after who?" she flung at him. "Didn't I mention I hate the multiple choice? Give me some short answers or I—"

"You'll what?" He gave her a look. "Stake me?"

"Maybe." She put her hands on her hips. "Spike, just tell me what you're trying to say."

"They rioted from fear," he said. "'Least, that's what we figured back then. But now I'm beginning to wonder if perhaps it was the fog. It was like this. Didn't affect me then, doesn't affect me much now. But you . . . Slayer, you're getting jittery."

He gestured to her hands. They had begun to shake. She put them behind her back and said, "Hurry up, Spike. I want to concentrate on looking for my friends. If you know something you'd better give it up pretty damn fast before I beat it out of you."

"Delicious thought." He put his hands in the pockets of his duster. "Here's another: The thing that walked in the fogs back then, the thing that made the people riot—it was Jack the Ripper.

"And I tried to help the Slayer kill him."

Buffy gaped at him. *"What?"*

"I have a strange feeling of déjà vu," Spike said dryly. "And I feel a story coming on." He pulled out a cigarette and lit it. Inhaled, exhaled. "That's better. Let me begin at the beginning. It was winter, and a moonless night. . . ."

Chapter Five

London, 1888

Whores and vampires sleep all day. In the aristocrat's mistress's flat, the company of four dozed and rested, waiting for sundown. Of all of them, Spike was the most eager for their night hunt to begin, and he spent the hours between waking and having sex with Dru scheming. By nightfall, he had an excellent plan . . . which required that he go out all alone.

It was not all that hard to manage. He took Dru with him, then found her an orphan's workhouse to devour. While she was distracted with the slaughter, he slipped away. He knew she wouldn't panic when she realized he was gone. Though quite the lunatic, she had a keen sense of direction. He had no doubt she would return home rather than face the streets alone . . . and that she would manage to keep herself safe, unlike the newly made vampires who had died by the hand of the demon who came in the fog. Those poor creatures had not walked long enough to learn how to survive. Dru had been a quick study, and there were many clever tricks she was still teaching him, Spike, about keeping himself from becoming dust.

His plan went well. While the little children screamed, he rushed off into the night. Soon he found himself at the crescent of white-fronted structures where the Slayer lived with her Watcher.

Cozy, that. I wonder if he calls her his ward. He snickered. *Or his niece. Always figured those Watchers for a bunch of nasty old men looking for a way to supply themselves with young girls.*

Too high 'n' mighty for Whitechapel bangtails, that lot.

Slowly he approached, looking over the property. He was beginning to think that this part of the scheme was a little off; that perhaps he ought to bugger off before he was detected, and—

"Good evening," someone said coolly behind him.

Spike turned around.

It was the Slayer, the same mousy girl who had folded up like a tent upon staking Barbara, Drusilla's get. He had no idea how the choosing of Slayers occurred, but he wondered if the Watchers Council had blundered this time round; this girl should be a governess, not a champion.

In her hand she held a stake, not at all steadily, and Spike folded his arms over his chest and grinned at her.

She blinked. "You're . . . you're a vampire."

"Per'aps." He gestured to the stake. "I come to talk to you about Jack the Ripper. He is a demon, and I want to help you kill him."

The look on her face was comical. He had never actually seen anyone's mouth drop open—save when one took the winding sheet off a dead man, if one were feeling peckish and chilly, and wanted a coverlet—but the Slayer's sweet little mouth did drop open, and if it had not been hinged to her jaw, would probably have clattered upon the cobblestones.

"What on earth would possess you to make such an offer?" she asked him.

"Because 'e's killing my babies," drawled a voice behind them.

Spike cocked his head and said over his shoulder. "Dru, luv, have you finished at the workhouse? Didn't expect to meet up with you until later."

"And I can see why. Playing with the mousie before you break her neck." Drusilla strutted toward the Slayer. Her eyes gleamed. "She's not much, is she, Spike?"

Cloaked in darkness, glowing like a Grecian nymph, she leaned forward, making come-hither motions with her long fingers. "Shall I make you walk into my teeth? They are sharp. They chomp down the hedgerows, seeking out the minotaur!" She opened and shut her mouth, slowly at first, then faster, until they were chattering.

"Leave off," Spike ordered her. "I'm offering her a deal." He looked sharply at the girl. "Here it is, then. We 'eard your Watcher going off on you. He's a right bastard, eh? And you know what they do to Slayers who don't deliver."

The girl paled. Spike grinned to himself. He wasn't certain that the Watchers actually killed Slayers who did not meet their standards, but given what blackguards they were, he wouldn't have been at all surprised that that was true. Seemed it was, given the unease evinced by the chit.

'We're 'ere to save your life. We want Jack the Ripper just as much as you do. We'll help you kill him."

It took her a moment to find her speech. "I . . . I can't. Sir James says that as he is a man, I can't hunt for him."

"Oh, your Sir James is a liar," Drusilla assured her. "Jack is demon, that is certain. We saw him. He tried to kill us." She looked affronted. "And he's killing my girls, my beautiful lil' children. And so, he must suffer and die." She whirled in a circle. "All his bits, chewed off and flung to the crocodiles!"

"Your days are numbered, pet," Spike told the Slayer. "Accept our bargain. We'll hunt with you. Then we'll go back to our respective sides of good and evil."

Drusilla swayed. "Shall we kill her instead? I'm still hungry. All those little ones . . . they were so little." She giggled. "Sweet and tender and fresh. But small."

"You attacked children?" the Slayer asked, aghast.

"Get this straight, and get it now," Spike declared, stepping forward. "We are vampires. We suck the blood of innocents. We'll work with you for this singular caper. That don't mean we're going to go all soft."

"I hate soft," Drusilla whispered. "Soft is squishy, and 'ard to eat." She smiled at her paramour. "Let's change her, the way we planned."

The Slayer held up her stake. Spike chuckled and grabbed it from her. Then he broke it in two and let the pieces drop to the ground. The young girl watched in fright. She was truly one of the most nondescript individuals Spike had ever seen.

"I'll think about it," she insisted, turning on her heel.

Spike grabbed her forearm, yanking her back around. "You'll do it," he said lazily. "Or you'll never see another sunrise."

"Never." Drusilla approached her slowly and began to circle her. She pointed at the moon. "You'll only see her. But not to worry, little one. She sings. She's singing now. She's saying, 'He eats time. He cheats time.' Do you hear it?"

"Actually, I almost do," the girl replied. She stared hard at Spike. "My name is Elizabeth," she said.

"Charmed," he declared. He held out his hand.

She did not take it. Nor did she smile.

She's got a bit more mettle than I gave her credit for, he realized. *Which is all to the good. She can kill that monster, and then we'll kill her.*

"Watch your back," Drusilla whispered.

"Oh, I shall," Elizabeth informed her.

Sunnydale

"And so . . . you and she . . . killed Jack the Ripper," Buffy said, as Spike's story came to an end.

"We didn't manage it," he told her as he tamped out his cigarette and pulled his duster around his naked chest. "But he didn't, either."

"Didn't . . . ?"

"He was trying to bring his people through to our dimension. The *Fomhóire*," Spike told her. "Faery. Bad faery."

As if by mutual assent, they turned right. Buffy saw the faint glow of the Sun Cinema, now almost completely blotted out by the thick fog. She heard someone hurrying past, heard a dog chuff unhappily.

"Go to hell!" a girl screamed in the distance.

"People getting anxious," Spike predicted. "It's what happened in Whitechapel. Not written down anywhere. Queen didn't want people to know her bully-boys hadn't been able to keep order."

"*You* go to hell!" a man shouted back.

"Went to hell, they all did. Bad doin's, that." He moved his shoulders. "Gonna get bad around here, Slayer."

"That'll be a change." She paused. "You should have told me about this before."

"Yeah. Didn't want to cop to helpin' a Slayer." He huffed. "Now you know my deepest, darkest secret."

"And you know mine," Buffy muttered beneath her breath. She hadn't meant for him to hear, but of course he did. He was a vampire.

"Luv, I *am* your deepest, darkest secret," he said proudly.

* * *

FROM THE DIARY OF SIR JAMES,
Watcher to the Slayer, Elizabeth.
London, 1888

As all good Watchers have written in their journals, so do I, this cold December night, as Elizabeth patrols.

Fog is common in Whitechapel—certainly nothing consequential enough to be feared. Even with this Ripper stalking the night, we English are a stout-hearted people who don't tremble at the mere presence of an atmospheric event.

But the fog this night is different somehow. I feel a strangeness in the air. The animals feel it, too. I watched as a man dressed in magistrate's livery was upended by his mare, which was desperately unwilling to press on. Dogs howl in the distance, the cats screech endlessly.

This fog billows, changing shape as objects pass through it, making them obscure and mysterious. Here and there I can make out the ragged corner of a building, the hard wooden edge of a cart, the slumped shoulder of a common drunk leaning against the side of a building. Other things pass at which I can only guess, my ears, eyes, and mind unable to make sense of the fog's wispy creations.

Its coldness seeps through cloth, skin, and bone. Like the chill of death delayed, no one is prepared for this, especially pathetic Elizabeth. Terror burns within her veins as surely as fire

> *burns paper. If only she weren't a commoner. If only she were of good blood, then she'd be of some account. What sad lot I have drawn to be the Watcher of one cast from such base material. . . .*

Elizabeth gripped the shawl tightly, eager for both the security and the warmth of the soft wool. The Slayer part of her was still a little stunned at the turn of events. She wondered if it was the influence of Sir James or her training as a Slayer that kept screaming for her to kill her two new allies. Or was it the influence of Sir James and her training as a Slayer that stayed her hand?

She was walking the streets of Whitechapel by herself, the vampires having vanished as if into thin air. They assured her they would be nearby, but she saw neither the white-haired male nor his mad, dark-haired mate.

What a terrible Slayer I am, she thought unhappily. *I have no sense whatsoever if they are near or no.*

"Eh. Who goes there? I got me ax, I do," came a voice from her left.

Elizabeth turned, but the man who had spoken was invisible in the fog. "Just a girl out to get herself some coins, sir." She doubted this man was the demon she was after, but she couldn't be certain. Everything seemed a little more evil in this night's fog.

"Best get back to home then, missy. This night's not one to be out in, and I surely ain't in the mood for giving coin to a bangtail."

She continued on, agreeing with the wisdom but unable to act upon it. Her quarry was still out there, torturing and eviscerating girls just like her. Girls who hadn't done a thing to anyone that wasn't asked and paid for. Girls whose only crime was to be lowborn and alley poor.

"You still with us, love?" It was the vampire, Spike.

Elizabeth hid a smile of relief with the back of her hand. So strange, it all was. Truth to tell, this Spike was handsome in a way that no man should be—if he hadn't been a vampire, she'd have fallen hard for him. As it was, his voice made her feel warm in the damp, cold fog. "I'm here," she said breathlessly.

"Dru's gone on up ahead. Should catch up to her in no time."

In fact, it had been his handsomeness that had kept her from staking him right away, and had allowed him to speak instead. When he'd detailed his plan for capturing the Ripper, her next impulse had been to dust him, anyway. As far as plans went, his lacked more than it offered. Still, he seemed truly eager to be as rid of the Ripper creature as she was.

Then she'd imagined what Sir James's reaction to the situation would be when she reported it to him. If she even told him the truth. Still smarting from his earlier debasing, she didn't want to give him the chance to lord over her again. However, it would be glorious that he should have to write in his book that it was she who'd captured and killed Jack the Ripper. And she thought how delicious it would be for him to have to write that it was with the help of two vampires.

Five minutes later, they heard their first scream, followed by the whinny of a horse.

Spike grabbed Elizabeth and threw her against the wall. The air left her lungs, bending her over double. She began to reach for one of the stakes secured beneath her dress when she heard the horse-drawn cart approach at a mad gallop. The driver shouted, but his beast ignored him, ignorant of all but its need to be somewhere other than where it had been.

As the cart careened past, Spike gripped Elizabeth's shoulders and pulled her to him. The back of the cart glanced off the side of the building where she'd been standing, showering her with fine pieces of mortar. Had Spike not pulled her to his spot deeper along the building's slant, she would have been badly hurt.

"That was a close one," he said. His lips almost touched her ear. "Your heart's beating fast," he added. "A wee bit scared, are we?"

Another scream followed by another, and then another, sounded from the direction they'd been heading, the same direction the horse had been heading away from.

"Your heart beats not at all," she snapped, pushing away from him. When he'd called her scared, it had infuriated her. She knew the depth of her own fear and didn't need someone like him to remind her of it. Sir James did enough of that himself.

"We'd better hurry," she added, surprising herself with her newly found courage. "Something's happening up ahead."

She began to move more quickly, gripping the stake in her left hand. Her right hand became her eyes as she felt her way forward. A man ran past, screaming like a child. A pair of women plowed into Spike, knocking him backward. He managed to remain upright, but one of the women sagged to the ground unconscious.

Spike cursed. "Damned people. If they can't watch where they're going, they shouldn't be allowed to walk the streets!"

Shouts of *"It's him! It's the Ripper! Run!"* and *"Get him!"* blared from everywhere and filled the night with their cacophony. Screams of triumph and fear rang between the bricks and wooden slats of the buildings. Windows shattered and doors splintered as people forced their way in and out. More and more people began to pass her now, running, weeping, shouting; it was like walking into an ocean wave. She slid to the side of the alley and continued her journey forward. Somewhere this hurricane had an eye, and that was where she was headed.

After a few steps, she noticed a lightening within the fog. The wisps and curls seemed as thick as they'd always been before, but the air had gained a strange bluish translucence. She could see her hands now, and she could make out the bricks of the wall she was navigating. A face propelled past her, lips drawn back trailing a scream. Several men followed carrying stones and a length of wood.

"Get him! Don't let him get away!" one shouted.

"The bastard kilt her—I saw it with me own eyes!" shouted another.

Spike reached out and grabbed the collar of the last man in line. He was a small bloke who carried himself with the confidence of a sailor, but now he struggled in the air beneath the vampire's grip.

"Bleedin' 'ell! He's gettin' away!"

"Who's gettin' away?" demanded Spike.

"Him! Jack the Ripper, you droolin' jape. Now, let me go!"

Spike released him and watched as the man disappeared into the swirling maelstrom. "Don't know what gin 'e's been swillin', but that fellow they was chasin' wasn't the Ripper." He shook his head. "I've seen the Ripper and that weren't him."

"Something strange is happening," said Elizabeth. "It's . . . I feel so . . . terrified."

"Not strange for *you,* pet," he reminded her.

"No. It's come on sudden, like a sickness."

She turned and felt powerful hands grip her right ankle. She could make out a darkness near her feet, but no features. She kicked, but was unable to dislodge the grip. The thing at her feet hissed, and Elizabeth understood what it was immediately. She raised her stake, prepared to cleave the dead flesh beneath her, but felt her wrist held in an even tighter grip.

"Dru, love, what are you doing?" Spike asked with amusement.

The vampire gripping Elizabeth's ankle began to sniff at her skin like a bloodhound. Elizabeth shuddered as she felt a tongue lap at her calf, tasting her. Taloned hands spider-stepped up her legs, past her stomach and bosom and onto her shoulders. From boot to brow, the vampire sniffed her, barked, then chuckled.

"You smell divine, Miss Bess. Your blood boils. I

can hear the moon singing your praises." She released Elizabeth and stepped back, her face a strange mixture of childlike innocence and base depravity as she raised her face to the night sky.

"Where've you been, love?" asked Spike.

"My minotaur," Dru said, straightening to her full height. "The demon."

"Any luck?" he asked.

"As you'll see, he's been a busy Ripper." Drusilla began to giggle. "Naughty boy."

"What do you mean?" asked Elizabeth with a scowl.

"You'll see," Drusilla said again, grasping Spike's head with both hands and kissing him savagely on the lips. She released him and grinned wickedly. "Now, come on." Then she disappeared into the luminescent fog, laughter trailing behind her like breaking glass.

Spike grinned just as wickedly and gave chase.

All Elizabeth could do was swallow her burgeoning fear and follow suit.

She entered the fog at a flat run. Five minutes of chaos and then she came upon them. Spike and Drusilla stood at the edge of a cleared circle devoid of all fog. They had reached what was usually a busy intersection, a place known for its fishmongers and tinkers. But what they saw now was as far removed from a fishmonger as could possibly be.

A tall, cloaked figure stood with his back to them, chanting in a strange, vulgar language, directing his words toward the center of the intersection. In one hand was an open book, in the other an open vial, a strange mist seeping over its rim.

In the very center of the intersection lay twelve very dead women, each with their chests ripped open. Arrayed to form the numbers of a clock, heads toward the center, twenty-four eyes stared sightlessly to the heavens. Someone had taken the time to place their feet together, and their hands were primly clasped and placed on their bloody chests as if in prayer.

The small circle within the center of the human-formed clock should have been made of the muddy cobblestone street, but by whatever magicks this man now cast, he had changed the space into the dark swirling of black-and-red clouds. It was like looking at hell in the sky rather than the ground.

Spike slid into vamp face and prepared to attack.

A large black dog that had been resting at the feet of the man got to its haunches and growled, white froth dribbling from its lips. It had an unnatural amount of teeth, so many that it was a wonder that it could raise its head.

The cloaked man turned slightly, but maintained his chant. His left eye slid from its socket. Pushed by the wormy tendril of the optic nerve, it crept onto his shoulder and stared at the three interlopers.

Shocked, Elizabeth pulled back.

"He shines so brightly. Don't you see it? He's so beautiful." Eyes rolling, Drusilla smiled wistfully for a moment, then her face melted into a vampire's countenance. "All the pretty girls' bloody hearts wasted for a spell," she lamented. "So sad."

Her eyes returned to normal as she focused on the Ripper. "Were you looking for dollies, then? You should have tried the workhouse. Lots of dollies there. But very soft." She sounded petulant.

The eye resting upon the Ripper's shoulder blinked in response. His chanting continued, unabated.

"I say we kill him just because of the eye," said Spike. "That's just not a proper eye."

As if to mock him, the other eye appeared on the Ripper's other shoulder. Then they both rose above the Ripper's head like antennae, their attention obviously fixed upon Spike.

"Spike, the wolf has teeth," Dru crooned. "It has—"

Before Drusilla could finish, Spike attacked. He was met by a roar as the dog transformed into something far more deadly and far larger. In an instant, the already large dog doubled in size. The beast's flanks rippled with enhanced muscles, and its normal-sized teeth were replaced by several rows of razor-sharp triangles like those from the mouth of a shark.

Spike and the beast met in a flurry of fists, fangs, and pointed teeth. The beast stood on its hind legs as it fought for an advantage, and its maw seemed capable of swallowing Spike's head in one deep gulp. But Spike wouldn't allow it—he gripped the thick neck of the creature with both hands and held the head aloft. Even with vampire strength, his arms shook with the effort.

Then, with a roar of triumph, Spike bit into the furry neck. The beast howled, brought up a claw, and swept Spike to the ground. The vampire tumbled backward, coming to a dusty halt several feet away.

The dog-beast pounced. As it brought its great

jaws to snap Spike in twain, the vampire kicked out with both feet, snapping its head around. It fell on its back with an earth-shaking crash.

Spike sprang to his feet and spit out a mouthful of bloody fur. The dog-beast rolled over and scrambled to its feet. Each regarded the other with newly found respect.

"There's a lad," said Spike. "Why don't you be a good little pup and fetch a treat for us, 'eh?"

A thunderous clap shattered the air, sending Spike, Drusilla, and Elizabeth to the ground. When the Slayer's vision cleared, she saw that the Ripper was no longer chanting and had turned his attention upon them, his eyes back in their normal place upon his face.

The twelve dead women who'd been arranged on the ground according to the numbers of a clock were no longer there. Now they were hovering in the air, their formation still the same. Instead of staring at the heavens as before, each pair of dead eyes stared at Elizabeth, as if to ask, *Why didn't you protect us?*

Slowly, the bodies started to rotate clockwise. Red-and-black clouds roiled within the center of the formation. An occasional lightning bolt cascaded across them as though illuminating another place, or another time.

"People and time, he eats them. People and time, he cheats them," sang Drusilla.

"Spike?" whispered Elizabeth.

"Yes, luv?"

"What is happening?"

"I've sacrificed to Nemain and Balor, and now their hearts have been eaten," the Ripper told them.

His mouth moved, but was slightly out of time with the words, as if they came from a great distance rather than from the twenty or so feet that separated him from Elizabeth and the vampires.

Biting back her growing fear, Elizabeth took a tentative step forward and held a stake out in front of her.

The Ripper's dog-beast had returned to his side, and his right hand stroked the fur on its immense neck. "There are things as old as vampires, Slayer. Things that have even been around far, far longer than you realize." He gestured toward the fog.

"The evil of the *Tuatha Dé Danann* still resonates in the land," he said. "I hate them. I shall destroy them all, delightedly."

"It's a fight of faery and faery," Spike translated. "Ey, then, are you *Fomhóire*? Has to be," he said half to himself. "They were the ugly ones."

"Both, and neither," Jack told him.

"A halfling?" Dru trilled. She clapped her hands. "A misfit? I remember those days, Spike! When Angelus hurt me so!"

"When the ghosts are fresh, they can be dangerous," the Ripper continued. "Your ancestors used to protect themselves from the *Tuatha* by torturing young girls. Druid men. It was their screams that kept the *Tuatha* at bay."

Elizabeth blanched.

"Spike," whispered Drusilla. Her eyes were closed, and movement danced beneath the fragile lids. "Darkness, so cold the darkness. I feel it seeping, leaking . . ."

Elizabeth stared into the center of the woman-made

clock and felt herself start to tremble. Misshapen beings, limbs growing willy-nilly from their chests, their foreheads, the backs of their heads, had formed just on the other side of the swirling center, arranging themselves into lines. Stretching behind them was a blackness deeper and darker than anything on earth.

Jack the Ripper grew two additional arms as Elizabeth watched. His neck had lengthened by several feet. His heavy head hung sideways.

From deep within herself, Elizabeth knew that it was time for her to act. She had to stop this monster.

She raised her stake and rushed the Ripper.

In turn, he raised his hand and cried, *"Kut Nool Smaggath!"*

A bolt of green energy shot from his hand and enveloped Elizabeth the Slayer in a green nimbus, crackling before it was absorbed.

Elizabeth screamed, but felt no pain as she slowed and eventually stopped near the base of the portal. *I'm blind,* she thought. *God help me, I can't see a thing!*

Worse than being afraid and in danger was being afraid and in danger and *blind*. There was little, if anything at all, that she could do to defend herself—she was totally crippled.

Then her ears were filled with the savage frenzy of the renewed battle between Spike and the Ripper's dog-beast.

"Klamath Ur Fomhóire!" shouted the Ripper. "And now my brothers and sisters, the world is once again ours!"

Like the door to a tavern opening during a storm,

the portal must have snapped open, an otherworldly ice-cold wind slicing through, chilling Elizabeth to the bone.

She heard Drusilla enter the fray again, attacking the Ripper on her left. The Ripper shrieked in pain as Drusilla growled and snapped.

On her right, the battle between Spike and the beast continued. The beast howled. Spike snarled. Each seemed to give as good as they got.

"Hello!" Drusilla shouted gaily. "Spike, Elizabeth! They're coming to play!"

Elizabeth began to pant with terror. She could see nothing. But then the memory of her clandestine observation of the Watchers Council rose in her mind. She could still hear the hated, painful words. *One can only hope she'll die soon, and we'll have another go at a brighter girl.*

She recalled Sir James, awash with anger and disgust as he berated her. *We both know what this is about, do we not? The same thing as always. Your fear. Your lack of heart.*

And more words from the Council and Lord Morchwood. *I've never heard of a Watcher that had more than one Slayer to look after.*

Your fear. Your lack of heart.

Your fear. Your lack of heart.

Fear and heart. Sir James had always spoken as if these were one and the same. One thing that Sir James had never understood was that fear and heart were different things entirely. The first was a limitation, the second was an ambition.

Spike's scream of agony was still echoing in the air as she lurched forward.

FROM THE DIARY OF SIR JAMES,
Watcher to the Slayer, Elizabeth.
London, 1888.

Perhaps it is my elevated status as Watcher, or simply the good breeding in my family, but it appears I was unaffected by this damnable fog. As such, I found myself incapable of understanding the behavior of those below, and especially those of good breeding. How or why at every turn could they became convinced that Jack the Ripper himself was there? It seems they saw him in the face of each stranger on the street, or hiding behind the previously accepted countenance of a neighbor. Even those of high birth rioted in the streets like animals fleeing from the slaughter, although I daresay the animals at least have reason to do so.

For fear some future reader believes I exaggerate, let me provide this example:

Four doors down from my own home was a gentleman named Bartholomew Madison. A banker by trade, he was a bit of portly stature and favored wool suits on the heavier side, perhaps because he must do his daily accounts in the draftiest of vaults beneath the Bank of London. I had occasion to speak with him only thrice; he is reserved and quite conservative, a fine and upstanding citizen. Yet I saw this same man, whom I might once have considered inviting to tea in my home, literally tear a fine leather coat from a stranger on the street, all the while screaming at the top of his lungs that the unfortunate object of his attention was concealing knives beneath his overcoat. Outrageous.

I also saw a crowd of well-dressed young people surround a beggar on the street and beat him quite senseless, all the while braying like asses that he was the Ripper. When the luckless panhandler no longer moved, they promptly began squabbling among themselves, pushing and cursing until it became a hideous free-for-all and their faces were bloody and swollen.

I had Mrs. Mead close the shutters in the lower part of the house early on for fear the commoners would shatter the windows, as the fools spent the better part of all evening throwing things at one another—rocks, sticks, and God knows what other types of waste. The upper floors were high enough to be beyond their range, and from there I could watch the chaos below, scene after scene that made me ashamed for my fellow man.

Elizabeth did not return that night, and the longer I waited for her, the more concerned I became. Against Mrs. Mead's wishes, I called for my coach.

I told my man to go to Whitechapel, for it seemed the proper place to find the Slayer. As we rolled into the filthy neighborhood, I was astonished to see the entire town in chaos. Through the fog, which smoldered like smoke from a funeral pyre, I saw the denizens of Whitechapel struggling with one another. There was much shouting and screaming, and men shooting at one another, going after each other with knives. Buildings were on fire. Women were running through the streets, shrieking.

Windows had been broken; men were racing down the street with hayforks, knives, and wooden beams. A man saw my coach, waved both his arms at me, and bellowed, "We're chasin' the Ripper! We've got 'im cornered!"

"I dare not stop here, sir," my excellent driver said, and I agreed with him.

The unholy fog had brought with it insanity, settled firmly upon the minds of men like a shroud over the cold body of a corpse. Tonight the streets of Whitechapel were awash with the mad, the evil, and the paranoid, and as God is truth, I fear there is no difference among the three.

We continued on, and on, and then Providence guided us to a small square. There I saw Elizabeth, and I was astonished.

"The Slayer Elizabeth propelled herself between what clearly was a vampire, and the jaws of the great dog-beast that threatened to consume him. She lunched forward, threatening the beast with her stake, drawing its attention away from the vampire and to her. The *beast spun, and she drew back her stake, rather like a Spanish matador preparing to plung in the ritual death-dealing sword, thus occupying its attention. Thus Elizabeth had saved the vampire—inadvertently, I supposed at that moment. I was astonished at this, but looked on.*

And then I saw a thing I shall never forget. Another creature, more man-shaped, leaped from the fog and shadows to the forefront of this terrible scene. It was hideous, with its eyes spinning in its cheek, and as I watched, its mouth transformed into a gaping maw, hair of blood, and boils and grotesque limbs all about it.

The thing was enraged, and had been battling a second vampire, this one a female with long, dark hair and very long fingers. This demon hurled the female vampire away from itself and sent her crashing into the one whom my Slayer had saved by distracting the dog-beast.

Shrieking, the demon bounded forward and grabbed Elizabeth from behind—two hands around her neck, one hand around her waist, and one hand gripping the arm that held the dangerous stake with which she had threatened its—his?—pet. Before either of the vampires could come to her aid—if indeed they had truly wished to, and that I shall never know—the hideous apparition snapped her neck and allowed his great dog-creature to sink its jaws into her chest.

Elizabeth never even screamed—probably never knew what took her. Her blood stained the hands of the monster. And she was dead.

He lifted Elizabeth in his arms like a lover and shouted victoriously, "Another sacrifice for Balor and Nemain!"

With fury, the vampires attacked him, and it was then that I truly understood that my Slayer had been fighting in concert with them. I was shocked to my very core.

The dog-creature dove into the fray, growling and snarling directly in front of its unholy master. The female vampire raked the beast deeply along its flanks, leaving furrows that filled quickly with blood. She raked again and again, frenzied with the success of her maulings.

"Stop!" the monster shrieked, unable to aid his pet with the Slayer in his arms.

The male vampire used his own hands to claw at the dog-beast's thick neck muscles. In a trice, the misshapen animal could only snap uselessly at the fog-clotted air—against two vampires, the beast was no match. Within seconds, it fell to the street, its lifeblood pouring from countless wounds.

Meantime, an airborne ring of women's butchered corpses gyrated above this chaos, and from the center of their perimeter, a *wirling portal foamed and frothed. From this swirling mass of fog another demon very like the first forced itself into our world in a hideous parody of birth.*

This new demon, much in appearance the brother of the first demon, landed at the feet of the being with my dead Elizabeth in his arms. The Slayer's murderer gave a cry of triumph. But that ejaculation shattered into rage as

the newly arrived demon collapsed, its body fetid and destroyed before it even touched the ground. Clearly, its attempt to enter our realm had failed.

The vampires seized that moment to press their attack, and the frenzied demon hurled the body of the Elizabeth the Vampire Slayer at the portal with unholy strength. I assume he did so in order to be free to fight the vampires. Whatever his reason, what happened next left me speechless.

The circle of dead women tumbled to the earth, and with a mighty and unholy scream of wind, the dark, seething clouds of the portal coalesced and collapsed. The demon and his pet were sucked through the portal, the creature shrieking at the top of his lungs, "I shall be back! I shall be back!"

His animal barked ferociously—it was not dead—and then the portal vanished as if it had never existed.

"Spike! They've all flown away, great

leathery wings!" shouted the dark-haired vampiress. She threw herself into his arms, all kisses and caresses, the like of which I shall not describe, as I am a gentleman. "Do we get to claim the death of the Slayer?" the vampire—Spike?—asked her, filled with himself. "Or does it fall to Jack the Ripper?"

I shivered. My Slayer had been killed by the Ripper. . . and at one time, I had forbidden her to go after him. He had been a demon after all, and I had not known it. Yet it was a simple enough mistake for me to make. No other man would have realized the truth.

And so it ended.

The life of the hapless Slayer Elizabeth, and my tenure as a Watcher. . . both are finished.

Would that I had been lucky enough to be charged with a true Slayer.

Would that I had been lucky enough to have had a Slayer with heart.

Alas, it shall never happen.

Chapter Six

Sunnydale

The guy, whose name was Paul Falkland, had run all the way to the cemetery. Whoever those bad boys on Main Street had been, they had not followed him.

Neither had Maeve, and he felt really, really guilty about that. But he was more terrified than he was guilt-ridden.

In the fog, the joint was jumping, and Paul wasn't sure that everybody in there was actually alive.

Crouched behind a gravestone, he bit his fist to keep himself from screaming as shapes lurched and darted through the mist; a mind-numbing cold spreading from them that made him shiver so hard, he was afraid they would notice him.

They spoke to one another in a strange language.

Then they started knocking over gravestones like they were looking for something . . . possibly him.

Go away, go away! Paul screamed at them in his mind.

One by one, they knocked the gravestones over.

Paul held on to the gravestone for dear life . . . and it was then that he turned his head toward the main gate and saw the words printed above it: SUNNYDALE MUNICIPAL CEMETERY.

"It's the wrong one," he whispered. "Oh, my God, I went to the wrong one!"

At Shady Hill Cemetery, Jack the Ripper paced. All was in place—he had brought the fogs, and panic was setting in. Below him, in a heap, eleven dead Sunnydale women would become the circle that would activate the portal. He had only one more to kill, and he was looking forward to making a grand Druidic spectacle of it.

No one knew how to maim and kill like the Druids, no matter how much they complained that the Romans had slandered them.

But the Sacred Fog had still not been brought to him.

Scowling, he scratched his hound behind its ears and grumbled, "Where's the vial? Where's the courier?"

Could it be that the *Fomhóire* no longer trusted him? Had they somehow learned that he planned to pit faery against faery, and then, at the last, unleash his own demon army upon the exhausted troops?

"Time is wasting away," he said, staring up at the weakened sun. "It is the Season of Osiris, when death holds sway. One night more, and it will be too late."

The dog chuffed. In reply, Jack the Ripper said, "I believe it's time to pump up the volume, old friend."

He began to chant. The fogs fell down from the heavens, covering the cemetery grounds with even heavier blankets of ethers and mists designed to confuse and worry whoever walked into them.

Faery, human, it mattered not. The fog would take them.

The fog would bleed them dry.

On the other side of Sunnydale, Gene Stone crept slowly over the redwood fence surrounding the huge brick house on Sonrisa Street, his senses sharp, his attention focused on everything around him.

He listened, and looked at the hodge-podge of equipment he'd strapped to his left wrist.

No nearby electric, no ultrasonics.

In short, nothing to keep him from setting foot on the huge lawn.

And then, Mrs. Stone's boy gets some goodies.

The burglar made his way toward the house, his B&E tools at the ready. If he was right, there would probably be a key hidden by the back door, which he could use to get into the house. The owner, a wealthy lawyer, had a collection of old silver coins that he was going to enjoy cashing in. Gene also had great hopes that he would find a wall safe.

There was no sign of life, and the burglar was grateful for the thick fog surrounding the building. It made this kind of work so much easier.

What was that?

He'd heard a click, a slightly mechanical *click* that sounded like it could be almost anything man-made, but that being the case, would mean that there was a man out in the fog with him.

Who could be watching.

He checked his gear again, noting that there still didn't seem to be any active sensors in the area. Which meant nothing, really, because a *passive* sensor would do pretty well. A thermograph would show him easily in the fog, or a parabolic microphone could detect the slightest rustling sound that he made.

And then it's up the river, third strike and you're out.

He froze, listening.

Nothing. Had he imagined it?

Doesn't matter.

He'd been in the business long enough to know that you trusted your gut before anything else. Twice before he'd used his thinking instead of his feelings, and he'd been sent away both times. His senses were screaming at him to get out *now,* and he was going to listen.

And then, a thought came to him, an idea that maybe it wasn't a man out there watching him, but something else. Some creature who wanted to catch him, punish him for what he might do, had done.

A buddy of his had been caught by a guy whose car he was about to steal. The guy had gone ballistic, shattered the buddy's knee, wrists, and fingers of both hands. Gene's buddy had told him that the nut had kept yelling that it had been *his* turn to suffer, and more was on the way.

No way.

But what if it was? The thief could feel it now, an angry presence outside the house, lying in wait, ready to kill him, mangle him.

I've got to get out of here.

Then he thought he heard another sound, closer.

Screw this.

He started to run for the wall. Several times on the run, he thought he saw something at the corner of his vision, which made him run faster.

There could be two *of them.*

Gene reached for his cell phone and turned it on as he ran. Still running he dove for a low tree limb and climbed up, fully expecting to feel an icy grip around his ankles.

There was nothing.

And he sure as hell wasn't going back down to the ground.

Terrified, the thief punched in 911 and hoped the police would be able to get to him soon.

Spike looked up at the sky and said to Buffy, "Going to be dawn soon. I have to get out of sun's way. Not sure it'll make too much of a noise with all this fog, but better safe than cinders."

"Yeah. I know. You will call Giles?"

"I will." Spike grinned at her. "On your dime."

"And you'll tell him what you told me."

"Every syllable. On your . . ."

"My dime. Fine. Go."

She smoothed her hair back with her hands. She

was exhausted. They had searched for hours and no Xander, Anya, or Tara. She didn't want to be thinking what she was thinking . . . that they were lying dead somewhere in a ditch.

That might be preferable to other fates she could imagine for them.

For the town of Sunnydale was waking up and wigging out. It was the fog. She was certain of that now. It was affecting her, too, but as she continually reminded herself that the fog was the cause, she was able to keep herself from breaking into a panic. Though her heart thundered and her hands shook violently, she was able to keep under the radar of falling apart . . . but just barely.

Spike, seeing her distress, gave her a grim half-smile and said, "You're doing a good job, Buffy. Back in London, I saw Whitechapel dissolve into complete mayhem. It was astonishing." His smile grew. "And fabulous."

"Of course you enjoyed it," she bit off.

"Of course I did. Every moment of it." He put his hand on her cheek. Strangely—or perhaps, not so strangely—she was more unnerved by his moments of tenderness than his . . . than anything else he did when they were together. She shook off his hand and looked away.

"I'm off, then." He stuffed his hands into his duster. On his chest, the scratch marks from her nails had already faded. Vampires and vampire slayers heal quickly . . .

. . . unless the wounds are inside, where no one can see them.

She watched him go, then loped wearily down the street. She had to find her friends . . . before someone else did.

Someone else who would panic in the fog, and hurt them.

Amos Lightburne looked out one of the many windows of his $550K-plus house and regretted his imagination. The imagination that had netted him numerous awards for various corporate advertising campaigns was also providing him with a sense of . . . worry.

It didn't help that he was alone, his ex-wife, Sheila, having decided that brawn beat brains—or at least imagination—when she'd left him for an aerobics instructor and moved to San Francisco.

He'd found that his mind abhorred a vacuum, so he spent many of his solitary hours suffused in layers of entertainment: A CD on the stereo and a DVD on the big-screen TV would provide the background for an afternoon of Internet research or e-mailing. The multitude of sounds, sights, and words would keep him from focusing on the fact that he was alone.

But not today.

He stared out at the gray fog surrounding his many-windowed house. There, too, was a double-edged sword. The many windows—facets, he liked to think of them on sunny days, facets of a huge jewel that he lived in—that let him admire the gorgeous landscape outside were, with this fog, the reverse.

Anything outside could look at *him*.

Now why had he thought of that particular word? Any*thing,* not any*one.*

Nervously he slid the blinds shut in the living room. He experienced a momentary doubt—by closing them off, he couldn't see if anything was coming toward the house, either.

Another trade-off, but he'd made up his mind.

In a rush, he started going room to room, blocking all of the windows. There were a few without blinds and he had to improvise, using some tacks and nails from his corkboard to hang towels, sheets, and blankets. The window over the front door was too small for even those solutions, so he used aluminum foil to block it out. The skylight in the bathroom was harder; he had to use one of the barstools to reach it, and by then he'd run out of pushpins, but he found some safety pins in a drawer.

As he worked, it got darker in the house; light had been coming from outside, even in the fog. But he didn't turn on any more lights. If it was darker in the house than outside, even if something could see *through* the coverings he'd blocked the window with, it *might* not see him in the dark.

After he'd finished covering everything, he still wasn't sure but thought that maybe the windows needed another layer.

Whistling anxiously, he headed toward the linen closet.

Chapter Seven

London, the Present

After Spike called and told them about his escapade back in 1888, Giles and Olivia had immediately motored down from Bath. Olivia dropped him off at Council Headquarters, then went on to her own London flat to wait.

The library looked like something out of a movie: Marble pillars made up the principal architectural elements of a room that included only the most proper Victorian moldings, wallpaper, and wall hangings. Large leather fender benches corralled huge fireplaces, and writing desks were scattered all over the vast room. The ticking of clocks was ever-present, each tick and tock counting toward the next time a gong, or bell, or animated clockwork would sound, all tasteful, all very refined and perfect for the setting.

Amid this old-boy's room, which had always made Giles think of the days when the British had had an empire so vast that the sun had never set on it, were the most protected treasures of the library, the *Watchers' Journals*.

The slot where Sir James' tomes should have been, probably had been, was filled with a leather-bound stick, cunningly crafted so as to appear to be the same as the other journal spines. Had he not been specifically looking for that one book, there was no way anyone could tell it had gone missing.

"Terribly sorry," the librarian said apologetically. "It seems to be . . . unavailable, doesn't it? I really must look into that." He sighed. "Things do go missing, you know. Have some tea?"

Even when he had been in charge of the Sunnydale High library, which was far less critical in the scheme of things than the annals of the Council of Watchers, Giles would have reacted far more strongly to any thought of one of *his* books going missing, than did this doddering extra from *The Pirates of Penzance*.

"It's been scanned into the database, of course," Giles said, smiling pleasantly . . . but firmly. "May I have the access code?"

The older man looked uneasy, but eventually he led Giles to a computer terminal. He booted it up and typed in a code while Giles looked on.

The screen read, NO DATA FOUND.

"My," the man said. "How very odd."

Giles was irritated beyond belief. He was also aware that Olivia was waiting for him in her flat, near the British Museum, where he had once worked. Yet he persisted with the aged librarian, scouring the library with him in search of the missing journals. They did discover an odd little box labeled HAIR OF WATCHERS. One of the Watchers whose hair had been collected was Sir James.

"I'll have some of that," Giles said, telling the man, not asking him. He took a few strands, glanced round and found the envelope, and carefully placed them inside. He put himself in the mind of a forensic scientist.

I have no idea what to do with this, he thought. *But perhaps we can use it in a finder's spell or something. It's the only link to Sir James that we have.*

By the time he left, terribly frustrated, he wasn't certain if the other man had helped "lose" Sir James's memoirs, or simply was so old and so near retirement that he had ceased to care about his position—or lack thereof—the Council.

And yet, by the time Giles had taken the Tube over to Bloomsbury and Olivia met him at the door, someone had brought round a note and tucked it into her mail slot. On a slip of paper, the text of which had been written in Latin, the message was simple: *His words are at St. Mary's Station.*

Giles had been shocked, although with what he knew about the Council he probably shouldn't have been. Someone in the Council of Watchers had removed part of their history, hidden it away for reasons unknown.

Someone else wanted it revealed.

While Olivia scrambled some eggs, Giles went on line and searched for references to a St. Mary's Station, but having then seen nothing, he had spent hours examining the archives of the London Transport Museum. There, he finally discovered that St. Mary's Station had been located on the Underground, just between Whitechapel and Aldgate East. "I'll be back soon," he'd told her, kissing her.

"Nonsense. I'll come, too." She hadn't sounded pleased. But she was game, and he loved her for it.

In 1938, the station had been closed and abandoned, and it had been used as a bomb shelter during World War II until a bomb had sealed most of it in 1940. They'd further learned that the station had been built on a section of the Underground known as a "Cut and Cover" line: one that had been excavated and then re-covered once the track had been laid.

Apparently the bricked-off rooms underneath the station still existed.

And if the book is there, we'll find it.

They'd taken the District line to Whitechapel and walked back toward Aldgate East, looking for signs of the St. Mary's Station. It had been an oddly unsettling journey, passing as it did through the area where Jack the Ripper had been operating in 1888. The weather had turned damp, and there was a light mist in the air. The amber streetlights saved electricity, but didn't give off much light.

It was easy for him to imagine a cloaked attacker walking through the narrow alleys that lined Whitechapel Street.

The two of them started searching for an entrance. It was Giles, with his years of Watcher imprinting, who found it. He'd noticed the dark doorway just behind a short brick wall, just out of the direct light from a streetlamp.

Now it was time to be cautious. For whatever reason, there was controversy in the Council about this book being in the library. If someone was willing to alter the record by removing it, who knew what other steps they would take to keep the secret hidden?

On the other hand, maybe the fact that it's hidden is enough.

He stepped into the dark room, turning on a flashlight he'd brought with him. Olivia stepped past, her hands pointing to the south. "That way, I think," she said.

Giles thought a moment. Then he said, "I do believe I have a use for the bits of Sir James's hair I nicked from the Watchers Library." He pulled the envelope with the strands from his pocket and showed them to Olivia.

"We can use the principle of contagion to track the book . . . if it's here. Both his journal and his hair contain bits of his DNA, which we can track. The journal from his having held it and written in it."

She looked mildly amused. "Linking his DNA. I like that better than talking about finder's spells."

Giles followed Olivia through the bricked-up corridors. They came to a blank wall. Giles scanned the wall, looking for some clue, some hint that would tell him how to open it. He looked carefully at the floor of the old space. There was a layer of dust covering everything, no easy tracks through it, no simple footprints leading to a switch.

But maybe there is.

He leaned down near the wall and shined the light he was carrying across the floor, parallel to it. His eyes, Watcher's eyes, had been trained to see the slightest variation in a surface, to note the smallest discrepancy.

He looked carefully across the floor, seeing at first only dust, and then *types* of dust, size differences in the motes collected on the floor. And then he saw patterns, levels of collected particles that told him a story.

There.

A shallow trench seemed to swing out in an arc from one side of the wall. It meant that the wall opened outward, a lazy way to do it. If it opened inward, there would be no mark left, a far better plan.

Why am I complaining? It helped me find it.

Knowing which side of the wall swung, and in which direction, made finding the lock a snap. He pushed several bricks in sequence near where he suspected it to be, and the wall swung out, noiselessly.

Behind it was a small room, maybe ten feet square. Within the room was a table holding a Watcher's journal.

He went inside, reached out, and grabbed it, just as Olivia cried out. "Giles!"

He spun around. Two gray demons stood there, one staring at him with his hand over Olivia's mouth. The other held a knife to her throat.

Giles dropped the flashlight, and the scene flickered wildly, the light spinning as it fell, throwing his orientation off slightly as he grabbed the knife from the demon and stabbed it in the neck.

"Aaah!" cried the demon, and the second one leaped forward.

The demon raised its free hand and muttered in Latin. A fireball erupted from its grasp. Instinctively Giles slashed with the knife, and as luck would have it, the blade deflected the ball of flame. Olivia saw it coming and dropped to her knees, dragging the demon to a half-standing position. It looked up, saw the fireball coming, and tried to let go of Olivia. But she held it fast, and the fireball caught it full in the face.

She covered her face as the creature whined in agony. Then it released her, and she scuttled toward Giles.

"We've got the book," he murmured, but he could see that it didn't matter to her.

The magick mattered. The horror.

I'm going to lose her when this is over, he thought dismally.

"Come on," he urged her. "We've got to get out of here."

He kept the volume hidden in his leather satchel on the Tube. Ever alert for whomever had sent the note—and then waylaid them with two demons—he and Olivia did not go back to her flat. Instead, they went down by the docks, and to a small flat of a friend of Giles's. As they walked quickly down the street, Olivia nudged him—they were hurrying past the London Dungeon, a popular and grotesque tourist attraction that hailed from the days of Grand Guignol.

"Rather ironic, don't you think?" she murmured.

"Indeed."

Once inside the flat, Giles blew a layer of dust off the musty old tome and began to page through it. His friend was at his job, and they had the place to themselves.

Olivia took a shower while he paged through the diary, saddened by the evidence of the man's extreme dislike of the young girl in his care. And he began to wonder if perhaps something had happened to Elizabeth, something early on, that had triggered the panic inside her. Something, for example, akin to the fog that now shrouded Sunnydale.

"This is painful," he said to Olivia when she came out, the grime of their adventure washed from her lovely skin. "It seems the two of them never worked well together. They both gave up hope."

"Terrible thing, for a Slayer," she mused.

"I agree." And right she was—hope was the thing that drove them all in the never-ending struggle against evil, wasn't it? He nearly laughed aloud at how prissy that thought was, even inside his own head. But really, wasn't it so? Without that elusive belief that things would, ultimately, work out in their favor, what did mankind really have on its side against the much more powerful beasties of the darker realms?

Why, the Slayer, of course.

And people like him, Watchers or former Watchers who still wanted to do good, who still wanted to give aid and fight the good fight. And a few—precious few, indeed—others such as Buffy's friends, who were determined to keep their own little slice of the world as demon-free as they could.

The journal had a fine, musty smell to it, a paper-and-leather scent that reminded him of age and, on a much more fleeting and melancholy level, of his long-dead love, Jenny Calendar. He'd told her once that the wonderful thing about books was that he could *smell* them, and that was something mankind would never be able to gain from the computers she'd valued so highly. It was a truism that still held, and only occasionally in his life, during his time as Buffy's Watcher or otherwise, had he held a book in his hands that bore the smell of unpleasantness.

"Here. I've got it. About the fog."

Olivia belted his friend's robe around herself as she joined Giles at dining table, he cradling the old volume as though it might break. And well it might—seldom were these books well preserved in the modern and much-coveted temperature-and-humidity-controlled environments now touted by librarians.

He began to read, and she with him.

After a time, Giles began to piece together what had happened. Adjusting his glasses, he muttered, "My God, Jack the Ripper may have been a *Fomhóire* faery." Nodding as he read on, he added, "My best guess from the description. They've always wanted into this dimension, to destroy the Tuatha. Perhaps the portal closed because Jack threw the Slayer in. Rather like Buffy when she dove into the energy thrown off by Glory's magicks. Her blood was spilled . . . there's a resonance there . . ." His Watcher's mind at full throttle, he read on.

Sunnydale

Candace Evans jogged along the trail through Waverly Park, as she did almost every morning shortly before dawn to keep her body in tiptop shape. The tight spandex and Lycra outfit she was wearing usually made her feel sexy as she ran, and provided a source of amusement when she watched guys trying to pretend they weren't looking.

But not this morning.

Maybe it was the murky fog that was hanging around everything, making the normally bright Sunnydale morning look like a shot from a horror movie, because there was no one out. The moist air was cold, and her workout suit was designed for the normally warm California air. The chill seemed to creep along her spine, a cold, clammy touch that promised worse.

She ran a little faster, rounding the corner toward Main Street.

Crank it up, Candy, she told herself. Burn a few more calories and she'd be just fine.

But it didn't work. Instead, contrary to all logic, she seemed to get even colder, the fog like deep water in the ocean, providing banks of colder air that she pushed through, chilling her to the bone.

And there was something more. She had the feeling she was being looked at, paced by another runner.

The girl glanced around, but could see nothing. The fog seemed to press closer, and her workout clothes seemed to feel even thinner as the cold worsened. It occurred to her that they would offer no protection against an attack. Knife or *claws.*

She shuddered, the cold feeling on her back joined by a sharp tingle up her spine. She hit the "off" switch on her MP3 player, killing the sounds of Madonna's thoughts on being a material girl, Candace's self-professed theme song. She tried running lighter on her toes, and *listened*.

Tap-tap-tap, went her Reeboks on the sidewalk, and she heard the sharp intake of her breath and the tight "huffs" she made as she exhaled. Nothing else.

Her unease grew.

Come on, girl, get a grip. There's nothing! You can't hear anything, see anything, nada!

But she *knew*.

She could picture watchers in the trees around her, looking at her, seeing her run from them, making them want to *chase* her, catch and devour her, like *prey*.

She suddenly realized that she was running at full speed, still a long way from home, trying to make it, running to *escape*.

She didn't try to slow down. She'd reached the place where she knew the hand was about to grab her, the hard claws reaching for her, inches behind.

Her breath came more and more ragged as she kept up the pace she used only for bursts at the finish line. The cold air was painful in her lungs as she gasped it in, huffing and pushing, her nasal passages aching from it. Her body was enveloped in a cold, clammy sweat as she cut sharp at the corner, seeing her house at the end of Dorinda Drive, the yellow porchlight gleaming like a torch in a medieval night.

She sprinted even faster, pushing herself harder than she knew she could, now that her survival was at stake.

She was going to make it—

And then she tripped on the cracked sidewalk just in front of the porch, her toes catching it, the rest of her body sailing past, on the way to the ground.

Her scream shattered the air as she rolled forward, knee scraped and tights torn. With a desperate cry, she hit the door hard, jamming her key in the lock, nearly breaking it off as she got the door open. She dove in, slamming it behind her, rushing to throw the deadbolt, sure that at any second there would be a huge thump as something hit the outside of the door.

She was inside, safe—for now.

There! Xander's car!

Oh, God. And a body. Someone lying next to it. Don't let it be anyone I know, anyone I care about. . . .

As the fog swirled around her, Buffy ran toward the inert figure at the side of the road. The car door had been yanked off its hinges; the lights tried to pierce the fog, couldn't manage it. Foul play to the extreme.

A fan of blond hair . . .

Tara.

Buffy dropped to her knees beside the Wicca and gently turned her over. Tara's face was ashen. Her mouth was slack. She looked . . .

. . . no, not dead. Please.

"Tara," Buffy said softly. "Wake up. If you can."

She rummaged in the car and got a blanket. She covered Tara up with it, warming her arms with her hands, and feeling the fog as it began to wig her out.

After a few eternities, Tara opened her eyes. She looked up at Buffy and said, "Willow?"

"She's okay. What happened?"

Tara licked her lips. "Something attacked us." She indicated that she wanted to sit up. Buffy helped her.

"I think . . . I think it took Xander and Anya." She touched her forehead. "Whatever it was, it took magick energy from me. My head is pounding."

"We'll get you home."

Tara nodded. Buffy helped her to her feet and began to walk her slowly toward the car. Tara hesitated. "You're going to drive?" she asked.

Buffy shrugged. "Unless you can."

Tara swallowed. "Let's walk."

"I can drive. Sort of."

Tara nodded and said, "Okay. I'll give you some help. Magickally."

"Good idea," Buffy replied. "Thanks."

"Self-interest." Tara managed a smile.

Buffy helped her into the passenger's side and then walked around, flexing her hands and arms kind of like someone who was about to lift eight hundred pounds. She worked the kinks out, then climbed up and slid behind the wheel.

"Wow, Xander's car is big," she said, scooting up the seat so she could reach the pedals. The keys were still in the ignition. "I hope the battery still has juice. The lights have been on for a long time."

Tara closed her eyes. "I'll give them a boost," she said.

Buffy turned the key. The car leaped to life—literally, as Buffy took off the emergency brake and put her foot on the gas.

"Goddess, protect us," Tara breathed, with her eyes tightly shut.

"Amen to that," Buffy murmured. Then she punched it, and they were off.

They had trundled down the road perhaps a hundred yards when someone stood in the center of the road, hailing them. Fog rose all around him; it was a tall, thin man, bluish white, with blond hair and blue eyes.

"Look. It's Elric," Buffy quipped, then looked at Tara's puzzled expression and said, "Xander loved those books in high school."

Tara was no more enlightened, but Buffy pulled over and got out. She could feel the cold coming off him in waves, knew what he was and who had socked a few of his buddies recently, and kept her distance. She folded her arms across her chest. "You must be Mr. Freeze," she said.

"I am MacNair," the man replied in an accent Buffy could not place, and did not care to. "We share a common enemy." He blinked his weird blue eyes. "Jack the Ripper."

"Willow, wake up."

Something crashed downstairs.

"Willow, wake up!" Dawn screamed.

Willow bolted upright in Buffy's bed.

Now Dawn could hear heavy footsteps stomping up the stairs. Whoever—or whatever—was on its way was definitely buying pants at the Big and Portly.

Willow was awake at once; she leaped out of bed, hurried across the room, and closed the bedroom door as quietly as she could, then came back and snatched Dawn's arm, urging her toward the closet. She was just pushing Dawn inside when the bedroom door burst open, making them both jump.

"Not a very inventive hiding place," the thing that stood in the doorway grated. "I can't believe you couldn't do better."

Dawn stared at it, wanting to scream, but her vocal cords wouldn't quite work on command. It was like nothing she'd ever seen before: tall and red—okay, so that was pretty day-to-day demony—but with a thick set of six bony ribs that lifted up and outward from each cheekbone. And teeth—how on earth did that thing manage to form human words with all those sharp things sticking from between its thin slash of a mouth?

Dawn's voice paralysis broke as the creature stepped into the room and she saw more crowding behind it. A line of disgustingly yellow drool slipped out of the side of the closest demon's mouth, snaking down its jaw and dripping onto its knotted, putrid-looking shoulder. What, were they waiting their turn at the fresh-meat buffet?

Willow yanked Dawn backward and stepped in front of her, then shouted a few magickal words and made a small but complex gesture at the advancing demon. The demon inhaled and coughed, then laughed at the bewildered look on Willow's face.

"Seems like someone has been overdoing things a bit. Your magick's weak." His tone was sarcastic. He took two great steps forward and snagged both of Willow's wrists in one thickly knuckled hand before she could try gesturing again.

"Let her go!" Dawn cried. She tried to step around Willow, but the demon shoved her with his other hand, hard enough to send her reeling backward.

Willow's dark-rimmed eyes flashed, and her mouth twisted into an angry line; before she could say anything—a word or a phrase that would make this ugly thing's head explode would be nice—a second demon, skinny and foul-smelling, darted forward and plastered a piece of masking tape across her mouth.

"There! Fixed her right shut, I did. Didn't I, boss, didn't I just?"

The little beast danced around like an insane ballerina, his voice half-shriek, half-scratched-blackboard sound effects. Bruised and occupied with clawing her way back to a standing position, its words still climbed along Dawn's spine like a metal fingernail. Before she was fully upright, she found herself hauled forward by the big bully who still had a tight grip on Willow.

"Mnmmmmmmmmft!" Now Willow's eyes were wide and clear above the thick piece of tape, but with her mouth sealed and her hands bound, there was nothing she and Dawn could do but watch helplessly as someone else stepped into the room.

"Hello, my two beauties," said a tall, human-looking figure. He bowed. "I'm Thak. But you may call me Jack the Ripper."

"Oh my *God*," Dawn choked. Instinct made her try to back away, but the demon held tight to the back of her shirt, pulling upward until she was almost on her toes and dangling like a loose marionette. Her legs worked desperately to help her escape, but the soles of her shoes found no purchase—she was barely touching the floor. In front of her, Willow shuddered visibly, trying without success to gesture with her clasped fingers.

"C'mere and let me have a look at you," the beastly man—if he *was* a man—said. His voice, clear and with a lilting Irish accent, seemed to be the only thing truly human about him. "Step on up," he encouraged Dawn. The demon holding her forced her to oblige. "You truly are quite the lovely girl."

"And you're not." The words tumbled out before Dawn could stop them.

But he only laughed. "So true. But when you're Jack the Ripper, it's what's *inside* that counts, not out. But I'm in need of tender hearts. Yours, for example."

He smiled and Dawn cringed and his mouth elongated until that terrible, toothy grin of his was nearly ear to ear. Something was wrong with one of his eyes, too—it was . . . drooping or something, sliding halfway down his cheek. Was it even *attached?*

Abruptly, his smile disappeared. "I'm afraid my fun will have to wait a bit, at least until that Slayer sister of yours returns."

He waved at the demon imprisoning them and turned to go back into the hallway. As the bigger creature yanked her forward, one soulless eyeball eased around the side of the Ripper's skull and peered back at her, bouncing lightly in the air like a ball on the end of a spring.

Forcing her attention away from his eye, Dawn tried to squeeze out of the creature's grip. She got her arm twisted painfully for her trouble.

"You leave my sister alone—and besides, she's not coming back here. She's . . . she's out of town!" Dawn said triumphantly.

"I think not," Jack said blandly.

Dawn and Willow were dragged behind the Ripper as he made his way back downstairs and into the living room. He moved through the house as though it were his own.

When he inclined his head toward the couch, the demon practically threw them both onto it; Dawn's immediate attempt to get back up got her an excruciating crack across the face from the little blackboard-mouthed demon. She glowered at him, thinking how much she'd like to stuff an eraser down his throat.

"You see," Jack the Ripper said, settling comfortably on a chair across from them, "I believe your sister may have something I have a need of. A little vial." He looked unhappy. "It's gone missing. I waited and waited at the cemetery, but no one brought it to me. And it occurred to me that a Slayer might manage to snatch it. Though Lord knows Elizabeth could never had done so."

"Elizabeth who? What vial?" Dawn asked. She swallowed hard.

He shrugged. "Just a final little ingredient to something I'm making, is all. If she'll just hand it over to me, I'll give you back to her. A fair trade for all involved." He shrugged again, then his heavy, black gaze found Willow. "I've really no need of the witch, though. Odds are I'll probably disembowel her."

That terrible, savage grin split his face once more. "I'll get the Vial of Sacred Fog, bring the *Fomhóire* through, and the *Tuatha* will rise to the challenge. The Last Battle will take place, as both sides want. And after they're wiped out . . .well . . ." He laughed. "Not to worry about that. Neither of you will be alive to see it."

"We don't have a vial," Dawn said. "Can't you just mix something else up?" Suddenly Willow's voice echoed in Dawn's head, and she knew the demons could hear the witch's thoughts as well.

He shook his head. "Tried that before, in London. Had a vial, but the mix wasn't right. The fog wasn't strong enough, and my brethren couldn't come through. But I'm given to understand that a courier was bringing me Nemain's handiwork at last. Except that I haven't gotten it yet."

Dawn raised her chin. "Well, Buffy doesn't have it. And if she did, she wouldn't give it to you!"

"She would," the monster assured her, "if it would save your life."

With that, he cuffed Dawn hard across the head.

Everything went black.

* * *

Spike was half-asleep when the door to his crypt swung open and royalty came calling. "Wha . . .?" Spike groused, rising up on his elbows. Then he smiled. "Banshee, old man," he said by way of greeting. "How's things?"

"If the Slayer has the vial, she should give it to us immediately," the faery monarch replied. His Blueness was in a mean temper, and Spike knew it was not wise to cross him when he was like this.

They'd done many capers together; why, back in the day, as soon as Jack had been forced back to his own dimensions, Spike, Dru, and Banshee had tried to brew up some Sacred Fog together, take over the human world. Hadn't gone right.

Ironic, then, that they'd all ended up in Sunnydale. Well, except for Dru decamping. That was not particularly ironic.

It was positively maddening.

No matter. Over her. Got Buffy.

"She doesn't have it," Spike told him. "'Least not that she's told me. But I gather it's around?"

"A *Fomhóire* warrior came through the Hellmouth. But then we lost track of him."

"Using old Maggie's eyes, eh? You still imagine you're on fire now and then? Could be the change of life, you know." Spike lit up a cig. Banshee came closer, looking angrily down at the vampire.

"If you value *your* life, you'll find that vial and give it to me," Banshee told him.

Then he swept around in all his blueness and wafted back out the door.

Spike tried to go back to sleep, but his mind kept drifting back and forth between London and Sunnydale, the Slayer then and the Slayer now.

Sooner or later, Buffy's gonna die, he thought. *And part of me will die with her. But for now . . . finding that vial might do me some good.*

He sighed for Buffy and the human race. Banshee hated 'em as much as he hated the *Fomhóire.* And if Jack found Spike without strong allies, he'd probably do him in for vengeance's sake. After all, he and Dru were the ones who had thwarted him the first time he'd tried to bring his people through the portal.

Maybe it's time to change sides, Spike thought.

He rolled onto his left side and closed his eyes.

Then again, maybe not. Tell you what, William. Sleep on it.

Despite the fact that the fog was getting thicker, Buffy drove home pretty well. MacNair had sat in the backseat, stone silent, while Tara had said "Look out" only two or three times.

Buffy had tried to call Dawn and Willow on Xander's cell phone, which was inside the car, and no one had answered. Hence, speed; she bumped the curb pretty hard when she came within distance of the driveway.

Grimacing, she bolted from the car.

She pushed open the front door, totally freaking when she realized it was unlocked, and ran into the foyer.

"Dawn! Willow!"

There was no answer. She began to take the stairs when she realized the phone was ringing. She raced to get it.

"Giles," he said. "Buffy, bad news."

"Giles, I think Dawn and Willow are gone. Everyone's gone," she said.

"Listen, Buffy. Listen to me quickly. There's a portal, or there may be one. There are two races of faery. One lives in our dimension, or sort of does. The others will be trying to come through a portal that Jack the Ripper will be opening. They're called *Fomhóire*."

"Spike's information," she said, taking the phone with her as she ran upstairs.

"The portal can only be closed with Slayer's blood, shed by an enemy," he said. "Sir James researched it after Elizabeth's death."

"Oh." She raced down the hall. "They're not here."

"Buffy?" Giles queried.

"Slayer's blood," she said. "Been there, Giles. With Glory, remember?"

"You died that time," he reminded her.

"One drop. Two, tops," she said. "Giles, they aren't here!"

There was no one in either of the bedrooms. But there were signs of a struggle, and there was a note . . . in blood, on her mirror.

Bring the vial, or they die.

Chapter Eight

In eight hundred years, Anya had never been this frightened.

She couldn't find Xander; they'd gotten separated somehow, and anyway this whole thing was sort of third-person strange. On the one hand, she was insanely, utterly terrified—so much so that she could hardly breathe, couldn't think clearly, couldn't reason; on the other, it was as if she could look down and see herself in her own body a la an out-of-body experience—there she was, blundering through the fog-choked streets of Sunnydale, running into brick walls with an almost blackly humorous sense of unerring direction.

This happened in much the same way that, in the cartoons Xander always watched on Saturday mornings, the boulders launched at the Road Runner by the Coyote always fell right back on top of him. If there was a wall within ten feet of her, by God she was going to hit it, usually with her face. By the time this was all over, she'd probably look like a boxer who'd gone six rounds in the ring.

And when *would* this be over, anyway? That was something else feeding her terror, this pervasive, never-ending suspicion that this noxious-smelling mist would be here *forever,* that she would spend the rest of her days running and running and running—

Anya heard a sound behind her and she whirled, then stepped back, promptly tripping over a trash can. Okay, so she was in an alley—that would be the trash can thing—although she hadn't a clue exactly where that alley was in Sunnydale. But that noise . . . was someone following her? If so, who? Friend or foe? Demon, devil, or—

"Hello?" Her voice sounded thin and tremulous, cowardly. That was the part about being human that she found the most annoying—they were so fragile and easily broken, and now here she was trapped in this damnable fog and nearly blinded by it, spinning around like some insane child's off-kilter top. Her heart was pounding, and she was gasping for air, nearly hyperventilating. The only thing faster than her breathing were her thoughts, tumbling over one another like the balls in one of those television lottery machines.

She heard another noise, louder than the first— kind of a *thump-shuffle,* like someone dragging their feet. Or a body, maybe they were dragging a body, the corpse of some poor girl who'd probably looked just like her, reddish hair and big eyes, pretty . . . pretty *dead* right about now. Because the citizens of Sunnydale were acting like vengeance demons, just going all barbarian like back when she was Aud and her village was attacked. She felt just as terrified now, just as human, just as helpless. She wanted the power to stop the madness, just as she had then.

Well, to do that and kill my unfaithful husband . . .

—*thump*—

"W-Who's there?" Anya sucked air into her lungs and got dizzy—she'd been holding her own breath during the entire duration of this latest of her ongoing mental rants. If she didn't start communing with oxygen pretty soon, she'd likely end up passed out on the ground, and then what would happen? Why, she'd be prey, that's what, unconscious and totally at the mercy of whatever demon or vampire or creature of the big bad night that came along. And wouldn't she just make the nice midnight snack, her with her milky white skin and top-of-the-line body hygiene—

Something tickled her ankle.

Anya screamed and leaped backward, lungs hitching as a small rat skittered away from her and disappeared into the fog. It had *touched* her leg with its whiskers, maybe even its tongue; what if it had licked her, or worse, *bitten* her? She might get the Black Death and thank you very much, she had *seen* what that could do to the human body. And it was all about going back to being human, wasn't it, trapped in this unreliable and soft shell, nothing but a big, delicious bite for who knew what might be lurking out there—

She heard another *thump* and could have sworn this one was closer, practically right on top of her. Panic filled her and she turned and ran, as fast as she could, swinging her arms in front of her like the feelers of an oversized beetle. Everything was suffocating in this fog, this nasty yellow glop that had swallowed up the regular air, and what was it doing to her lungs right now, even as she catapulted through it toward the unknown?

Maybe she should try to hold her breath, maybe every inhalation was giving her cancer, or filling her chest with poisons that would make her hair fall out and double her over with a bloody cough for the next thirty or forty years before she finally passed away from this oh-so-miserable human existence. Or her skin—it could be killing that thin little surface covering with every second that passed. Maybe it would turn her into a crumpled old woman with oozing, nasty sores all over her body, and broken blue-and-red veins running in every direction beneath her cracked, translucent flesh. . . .

Out of breath, sucking in more and more of the revolting air, Anya had to stop. Before she could take her current train of hysterical thought any further, something dark and big lumbered at her out of the fog.

For a moment, Anya froze. Then, without even focusing on whatever it was, she shrieked and turned to flee. The creature behind her made a noise, but it was muffled by the fog, the sound deformed into something between a grunt and a gurgle, as though it was hungry. She careened along the alleyway—at least she thought she was still in the alley—with her mind unable to let go of the idea that for a human it always came down to that, didn't it, the hungry thing, where something bigger and badder and with a whole lot more teeth was constantly trying to chew on you—

Something new rose up in front of her and she plowed into it with a painful yelp, sliding down until she hit the ground. It was a car—something purple, one of those trendy-looking PT Cruisers with darkly tinted windows that anything could hide behind, there was no telling what was inside it, probably vampires or worse, maybe even zombies, that whole flesh-eating thing all over again. This fog gave creatures like that, the really hungry ones, the perfect cover, of course. What better way to skulk around and search for a fresh, hot-blooded meal, something tasty and juicy, like a lithe young woman running all alone at night in this demon-riddled town—

And oh yeah—whatever had been behind her in the alley was still coming for her.

Anya dragged herself up using the handle of the passenger side and was horrified when the door opened. To her, it looked like the mouth of a big, ravenous animal, all black and bottomless and waiting. She slammed the door closed again before anything horrid could burst out of it and attack her, then bounced off the fender and ran to her left. If only she could see something, *anything,* but the fog wasn't letting up, it was still thick and grotesquely insidious, snagging at every step she took, poking misty fingers everywhere she had exposed skin.

She'd gone maybe twenty feet at the most when she tripped on something and went down, scraping the palms of her hands and one knee along the filthy concrete. Anya was on her feet again instantly, bouncing upright like a frenzied doll on a spring. Oh no—her hands were bleeding! What if she got some kind of infection, or blood poisoning? What if there'd been mouse droppings on the street and she'd gotten *that* into her bloodstream through the cuts? Instead of being the star entrée of some monster munchfest, she would die a horrible death because of that virus that was so like Ebola, what was it called—

Crash!

She shrieked again and plowed into the mist, not caring where she was going, not caring that she couldn't see. There was a monster after her, there had to be! It was probably big and hairy and red, or maybe it had a club and pounded on people and ate babies like that one man she cursed, the one she'd turned into an ogre—yeah, maybe it was *him,* finally come to exact his revenge! He would beat her into a bloody pulp and leave her to die a slow and terribly painful and lonely death, all her bones shattered until she was silent and not even able to cry out—

Everything in front of Anya suddenly tilted.

Her arms pinwheeled wildly as she tried to maintain her balance, but there was nothing in front of her, no solid ground on which her feet could find purchase.

In that long but instantaneous moment before death that legend claimed drowning people experienced, she felt, not saw, her life—all eight hundred-plus years of it—zip across the surface of her brain. With it came the realization that she had traded the comparative safety of a monstrosity-filled Sunnydale alley for the edge of an abyss, and while she'd never known such a thing to exist in Sunnydale, it was surely here now.

And she was falling over it.

So be it.

She felt herself start to float and she stopped spiraling her arms, stopped fighting. She surrendered herself fully to her fear and just let herself go.

But as the last of her body dropped into the blackness and the thundering of her own heartbeat filled her ears, a hand snaked forward from the fog behind her and closed fiercely around her ankle.

Anya's body lost the graceful dive she believed destiny had assigned her. Instead, held by the last-minute death grip, she made a sharp half-circle and slammed front-first into rock-strewn dirt, the vertical face of the unseen cliff. She howled in pain and shock, then wailed anew as she was dragged back up. Grit filled her mouth, pebbles grated along her skin and worked their way inside her blouse as it was pulled up to the middle of her rib cage. When her hips finally came over and she was bent double, her rescuer's other hand latched on to the back of what was left of her blouse and hauled her the rest of the way.

She rolled away from the cliff's edge, then

scrambled around with her fingers twisted into defensive claws, ready to face whatever monster had saved her from death's hand to claim her for itself.

Xander leaped on Anya before she could try her skills at cliff-diving again.

"Anya! Stop it—it's me! It's Xander!"

"Let me go!" she screamed. "You're not Xander! You—you're a shapechanger or something, some kind of thing that's going to eat me—"

"I am not!"

"Are too!"

"Am *not!*" She was fighting him like a hellcat, and it took everything he had to avoid having his eyes gouged out. "Anya, *stop it!*"

Xander wrapped her in a bear hug and kissed her.

She struggled for about two more seconds, then the fight went out of her. Another second, and she was kissing him back, holding on to him as though her life depended on it.

Then she pulled her head back and stared at him. "Xander?"

He gave her a crooked grin. "You'd better hope so. I'd hate to think you'd kiss like that with just anybody you meet at a cliff's edge."

"Xander, this fog—I'm so scared. I can't think straight, I keep thinking that things are after me! I think I'm going crazy!"

He brushed her hair out of her eyes and thought he'd never seen her look as beautiful as she did right now. Maybe it was the fog, and the way it shrouded everything with soft edges. Or maybe it was just that he loved her so much and had come so very close to losing her.

Xander stood and pulled Anya to her feet. "I think it's a good possibility that things *are* after you. And me, and everybody else in Sunnydale. I'm scared, too, and my wisest suggestion is that we go back the way we came and see if we can find our way to a fog-free zone."

The gaze she sent toward the yellowish layers drifting in front of them was frightened, but at least she'd shaken off the full-blown panic of a few minutes ago. Finally she nodded and, arm in arm, they crept cautiously back into the fog.

Back out they went, Buffy, Tara, and MacNair.

The fog was everywhere.

Thick and noxious, like some sort of nuclear accident tinted an ugly pale yellow instead of the green that television had always made people expect. It had a weird sort of substance to it, too, there but not there, a tangible touch of evil that was too elusive for her to grip. It curled in the strands of her hair and made it feel greasy and limp; it slithered between her clothes and her body like the unwanted touch of a dirty stranger. For a fleeting moment, all Buffy could think of was going home to where it was warm and safe and light, where she could climb in the shower and scrub away any remnants left by the filthy mist surrounding her.

A nice thought, very warm and homey—

But not an option.

Somewhere in this mess was Jack the Ripper, and he was a whole lot more of the big bad than anyone had ever dreamed. In fact, also somewhere in this big bowl of vile yellow soup that had become the air around her were Spike, Willow, Dawn, Xander, and Anya.

God, let them be okay.

"MacNair?" Buffy's voice was loud in her head, but the fog swallowed it up and minimized it, as though it could turn the volume down at the source—her own vocal cords. "Tara?"

Out of the corner of her eye Buffy saw a shadow and she spun toward it and crouched defensively. But the shadow was gone a millisecond after it had been there . . . if it'd ever been there in the first place. The layers of heavy mist were nearly suffocating her, muffling all sound, dimming everything in front of her eyes. She had the creeped-out notion that Jack was just out of range, that he could easily see through this creamy-looking air while she could peer only a couple of feet in any direction. That was an advantage she didn't want him—or any enemy—to have.

A noise slipped through the mist and she shuffled toward it, moving only about a yard. Was it . . . yes, definitely Tara's voice. She tried to move closer to the sound, then abruptly lost it as a fresh, infuriating cloud rolled in front of her.

Her impatience boiled over, and frustration got the better of her. She balled one fist and swiped uselessly at the air, wishing she were connecting with flesh and bone on the Ripper's face. "Come on out, you coward!" It was a shout but not, nearly powerless against this amorphous wall. Even so, she thought she heard a repulsive chuckle somewhere to her left.

"He is close."

Buffy whirled and instinctively recoiled when she saw MacNair standing nearly close enough to touch her. As if the fog wasn't bad enough, his nearness was washing her with swells of cold. It made her want to shudder and her teeth try to chatter, but she'd be damned if she'd let this blue-skinned faery see that and interpret it as a sign of weakness, or worse, fear.

"We must get the vial, else we are all defeated."

"This is the best pearl of wisdom you can manage after being alive for centuries?" She eased forward another yard, stepping along the rough surface of the street like a blind person without a cane. She could tell MacNair was following her by the sense of chilliness that hugged her spine and stayed with her as she moved; at least he was considerate enough—for now—not to make contact with her. That whole liquid-nitrogen-on-contact thing was kind of too bad—if he'd had a little color in his cheeks, MacNair would've almost been eye-candy. Tall and very slender, his white hair and nearly transparent eyes vaguely reminded her of Spike and—

Despite the damp fog and the cold emanating from MacNair, warmth washed through her, and Buffy felt her face flush. "Hello, body heater," she muttered.

"What did you say?"

She shot a glance over her shoulder and saw only confusion in MacNair's gaze.

"Nothing. Let's just keep searching. Demon Jack's gotta be around here somewhere. He's too ugly to hide for long."

MacNair said nothing, just shadowed her as she inched forward. Every now and then she would get a sound flash—a few words that she was positive were from Tara's smooth voice.

"My king and his soldiers are near," MacNair said suddenly. "I feel their presence."

"I'm surprised you feel anything but cold," Buffy retorted.

"I'm quite comfortable, thank you."

"I wasn't worried."

"There!" MacNair shouted excitedly. "I see him!"

Buffy squinted in the direction he pointed. "Who?"

"*Thak.*"

A chill sped along Buffy's shoulder, one far colder than warranted by the fog and MacNair's presence. *Thak* . . . Jack the Ripper's original, ancient name, evolved through the centuries into something modern man could accept. For over a hundred years the men and women of London, no, of the *world,* had thought themselves safe from this bloody monster, rescued from his atrocities by the inescapable kiss of Death. Blissful fools—naive and innocent—they had no clue that Death could be recanted or avoided altogether, and that time itself could be twisted into a tool for renewing age-old battles.

And suddenly the fog was alive with movement.

It thinned enough to give Buffy flash pictures, like strobe-light shots taken during a bad horror movie. Someone ran past on her left, screaming—a woman wearing slacks and a sweater, crying and pulling at her own hair. Her words were garbled and filled with panic—

"They're in my hair, oh God, someone help me get them out, please get them out, they're sharp—"

She was gone before Buffy could do anything for her, then two more people staggered into the limited range of her vision. Older men, one struggling to escape while the other held on as if his life depended on it, and both shouting a different story into the other's face—

"Let go of me, I know you're trying to steal my wallet, you'll kill me, you'll rob me—"

"Anthony, stay with me, Mom said you have to watch over me, Mom said we have to go to the store and you can't leave me, you can't—"

And more—everywhere she turned, Buffy saw people, everyday, ordinary Sunnydale *people,* turned into paranoid, raving lunatics. They spun through the streets like mad spirits, punching at the fog swirling around them, raging at one another, all trying to escape the inescapable: the yellowish mist that would not stop following them, could not be kept at bay, and could not be beaten.

There was movement behind her, a rushing sound. Buffy instinctively ducked and something spun past her head—a battle-ax with an admirably long and sharp point. As she crouched, a demon lumbered from between the swirling fog, and for a moment, all Buffy could do was gape at the creature, a weird cross between a Vahrall demon and a grown-up Gachnar.

Lovely.

The thing saw her and raised its ax a second time, intent on making two Buffys from one. She started to roll to the side and realized too late that she'd chosen the wrong direction—she hadn't been able to see the brick wall that was right there, and now she had nowhere to go. Being trapped at ground level was a definite undesirable thing; the laws of gravity gave the person on the receiving end of an ax blade a distinct disadvantage.

The demon had arms bulging with knots of muscle, and Buffy braced herself, wondering if she could survive the coming blow. The thing grunted with effort as it aimed, then the ax came whistling down toward her head.

A figured stepped out of the fog and directly into its path.

MacNair caught the demon's downward stroke at its peak, wrapping his freezing fingers solidly around the thickly structured wrist. At the same time he slapped the flat of his other hand against the attacker's chest.

The ax never descended the rest of the way. The demon bellowed as his arm froze in midair, faster than Buffy could blink. It tried to pull away, and MacNair's hand trembled with the effort it took for him to hang on. A crackling sound filled Buffy's ears, like winter pond ice splintering from the weight of someone walking on it. An instant later the creature's cry died in midwail as a ring of bluish-white frost spiraled out from where MacNair's hand was pushed against its chest. MacNair twisted his upraised hand, and the demon's arm literally broke off, shattering when it fell to the ground next to Buffy. A fast two-second count—

One—

Two—

—and the creature itself toppled over backward, its chest and lungs as dead, cold, and solid as petrified wood in an ancient winter forest.

Buffy didn't bother saying thanks as she leaped to her feet and snatched up the creature's heavy weapon, letting the feel of it sink into familiarity. She would definitely need more than a stake tonight, and this nice, heavy war ax would make a darned good start. She turned and saw another demon in the fog, this one chasing some poor college girl who seemed able to do nothing but run in ever-smaller circles; sooner or later she would run right into the thing's grasp, and the grinning demon knew it.

Before that could happen, Buffy stepped between the two of them and gave the girl a hard shove, sending her off in another misty direction. "Hey, dungeon breath. Care to try your hand with someone a little more sane?"

Surprised, it hesitated. No slouch she, Buffy grabbed her chance to bury the point of its dead companion's ax deep into its abdomen. This one hit the ground with a worthy crash, and she promptly availed herself of a second weapon. One for each hand, a nice matching set. Speaking of sets, this was two down, so how many to go?

More shapes spiraled around her, too many to count. A voice was droning on and on and on somewhere close, and Buffy aimed for that, following words that bore the lilt of an ancient land and flowed like an ugly incantation. She lost track of MacNair, saw him fleetingly as he swiped at another creature far faster than the previous demon; before she could help him, the fog moved in front of her and took him and his opponent away. She saw more *Tuathans* like MacNair, their blue-white skin momentarily gleaming amid the suffocating mist. Some fought and won, others died and left this world in a whirlpool of mist that was immediately swallowed by the hungry, unnatural fog.

"Buffy!"

Relief swept through her at the sound of Tara's voice. She reached out a hand and found Tara's arm, locked onto it like a drowning man grips a life ring. "Are you all right?" she demanded.

"I'm so scared."

"It's the fog."

Tara looked around a little wildly, and Buffy had the nerve-wracking suspicion that perhaps the only thing between Tara and the craziness of the rest of Sunnydale's townspeople was her wellspring of magick.

Buffy glanced back at Tara and saw her eyes widen as she focused on something behind Buffy. Buffy spun, ready to strike or defend, but too late; someone or some*thing*'s fist whacked her solidly on the jaw. She tumbled over and rolled, still maintaining her hold on the two axes she'd confiscated from the demon-deads, but before she could regain her footing, Tara mumbled something and drew her hand in a downward motion. A second later the demon, a squat thing that looked a lot like a walking frog, forgot all about Buffy and Tara and everything else as it began to scratch madly at itself, twisting and turning and trying in vain to reach unreachable places along its somewhat lumpy back.

Buffy scrambled up and watched it stagger away as Tara shrugged. "A little mystical itching powder," she explained. "Really, it's more a party joke than anything else."

"Seems to do the job," Buffy said. "Come on—we need to find Jack and show him the real meaning of the word 'rip.' Can't you do anything about this fog?"

"Well, I can try . . ."

Whatever the rest of her sentence was, Tara didn't remember to finish it.

Swirling through the fog, some rat-faced little demon guy tried to grab Tara, and she backfisted it in the nose hard enough to break bone; not very sturdy, it howled like a baby and ran the other way.

"Rock it, Tara!" Buffy congratulated her. She offered a high five, and Tara shyly but proudly tapped her palm with hers.

More fog washed over them, dank and smelling like very cold but well-used gym lockers . . . *and cold does too have a smell.* Buffy gripped Tara's wrist and said, "Don't lose contact."

"God, I hope Willow's okay," Tara murmured.

"Me too," Buffy replied.

The fog became so thick, Buffy could literally cut it with an ax . . . and she did so now, hacking it out of her and Tara's way. It floated away in thick wedges that looked like moldy sponges. It was exceedingly weird, and Buffy gave a murmur of thanks to her closet guardian that she had not made the same mistake twice and worn her black leather pants.

Then, as she hacked more and more of the gray matter away from her path, Jack the Ripper floated about fifteen feet above her, like some overpriced Halloween projection in Westwood in L.A.

Here we go, she thought, moving into major climactic battle mode. *I'm going to kill this sucker once and for all, and he is gonna be so sorry he thought he could come to my town and threaten my family . . . sorry before he dies, that is. Because he is so gonna die.*

From his invisible perch he smiled at Buffy, and it was a hideous thing to see. He was built . . . *wrong*. Proportions were off, placement of vital bodily features was skewed. Was he human? No . . . but had he ever been? Probably not. He had curly brown hair and some human features—eyes, nose, mouth—but he was . . . *empty* or something. It didn't matter, anyway: Whatever he was now, there was something so pervasively and unavoidably evil in him that he was one of the most terrifying things Buffy had ever seen. plus he had a very, very ugly dog-thingie panting and drooling beside him.

But she just wasn't the type to duck and hide.

Instead, she glared at him. "Hey, JR. Come on down. We'll play a game." She twirled the two long-handled axes like cheerleading batons. "It's called role-playing. I'll be the Slayer-Who-Kicks-Your-Ass, and you can be Toast. And your little dog too"

Buffy wouldn't have thought it was possible, but that tooth-filled leer of his widened even more. "Oh, I do so love games, Slayer. I've been playing them for centuries."

Buffy grimaced—she couldn't help it—but stepped toward him, anyway. Instead of retreating, he went sideways, like a crafty animal thinking it could sneak up on its prey. "And his icky animal came with him Great," she said. "When do we start?"

"Just as soon as I read you my rules."

"What—" she began, then her voice fell away, swallowed by a renewed layer of fog and a momentary sense of *sludginess,* as if she and everything around her had been encased in warm goo.

Through it all came the Ripper's voice, grating while at the same time strange, insidiously melodious: *"Shuggoth ir orbis!"*

The heavy wrapping of air abruptly dissolved, and Buffy hefted her axes and started to step forward.

Blackness.

She stumbled and went down on one knee, then instinctively brought one ax up to rest along the ridge of her shoulder and the top of her skull, scant protection against a blow but better than nothing. The fog was gone, the ground was gone, the *world* was gone, and finally the full impact of the Ripper's incantation sank into her brain.

She was *blind.*

She strained to see, but there was nothing there. Actually, there *was* something now; the initial blackness was gone, replaced by a sort of dull yellow background color that was the same as the fog twisting through Sunnydale. So *was* she blind, or was this just the fog? But if it was just the fog, why couldn't she see the ground when she leaned over and practically put her nose to the street's cold concrete?

She heard Tara calling out to her, but she was helpless—she couldn't even find the direction of Tara's voice. For a single, eternal second, she was tempted to sink into hysteria. To be so vulnerable—

No, she wasn't.

How many times had she and Giles trained for just such a situation like this? And had she not gone through exactly the same sort of test at the hands of the Council? She might not have her eyes—*temporarily,* she told herself—but she still had her training and her Slayerness. She was still *Buffy*.

Instantly her other senses increased tenfold, maybe a hundredfold. She could hear the townspeople much more clearly all around her now; they were screaming, more and more of them running along the streets in fear and panic.

Bushes rustled, night birds shrieked along the treetops, driven to a bit of insanity themselves by the chaos below. She heard a car crash into another one street over, caught the driver's curses as he got out, smelled the exhaust and fumes of hot metal. Two hundred feet away, a child sobbed in the bushes, separated from his mother and too terrified to come out—she wished she could get over there and find him, but she had more important things to give than comfort right now.

"Come out, come out, wherever you are," Buffy said softly. The axes were solid and weighty in her hands, good anchors to a world she could no longer see. But she would not worry about trivial things such as sight right now. She would only worry about the survival of herself, and the killing of Jack the Ripper. "Surprise—I'm still in the game."

"Of course you are," said Jack. His voice seemed to come from all around her. "I never doubted it for a moment. But did I mention that it's a very *short* game?" He paused, then continued. "And, of course, I can be the only winner."

Centuries of skulking around had honed his skills of silence and speed, so Buffy sensed his movement more than anything else. He made no sound, not even a telltale exhalation of breath—he was demonic, anyway, did he actually breathe?

She swung one of the axes around as a cover, then sliced outward with the other; her offense missed, but at least her defense held. She felt the impact of his weapon with the handle of the ax in the way his blow, strong and hard, made her body vibrate right down to the bone; with it came a long *screeeeeeeech* as a metal edge met more metal—that would be the part where he had tried to carve her up like a holiday turkey with one of his fabled knives.

She pushed outward with the ax handle, then pulled down, hoping to hook his wrist and knock the knife free—a risky proposition since she couldn't see who or what might rush in to pick it up. She sensed him getting ready to strike again and she paused, letting her ears and sense of smell tell her from what direction the blow would come. She knew the instant he left, melting back into his fog; she also knew that whatever advantage her heightened other senses had given her would never hold against the half dozen or so demons who had moved in to take his place.

Jack the Ripper had moved on, no doubt intent on getting the vial some other way. But how?

Buffy didn't have time to contemplate that. Something grunted behind her and she ducked, narrowly missed getting hit or beheaded or God knew what by something swinging through the air. She sidestepped a charge from her left and heard her attacker crash into the one behind her, both of them spewing invectives at each other as they scrambled to regain their footing.

Meanwhile, something else grabbed for her on the left; she pulled away but felt the sting as its sharp, long claws grazed her skin. Another grab, and another, and then there were blows raining down on her from all directions and before long it was all she could do not to end up being beaten into a bloody pile on the street. There were too many of them, and heightened senses and Slayerdom skills or not, she was at a distinct disadvantage here—

"What the hell is this?" a familiar voice demanded. "You're 'aving a game and I didn't get an invitation to play?"

Spike!

More crashes and thumps and curses, too many for her to keep track of, but this time the blows lessened; soon her body responded on its own to the call for battle. Blinded or not, she couldn't *not* fight, or at least try, on her own behalf. If she let Spike do this all by himself, she'd probably never hear the end of it.

She heard something hard hit flesh, and Spike hissed. "Bloody hell!" he snapped from somewhere in front of her. "Big dog bit me! That *hurt*—you'll pay for that, rot-breath!"

She heard his return blow to whatever had injured him as a whistling through the air, and while she'd never admit it to him or anyone else, she had to admire his speed. She threw in a few whacks of her own, still running on the same unseen sensations that had pulled her through the Council's tests not so long ago. She connected, but it didn't seem to help; for every demon she and Spike beat back, she could hear another—and sometimes two—arrive to take its place.

Spike yelped as something hit him, or maybe bit him. Buffy took a hard blow along her left back as she tried to defend herself from two unseen somethings in the front, and for the second time in this battle, she went to her knees.

"Tara!" Spike barked. "Don't let me hold you back if you feel like tossing a bit of that Witch-a-Roni into the kettle here!"

Is Tara here? Buffy couldn't tell. There were too many demons on one side and not enough optic nerves on the other—hers. Then she heard the Wiccan's voice, chanting so softly that even with her heightened sense of hearing, Buffy could barely catch the words.

> *"Demon flesh of foggy night,*
> *Creatures hear my call,*
> *You'll find you cannot stand and fight,*
> *But only fall and fall and fall. . . ."*

A creature of some sort thudded heavily to the ground next to Buffy, who promptly slammed the butt end of the ax handle in the direction of its head, hearing a satisfying *crack* for her effort. The thing wailed and scrambled in the other direction at ground level, apparently unable to stand. Curses and growls cut the air as more of Jack's demonic force got cut down to size by Tara's incantation, but Buffy's relief was shattered when she felt Tara grab her by the arm and haul her upright.

"Come on! We have to get out of here—the spell will only work on the ones who were in earshot when I said it!"

Buffy stood and felt herself wobble. Her balance was whacked out without sight, and the faster she moved, the worse it got, like trying to run in a void where she couldn't feel the ground. She hoped that Tara could undo whatever Jack the Ripper had done to her sight, or she was going to be the first visually challenged Slayer the Council had ever had.

Tara started to lead her away, and something hit her viciously across the backs of her knees. She yelled in pain as her legs buckled; one of her axes went flying, and the other jammed into the ground as her weight pushed it down. She could *feel* the demon that was bearing down on her—its size and its strength, like a smaller version of the ugly Gingerbread monster she and Willow had once faced. Weaponless, there was nothing to do but throw up her hands and wait for doom to fall—

"Not bloody likely!"

Spike sprang in front of her and took the blow in her stead.

It drove him to his knees beside her, then he was up and growling in fury. Buffy was glad she couldn't see him, because she knew that sound and the quickness of his movements, knew the *smell* of him now— so different from that of the undead man that none of her friends knew she'd held in her arms time after time in an underground tomb. Undead, yes, but during those times he had been, most of all, a *man;* now he was a vampire, a beast of the night who was full of deadly rage.

Drafts eddied around her and Tara, and Spike's snarling filled their ears. Moments later, the currents carried the smell of blood to Buffy's nostrils, and she hoped it wasn't Spike's. It seemed like an hour, a day, a *month* . . . and then he was between her and Tara and his voice had lost the guttural rasp of the vampire as he morphed back to human form.

Now it was filled with urgency instead. "Let's be on our way, ladies. I don't think that bloke can actually die—leastways not by anything *I* can do to him. Best bet's just not to be around when he gets up . . . or more of his mates show up to join the fun."

"But the fog—" Tara started to say.

"Not to worry your little Wiccan head," Spike said. "It's not much different from walking around in the dark."

If only that were true, Buffy thought as she linked arms with Spike and Tara and let them lead her through the choking fog.

* * *

Paul Falkland was a gibbering idiot.

He had somehow managed to crawl into a crypt without the Blue Men noticing him. Hiding in the corner, he had finally lost his mind. The vial the weird chick had given him lay on the floor in front of him. He wanted no part of it.

Which was a good thing . . . because otherwise, he might have had to acknowledge the presence of the hideous little man who had dropped without warning from a window ledge and waddled toward the vial. With one miniature, fat-fingered hand, the escapee from *Freaks* had grabbed it up and clutched it to his chest.

Then he'd said to Paul, "Thank'ee, lad," and scrabbled up a moldering stone bust back to the windowsill. The grate had long since fallen to rust; the little man climbed around it. Then he hoisted himself out of the window and disappeared.

Paul gibbered on.

Chapter Nine

Willow figured a couple of hours had passed since she and Dawn had been kidnapped. But it still wasn't enough time for her magic to recharge. She looked up at the demons who had captured her and Dawn and thought, *I could take these guys easy, if I wasn't so burned out. I'm in withdrawal. And it ain't pretty.*

She felt weaker than ever, tired and sick from more dry heaving. the getting sick part must have been why they took the tape off her mouth. But now they had taped Dawn's mouth shut. Willow wondered uneasily if they had done that because Dawn was making too much noise. As in, screaming. The room was spinning. Dawn was unconscious, and Willow envied her.

The two of them had been taken to the same cavern

in which she and Buffy had fought the Riencosta demon and the troll. Willow now understood the reason there had been so much demonic activity belowground: Jack the Ripper had been conscripting an army, preparing for a huge battle—*let's call it a war*—and he needed soldiers.

Waking nightmares were popping in from all over this dimension, and other dimensions, too. Red ones, green ones, leathery ones, and feathery ones . . . it was like Dr. Seuss on a terrible, horrible, no-good, very bad day.

Yay, Sunnydale, home of all the evil that's able to exist.

Willow looked over at Dawn and said softly, "I'm so sorry, Dawnie."

Then Dawn's eyes opened, and Willow saw the terror in them, above the masking tape they had recently put over Dawn's mouth.

Then suddenly, a tiny head popped up from behind Dawn, a truly ugly little thing, and Willow couldn't help a grimace of distaste. She had no idea what it was, but it put its hand over its mouth, indicating that she should remain quiet. Then it set to work cutting Dawn free.

Once it was finished with Dawn, it scuttled over to Willow. Their demon guards were discussing the merits of beheading over eviscerating, and neither noticed what was going on.

"I'm Flinn. I'm saving you, me lovely lass," the creature whispered. Then, almost as an afterthought, it added, "'Tis a leprechaun I am."

"Okay," Willow whispered back.

"We must hurry. It's the Last Battle, and I've thrown

me lot in with himself." He gazed at her. "You're so lovely."

"Okay," she said again. "And escaping is done how?"

"They're suggestible," he suggested, indicating the demons guards who had grown tired of watching two scrawny human females and had turned themselves to the more important task of working the room, making friends with the throngs of newcomer demons showing up for war duty. "Perform some magicks on 'em, girl."

"How did you find us?" she whispered, and then one of the demons in charge shouted to the others, "Hey! Pipe down, youse!"

"Yikes," Willow muttered. Quickly she searched through her memory for something to cloud his mind . . . but she was tired and frightened, and there was just too much to keep track of. "I can't remember how to," she confessed.

A mind is a difficult thing to waste.

"Then just kill 'em," the leprechaun told her. "Take out a couple of them to confuse 'em, and I'll get you out of here." He pointed to where the guards loitered. "Just beneath that big brute's feet is an underground passage," he told her. "Take them out, then run like hell and I'll magickally open the passage."

Willow closed her eyes and conjured fireballs, lobbing them at the guards. Before the two demons realized it, they were both on fire.

"Gaaah!" one yelled. They raced around shrieking, then tried to bat each other out. the other demons just watched She kept making fireballs, kept throwing them, until they were both in such pain that they were unaware of anything but that.

"Come on!" she shouted to Dawn.

The leprechaun hitched a ride on Dawn's back. Flinn made magick, and a hole opened up in the floor. "Jump in!" he shouted.

Then, as Willow dove for it, Jack the Ripper appeared before them in the cavern, surrounded by a rolling blanket of fog. The noxious odor of way too many strawberries wafted around him, and Willow's stomach churned.

We were so close to freedom, she thought desultorily.

"What are you doing?" Jack thundered. He pointed a finger at the leprechaun named Flinn. "Who are you?"

"Flinn, Your Lordship," the leprechaun said grandly, sweeping a bow. "And I got something you want."

With a big smile, he held out his stubby hand, revealing the vial.

Jack the Ripper burst into delighted laughter.

Flinn joined him. "I was bid by Banshee to bring it to him," he said. "But you and me, we both know who's going to win this great battle."

"Wise of you," the Ripper said. He frowned at the demons who were still ablaze; the creatures were running in circles now, lost in the pain and the fog's disorienting power. He flicked a hand in their direction and said to some of the others, "Put them out or put them down."

A green-scaled demon said uncertainly, "How?"

"Don't we have a fire extinguisher?" Jack asked. "Or at least a bucket of water?" Apparently seeing none, he shrugged. "Just let them burn."

More fog roiled around him. Then he clapped his hands, and it began to dissipate. Willow stared in horror as the bodies of perhaps a dozen young women were revealed, stacked around the Ripper's feet. A hideous doglike creature was sniffing at the corpses.

"Yes. These are the sacrifices for the portal," the Ripper told her, looking very proud. "I took their hearts."

"Oh, God," Willow murmured.

"I need one more." Jack the Ripper began to advance on her. Willow clamped her mouth shut, forcing herself not to scream. Instead, she looked inside herself for magicks . . . but again, she was too drained.

I've been wasting my power. I won't do that anymore, she promised herself.

The leprechaun stepped in front of her, shielding her more symbolically than literally.

"Wait. She is my prize. She's what Banshee offered me, and seeing as I gave you the vial . . ."

The Ripper looked touched, which on him was a sinister thing. "So she has taken your heart."

The leprechaun nodded.

The Ripper shrugged. "What about the other one? The younger one?"

"I've no claim to her," Flinn replied.

Jack rubbed his hands in a horrible parody of an old melodrama villain, the black-hatted landlord preparing to collect the rent from the hapless widow.

"No," Willow said.

Jack and Flinn both laughed at her.

And Dawn began to sob.

* * *

Half an hour later, all was ready. Jack's hour of triumph had arrived at last . . . under the the Osiran Moon. "And now . . . now it shall come to pass," Jack the Ripper announced. He stood on a vast plain outside Sunnydale with the vial in his hand. His demon hordes were behind him, clanking their armor and flourishing their weaponry. Bound to the leprechaun, Willow stood silently, sick to the pit of her stomach over what she had done.

No one will ever know, she thought. *If I hadn't done it, they would have killed Dawnie.*

Still, she had skirted so close to the line that she may as well have crossed over it.

The magicks I just did . . . so evil . . .

She doubled over, feeling ill.

Then Jack opened the Vial of the Sacred Fog.

And hell came to earth again.

"Anya, look," Xander said quietly.

As they both looked over the cliff Anya had seriously considered jumping from, Xander saw a sight that made his blood run cold: An enormous portal, maybe the size of the entire Sunnydale Zoo, had formed in the air above the plain that lay just beyond the town. Go far enough and one passed the old drive-in, once the secret headquarters of the Sons of Entropy. Now there was a way different kind of screen to watch: Emergo-Demon, in living gory color.

Demons of all sorts were emerging from the portal, some Xander had crossed before, and others designed especially for the sequel—leathery green ones, purple ones covered with bristling quills, and some really cool dragons like in *Reign of Fire*. More startling than the variety was the sheer number, tumbling and floating and flying out of the magickal ring. They appeared to be buoyed by the fog, and they took it stairstep-style to join the ranks of their brother and sister demons grouped behind a lone figure . . . in an opera cape, for God's sake. And he had a really, really ugly dog.

That guy's gotta be Jumpin' Jack Slash.

The bad kept popping through the portal, while the others roared and shouted and clanked stuff. These were the millions of extras no movie, not even *Lord of the Rings,* could afford. Real life was ostentatious that way. Never send in five demons when you can afford five million.

Floating and bobbing about ten feet above the ground, fog swirled around Opera Cape. Screams of bloodlust and terror both erupted from the fog, and a wind whipped up, answering them.

The sky lowered, darkened, blackened as the sun vanished. More demons appeared as if by magick. Lightning zigzagged.

The air stank of rotten corpses and strawberries.

"This is bad," Xander said. "Really bad."

"Yes," Anya agreed. "Let's run away now." She smiled sadly. "That's a joke, Xander. I know you won't run. I know I will probably have to die at your side." She frowned. "I never thought I would say this, but sometimes I hate being engaged."

* * *

Screams whipped in the wind, and in the town of Sunnydale mayhem and murder gloried just beyond the field of battle.

From his position beside Buffy on the far end of the plain, Spike saw the glow of burning buildings, illuminating the nightmare sky. He smelled burning human flesh.

He had been in Whitechapel. He knew it was happening in Sunnydale—the sheer panic, the rioting that the British government had managed to keep out of the history books.

"What's happening?" Buffy asked, still blind.

"Preparing for battle," Spike said curtly. "The really big, nasty one."

"As opposed to all the other really big, nasty ones we've fought in the past."

His voice was tinged with sadness. "This one is the real one, Buffy."

He slipped his hand through hers, lacing their fingers together, and it was another one of those tender moments that made her feel awkward.

"Buffy," he murmured. "I'm really going to miss you, Slayer."

Flanked by Jack the Ripper's demon guards, Willow stood with Dawn. The young girl was sobbing and vomiting, and Willow was too numb with horror and self-loathing to permit herself any kind of release from the screaming inside her head.

She had helped the Ripper acquire his twelfth sacrifice.

The twelve dead girls hung suspended in the air. Eleven of them were people Willow did not know. But the twelfth . . .

. . . the twelfth had been a classmate named Eileen. Thak had plucked her name from Willow's memory, which she had allowed him to do, and tracked her down.

A long time ago, Death's own nightmare had stalked children in the ward of Sunnydale's hospital, and murdered them one by one. Thanks to Willow's compliance, Jack the Ripper stole to Eileen's bedside in the Oncology unit at the same hospital—no child she, but just as vulnerable—where, weak from chemo, she had been completely helpless to stop her own evisceration. She had not flatlined until it was nearly over."

Eileen had come without question, knowing only that in these desperate times, a friend had called.

And she had shown.

Jack had demanded a substitute for Dawn. And to save her . . . to save her . . .

I didn't kill Eileen, Willow told herself over and over again.

Dawn had been taken to a place of safety. She had not seen, would not know.

But Willow did.

And now, Eileen's body circled slowly with the other corpses, bound and gutted, the fancy work of Jack the Ripper, who, with Willow's help, was probably going to rule the earth.

* * *

Banshee, king of the *Tuatha Dé Danann* was carried to the killing field on his throne of bones. MacNair, in full *Tuathan* battle gear, stood beside him as together they brought the army within arm's length of the Slayer's ragged band. Spike the vampire was with Buffy Summers, and he saluted Banshee with a nod.

The eyes of Witch Maggie told a terrible tale: Jack the Ripper had the vial, and he was using it.

Spike smiled thinly at the fearsome faery lord and said, "I'll fight long as I can."

"As will I," Banshee agreed.

"And I," MacNair chimed in.

"'And I'll do it myself,' said the little red hen,'" Buffy riposted.

"To the end, a courageous warrior, who mocks her own death," Banshee allowed.

"That's me. Bunny," Buffy said. She was still blind—Tara couldn't lift Jack's spell but she was ready to give her all in the big mosh pit of doom.

The army of Jack the Ripper was cheering and screaming, hot blood coursing, battle bravery stirring. They were perhaps a half-mile away . . . and when one is staring death in the face, a half-mile is as close as half an inch.

Then *Thak* the mad faery halfling gave the signal to attack. He raised a fancy Victorian walking cane and plunged it into the ground in front of him.

All hell broke loose.

Thunder clanged around Buffy as if she were inside an enormous drum. Pandemonium erupted, screams and yells; the panic of ordinary citizens and the war cries of the *Tuatha*. King Banshee's forces surged forward, their footfalls shaking the ground. Skyquakes shook the air, and Spike started yelling out the action to her:

"They're coming now, out of the sky!" Spike said. "The great *Fomhóire* themselves, not just all those other demon hangers-on. God, they're ugly!"

"Glad I'm blind."

"They're coming for the *Tuatha*. Banshee's raising his greatsword to tell our side when to break formation and do the fightin'. Pity you can't see it. It's massive, got all these runes." He sounded covetous.

"Jack'll rune the day he tried this stunt," Buffy muttered.

"Really, pet, you've no sense of humor," Spike said fondly. "Best to leave the stand-up to the professionals."

"Yeah, right," she said harshly. "Like you do." She imitated Spike's street-British accent: " 'Two vampires walk into a bar, one says, I hate to be negative. Got any universal donor?'" Then she changed her voice, mimicking the Buffybot that Warren had created for Spike: "'Oh, Spike, you're sooooo funny! Ha ha ha ha ha.'"

"Sword's down!" Spike shouted, as behind them, row upon row upon row of *Tuathan* warriors yodeled high and shrill, a cross between Xena and something scary, fierce, and deadly—*okay, like Xena*—and all around them, the icy soldiers pressed forward.

Each side blazed with hatred, each side eager for deathdealiing, the faery massed on one another, eager to settle the old score and obliterate their nemesis.

"It's a great day to be a Klingon," Spike yelled to Buffy. "Too bad we're not."

"Speak for yourself," Buffy retorted. "If I had any free time at all, I'd watch *Farscape,*"

"In reruns, luv."

"All the good shows move on eventually."

Buffy and Spike moved forward with the *Tuatha*. Tara had still not reconnected, and that worried Buffy big-time. One false bump into the *Tuathans* could seriously harm or even kill the Wicca.

And where are Xander and Anya?

This is all happening because a bunch of interdimensional-hopping wanna-bes came to my town. And it was so nice of Spike to never mention that a bunch of faery had built their stupid faeryland underground. Can't fool me; the Tuathans *are not much better than the* Fomhóire. *As I recall from my pre-blind attack, they look a little more like Legolas than Jack the Ripper and his brand do, but let's don't kid anybody. The* Tuatha Dé Danann *are not cuddly little pixies. According to Macnair, their king sits in a chair his skilled craftsmen made out of human skin and bones.*

And besides, I'm a Viggo girl. Legolas is a Nancy-boy.

Spike knew the *Tuathan* "Big Noise," as only Spike would put it. Spike and Banshee probably played demon poker together. It made sense that he'd fight with these guys, and she was glad that, for once, Spike's cronies were the lesser of two evils.

But as this was a war, the Slayer was being forced to pick sides, too. Buffy was a practical gal—okay, except during shoe sales. As a champion of the good, she had to go with someone a little less interested in doing bad damage to the world than the other guys. But fact was, she was also buying time while she decided how to get rid of all the faery.

And get my sister and Willow back. Jack's got the vial; he didn't need them to deal with me after all.

Has he killed them?

"You know the part about closing the portal with my blood," she said as they loped forward, Buffy unwillingly clasping Spike's forearm. It was creepy to be blind in the middle of a battle, but even creepier to have to depend on Spike for anything except feeling ashamed of herself. "An enemy spilling my blood."

He gave her hand a pat, as if she were his maiden aunt or someone else he had to help along. "Yes. Shouldn't be too hard to accomplish. Little slice, dribble dribble, and we go home happy, as Xander likes to say."

She licked her lips, not really wanting to say what came next. "Given this some thought, Spike. You're not my enemy."

"Don't worry, pet, I am. I'm every human's enemy. I'm evil, Buffy," he reminded her. "Get this chip out of me, I'd tear your throat out."

"Well, yeah," she allowed, "but still . . ."

There was an abrupt shift in the force. The air around them hardened, as if it were made of flimsy plastic or very thick pudding. The *Tuathan* warriors liked it no better than she did, and began to grumble in faeryspeak.

"What's happening?" Buffy demanded.

The ground shook so hard that fissures opened up.

Rocks flew upward from explosions deep underground. The earth split between Buffy's legs, and she leaped to one side, taking Spike with her.

Is the Hellmouth opening up? 'Cause that's just great, that's all we need right now . . .

. . . probably something Jack prearranged, with all his magicks and his plans. He must be just the best date, gets the movie tickets through Fandango way ahead of time. . . .

"The portal's getting bigger," Spike told her. "It's gonna be easy to spill your blood into it. We won't even have to call a taxi to get to it."

"And the vampire's back in the house with lame stand-up."

"Speaking of lame . . . I'm just gonna nick you. You bein' the Slayer and all, you might not even notice it. 'Course, you've yet to not notice anything I do to you."

"Let's skip the sordid details," she said with asperity. "But it won't work. You don't fit the classic definition of enemy."

"There's right optimism for you, we can hope," he said.

The battle had commenced. The noise and darkness were terrifying. Any living thing with half a brain would run. Dogs were streaking down Main Street; cats were scrabbling manically into treetops; birds in their cages were screaming to get out.

As for the human population, they were running amok. Xander knew that at the end of this Scooby's working day, it was going to be easier to find a parking spot just about anywhere in town. Because a lot of people were dying, by the scream of things. . . .

Coyotes, possums, and skunks fled the battlefield. As a chipmunk skittered around her ankles, Anya screamed, "Look out for the bunnies!"

"I'll save you from the bunnies," Xander promised her. "I'm just not certain I can save you from all the demons."

"That's okay, Xander," she said. "Well, actually it's not. But you're only human, after all."

Xander and Anya ran down the steep cliff, falling and tumbling, helping each other up. They were a mass of cuts and bruises.

"Why are we hurrying?" Anya demanded. "There's nothing we can do."

"We can be there," Xander said grimly.

"It looks hopeless." Anya looked pensive. "We'll all be killed."

"Not if I have anything to do with it," Xander said.

Anya sighed. "You're so romantic."

"Buffy!" It was Tara. She touched Buffy's hand.

"Tara," Buffy acknowledged, flooding with relief. *Okay, one person I care about is not dead. That's progress.*

"We got separated," Tara said unnecessarily. She was panting hard. "I'm not sure I'm going to be able to keep up. These battle guys are in . . . battle shape."

"Can you do magicks from the sidelines?" Buffy asked. "Give us strategy magicks? Kind of like the Raiders' coach?"

"I-I'll try."

"Not the Raiders, luv," Spike said kindly. "Raiders keep losing." To Tara, he said, "Listen, blondie, all the supernaturals are levitating above the battle. Whyn't you do that, go float around and tell us what you see?"

"I'm just a witch. I *use* magick," Tara protested. "I'm not supernatural."

"Just rise," Spike groused at her.

"Don't let him bully you," Buffy said. Then, after a beat, "Can you rise?"

"Trying now," Tara said.

After a moment, Spike said to Buffy, "She's going up." He chuckled. "Bird's wearin' a thong. Who'd have suspected she was a bit of a player?"

Then over the plain, in a large, echoic voice not unlike someone testing the great P.A. system in the sky, a demonically accented voice bellowed, "Slayer!"

"That's my name, don't wear it out," Buffy said grimly. "What's he doing, Spike?"

"Well, he's about as tall as Big Ben now," Spike said. "Shapeshifter, you know. Growing."

"Been eating his Wheaties," Buffy yelled back.

"Just devourin' the hearts of girls. Lots of magick in hearts. Valentine's Day used to be this huge Druid mass sacrifice thing. It was actually quite fun, all these girls on altars. Druids, nasty lot. Certainly have had a lot of spin on their magickal practices. It's you Yanks with your Renaissance fairs cleaned up their image—"

"Whatever," she cut in. "Tara, can you hear me? What do you see?"

Tara's voice filled Buffy's mind. *Just . . . lots and*

lots of demons fighting. The battle will reach you in about ten seconds.

"Okay, thanks," Buffy said aloud. To Spike, "Got a plan?"

"Slayer!"

Buffy narrowed her unseeing eyes. That was the voice of Jack the Ripper ringing above the melee again.

Buffy, there's not much I can do, Tara reported.

"It's okay." asked again, "Got a plan?"

"Why should I have a plan? *You're* the Slayer."

"Then you really are my enemy," she said. "We close to the portal? Wanna do it now?"

"I always wanna do it." Then he yelled, "Oh, my God!"

"Slayer!" Jack's voice shook the ground, the sky, the world.

Tara screamed.

Then the hordes descended on Buffy and Spike. She heard *Tuathan* soldiers going down; bellows of agony and fury raged around her as the earth shook and split again and again.

Not a problem.

She was blind, but she wasn't defenseless; she went into attack mode just as Merrick and Giles had taught her—and Angel had shown her some great moves, too—all the attack postures on her Slayer menu were activated in rapid-fire sequence, and she was kicking and slicing and dicing like the hot warrior chick she was.

I wish Mom could see this, she thought wistfully, then realized that maybe her mom *could* see her. And that wherever her mom now resided, her fate might lie in Buffy's hands.

There was wind all around, and quakes; fissures split the ground where they fought, and at one point she was about to fall in one when Spike hauled her out.

"Slayer!"

Jack's voice eerily rode the storm of battle.

And if ever there was a time to step up to the plate, Buffy knew this was it. She was going to take Jack out and fold down his tent if it was the last thing she ever did. No reruns, no instant replay. This was the real world, she was the real Slayer, and this was going to be real over, real soon.

She was a whirlwind, kicking and thrusting and killing; she kicked and fought and raged like a crazy person—

—*the fog?* she wondered. *It's filling me somehow, with more adrenaline than I've ever had before. More energy. It's like all my fear has been channeled into aggression; it's kind of cool.*

I wonder if this is what Willow's been dabbling in. I can see the attraction. . . .

And Tara looked across the oncoming army and saw Willow standing with the *Fomhóire* army, who had done something to the fog around Buffy. It was glowing with a light crimson hue, like blood. Blood and fog.

"Willow!" Tara cried, knowing Willow couldn't hear her. If today was the day to die, she wanted it to be with Willow.

The battle raged. For hours and hours it wore on. Faery forces were decimated on both sides. For a time, the *Tuatha* scored more deaths, and then the *Fomhóire* would steal back the battle.

Both sides were acutely aware that the Slayer was on the field, and that she—like justice—was blind. Demons were dying by the hundreds, battling one another as the lines were drawn.

Rain poured down, sizzling in the fog, making the ground slick with mud and gore. Buffy fought as she had never fought before—roundhouse, sidekick, doing complete three-sixties in the air.

Then, as faery races began to fall each to the other, Jack the Ripper unleashed his full army—more demons than had ever been gathered together in one place. The carnage was terrible.

But Buffy was up for it all, ready for it all. She reached forward with arms stained with demon blood, wresting weapons from dying creatures and stabbing others with them. She slashed and hacked and fought . . . and then she started all over again.

"Getting near the portal," Spike advised, and she nodded. She knew they were frequently fighting back-to back.

"Finally."

"This group knows what's doing," Spike said with grudging admiration as the two fought a Varhall together. "Lettin' the demons out, not lettin' you near the bloody thing. Hey, cool! It's a real Congara. On your left!"

"Got it!" She drew back a spear she had yanked

from something's slimy tentacles, and rammed it into some gooey, stinky flesh.

"Brilliant," Spike enthused. "Trolls!"

"How many?" she demanded.

"More'n I can count. Coming straight for you."

"So, more than ten," she shot back, turning the spear sideways and small, hard bodies out of her way like, well, like sweeping small, hard bodies.

"'Least I never flunked math. More coming!"

"You never took math!" She swept back the other way, then executed a rapid-fire series of snapkicks that contacted with a number of chins and sternums.

Speaking of shoe sales, I am gonna need some new ones after all this.

They battled on for about two minutes. Then Spike shouted, "Oh, *wow!*"

"Wow?" She kept up her kicking maneuvers. "Not liking the sound of that wow!"

Spike was too stunned by what he was seeing to describe it to Buffy. It had happened at last, the moment foretold in songs and video games: Banshee, king of the *Tuatha Dé Danann,* squared up against Balor, the king of the *Fomhóire,* as Balor emerged from the portal with a fanfare of fireworks, starbursts, and lightning. Skyquakes were nothing compared with the way the sky shattered as he stepped from his exile, and touched the human dimension.

Banshee, the ice-blue *Tuathan* of approximate human size, rose into the air. He held his runesword in his hand. It was magickal, Spike knew that, but the great

king seemed puny when compared with the massive—
and very ugly—Balor, who loomed over him by perhaps
ten feet.

Balor held in both hand an incredible sword of his
own, and Spike found himself thinking, *Gotta steal
me a very good sword. All the Big Bads have 'em this
season.*

"To the death," Banshee proclaimed. Balor's answer
was a contemptuous laugh.

Both held their swords high. Beneath them, the
demon armies of the plains erupted into shouts and
shrieks. The wind whistled, nearly slicing Spike's
eardrums, heralding the deaths that Banshee was said
to bring.

"Spike? What's happening?" Buffy shouted.

"They're gonna fight. The two faery kings," Spike
told her.

"Okay, then while everyone is distracted," she
said, "stab me or something. Tara, can you hear me?"

"Yes," she said from high above them.

"Once he nicks me, levitate me, if you can."

Okay, Buffy. I'll try.

"Okay. Spike, go ahead." But his gaze was glued to
the impending battle.

There was a pause. Buffy said impatiently, *"Spike?"*

"Sorry." He turned and grazed the back of her hand
with his nails. "You're bleeding."

"Beam me up!" she shouted to Tara.

"Okay."

Wind rushed around Buffy as she was whooshed
upward. It was exhilarating. She touched the back of

her hand and felt her blood; she flicked it away from herself in hopes of it sprinkling the perimeter of the portal as quickly as possible.

Nothing happened.

They went at it, Banshee and Balor, and Spike watched, amazed at the ultraviolence and the strength of the two legendary kings. The armies all stilled, watching with horrified fascination. In the distance, Sunnydale still screamed and died. Spike was dimly aware of Xander and Anya fighting demons along the perimeter of the battle, working their way toward Willow.

With each arc of their great swords, the sky sort of flickered, reality being sorely tried. Strange shapes, black patches with stars falling in them; spinning portals swirling with mists popped into and out of existence. More monsters spilled from the dimensional connections.

The earth beneath Spike's feet was actually *hot.*

Hell's coming to earth, he thought. He wished he could be more upset about it. "Neat."

Banshee swiped at Balor's midsection, then drew back as Balor raised his weapon over his head and tried to bring it down on Banshee's helmeted head. Banshee raised one arm up, rather calmly, and grabbed the blade.

His hand was severed and fell tumbling toward the plain as his army gasped.

And Balor's sword immediately froze, and shattered like a rose dipped in liquefied oxygen.

With an oath known only to those who had studied *Fomhóire* as a second language, Balor advanced on the wounded ice king. From Balor's side another arm grew, and as Spike watched, the arm became another sword.

And before Spike could say "Manchester United," Balor ran Banshee through, directly in the region of his frozen faery heart.

Mist blasted from the great *Tuathan* king. As shrieks of despair rose from his troops, he put his handless arm into the hole, but it was no use: The *Tuathan* lost shape, lost form, lost essence . . . and within a few seconds, it was as if he had completely evaporated.

Balor threw back his head and uttered a war cry. His troops took up the sound, and Spike blinked himself back to reality; this was not some show on the telly. This was the next big step in what was going to happen to *him*.

"Gonna be a massacre now!" Spike shouted. "Bleed on the damn portal, will you?"

Then Jack's voice rang over the throng. "I am your new god!"

His voice was like thunder; The electric zing of lightning bolts shooting downward, ripping the earth apart.

Huge geysers of flame shot from the gaping chasms in the earth, and all manner of uglies poured from the fires, crabbing toward all living things and overrunning them.

The portal was not just the sky now; it was the earth below. It was everywhere.

Then Spike realized what the matter was, why Buffy's blood was ineffectual against the imminent arrival of the sequel to the human race. He shouted up to Buffy, "You were right! I'm not your enemy after all! Me cuttin' you don't close the portal."

"Oh, *great!*" she shouted back.

Then Tara's mind was filled with the essence of her beloved. Her heart clutched, and she thought, *Is she entering me to say good-bye? Will we be together again, in death?*

Willow said, *I gave her a rope, Tara. A Sailor's Eye, you remember them? For patrol. To help her.* She sounded very frightened, very defensive.

Even as they were about to die, Willow was afraid that Tara would pull herself even farther away from her.

"Tell her," Tara urged.

There was a huge booming noise. Then the sky went completely black.

Tara cried, "Willow? I can't see anything!"

With much sudden screaming all around her, Buffy yelled, "What happened?"

"We're all blind!" Spike cried up to her. "All of us! It's pitch black!"

Then sharply into her mind, Willow spoke: *Buffy, do you have the rope? Maybe in your pocket? The one from patrol?*

"The rope . . . ?"

The one I gave you for seeing in the fog, Willow explained.

Buffy felt in her pocket, located the rope. *Will, where you been? Coulda used this a while ago, you know?*

You did fine without seeing, Willow informed her.

You been watching?

Watching you, watching over you. She paused. *Dawnie's fine. So far.*

I gotta finish it then, Will, Buffy said. *I need to get wounded. I need an enemy to spill my blood.*

Put the rope to your forehead, Buffy. Willow sounded very sad, very regretful. *All will be revealed.*

Okay.

Buffy did as Willow said.

Buffy put her fingers around the bit of braided rope and put it to her forehead, and suddenly she could see . . .

The sky was nothing but a vast, unending ebony plane. Layers of black darkened to something beyond black, the epitome of evil. Hideous beings that flapped and whummed with wings the size of buildings lined up to come through; and behind them, even more massive creatures of utter shadow and blackness silently waiting their turn. Stars dripped from their maws as their black, spinning eyes surveyed the landscape.

Then Jack was there, Jack the Ripper, in all his Victorian finery-fancy clothes and a black top hat, and a cane. His adoptee from the humane shelter of planet zero panted beside him. He hung in the black void with a clocklike circle of dead girls spinning around him, each disemboweled, blackened eyes opened and unseeing.

Wait a sec, I know some of them, Buffy thought, sickened.

"It's been fun," he said to her. "I enjoyed it. But it's time for you to join Elizabeth. You lasted longer," he added, "but you still failed. And this time . . . I win."

Then he pointed at Buffy with his cane.

She fell back down toward the earth, hundreds of feet below her.

"No!" Willow cried, realizing that Buffy was falling to her death. She opened both her hands and ran forward.

"Hecate, protect and guide her to my side," she murmured. "Give the Slayer protection through my aid."

At once Buffy was surrounded by a field of blue energy. As it crackled and sizzled around her, her rate of descent slowed.

A trio of leathery-winged demons flew at her, circling around her. But the energy field kept them at bay.

"Hecate, bring her safely to me," Willow begged. "I am your maidservant. This I plea, this I demand."

The field of blue around here became a sphere, and then an enormous cloud. As other demons attempted to penetrate it, they erupted into blue flames.

And then Jack whispered to Willow from the void, *Your heart has sheltered me, sweet Wicca. You gave me my twelfth victim. Your magicks fed the confusion of all those around you.*

"You have done well by me."

"No, she's mine!" Flinn the leprechaun shouted. He stood at Willow's knee and turned around and around, obviously hearing but not seeing the shapeshifter. "I helped you!"

Willow felt rather than heard Jack's contemptuous laughter; then the leprechaun fell dead beside her.

"Hecate help me," Willow murmured. "Help me, I demand of you!"

The wind that rose around her was cutting. Her heart began to pump oddly; she grew dizzy. She started to stagger left, then right, unable to stand up. Falling to her knees, and then onto her right side, she lifted up her left hand and willed the blue sphere of energy to her side.

Her heart was thundering. She could feel fingers around it, beginning to yank . . . it was Jack the Ripper, about to destroy her.

Willow? Tara's voice sounded as if she was terrified out of her wits.

Willow made no reply. Her focus was on Buffy.

Willow ran into the blue cloud, throwing her arms around her friend. As she did so, she raised a hand and, nearly sobbing aloud, deliberately scratched Buffy's neck.

"Buffy," Willow cried. "Buffy!"

A single drop of blood welled on the Slayer's skin.

And fell.

At once, it all ended:

demons,

lightning,

rain,

skyquakes,

and portal—all of it—all, swirling and collapsing

into the fog, becoming the fog, sinking to the ground and compressing into water, and then into blood.

Jack turned his enormous head in their direction. From his eyes twin beams of magickal energy geysered like flame. His Hellhound threw back its head and howled with the force of a whirlwind. And then . . . they exploded.

Jack the Ripper and his fiendish companion were no more.

None of it existed any longer.

It was over. It had raged so long that it was night again, and the stars were coming out.

Buffy stared at Willow. She said slowly, "Will?"

Willow swallowed. "I stopped it. I saved you."

"The portal could only be closed if an enemy spilled my blood," Buffy said quietly. "Will?"

Willow didn't answer. Instead, she burst into tears and sank to her knees.

Buffy stood over her. "Willow?"

Wind blew on the battlefield as the corpses of the vanquished winked out and disappeared, one by one. In the distance, the town of Sunnydale still burned.

"I'm not your enemy," Willow sobbed. "I'm not."

Spike came up behind Buffy. "Come away for a while," he murmured. "You deserve it. We deserve it."

Saying nothing more, Buffy turned to go with Spike, aware that her world was not clear, but very dim, very clouded, and very foggy.

They walked a few minutes in the burning, black silence, and then Buffy blurted, "Willow's right. She's not my enemy. So how come it worked?

Spike gazed hard at her, his pale, sharp face etched by moonlight, firelight. "When you're as old as I am, Buffy . . . okay, not, because you're the Slayer, and human to boot, so, dying rather young." He took another moment, then tried again.

"the world is all fog, Slayer. It's never clear. and blood . . . it's not any thicker than mist. Relatives betray relatives. Mums turn on their young." Before she could speak, he went on.

"and sometimes, friends become enemies. Maybe Willow's not your enemy now, but in future, perhaps . . .

"Never." Buffy glared at him. "Willow will never be my enemy. She's my friend."

His gaze was almost tender. " As I said, you're very young."

"And you're . . . you're just evil," Buffy flung at him, her voice beginning to shake. "Evil."

"I am." He took her hand. "I'm evil, and I say things calculated to wound you."

She took a breath, held it , let it go.

"You're very bad at it," she informed him.

"I know." His voice was a whisper on the wind, one last tendril of panic-inducing fog. "I know."

Epilogue: London

Watchers Headquarters

Giles was alone with a pint, in a pub just around the corner from the British Museum.

He was alone.

And as he feared, Olivia had left him.

Buffy had called to let him know that, once again, the world was saved.

His private world was shattered.

But it was worth it, he thought pensively. "Long live the Slayer," he murmured, drinking alone.

And outside, on the street, the great-great-great-grandson of Sir James watched Rupert Giles and murmured, "Well done, old man."

It was true that the government wished the world to

know nothing of the terrible riots of Whitechapel, nor about who and what Jack the Ripper had really been. And so the diaries of Sir James had been expunged from the record.

But Alexander was a Watcher himself, and he had been in the library when Giles had come looking for Sir James's diaries. Alexander had understood what truly lay at stake.

Therefore he had slipped the note into the letter box of Giles's lover. He'd hoped his single act of courage would one day merit his overseeing a Slayer, as his ancestor had done.

I pray to God to do a better job of it than Sir James did, he thought. And then, watching the sad, older man, he added, *And I pray God it doesn't take so much from me as it has from you.*

This world, this sad world of blood and fog. How do we stumble through it?

There was no answer, nor did Alexander expect one. Silently, he walked away.

ABOUT THE AUTHOR

L.A. Times best-selling author **Nancy Holder** has sold approximately fifty-five books and over two hundred short stories, many of them set in the *Buffy The Vampire Slayer* universe. Her work has been translated into more than two dozen languages, and has appeared on the ALA and ARA Notable Book lists, among others. She teaches creative writing classes through the University of California and at the Maui Writers Retreat and Conference. Her Web site address is www.nancy-holder.com. She lives in San Diego with Belle "Little Heart" Holder, their two cats—David and Kittnen Snow Vampire Wacky Holder—and Dot the Psychodog.

As many as one in three
Americans with HIV...
DO NOT KNOW IT.

More than half of those
who will get HIV this year...
ARE UNDER 25.

HIV is preventable.
You can help fight AIDS.
Get informed. Get the facts.

KNOW
HIV ▶ AIDS

Edison Junior High Library

www.knowhivaids.org
1-866-344-KNOW